MW01222481

# RUN PLANT FLY

## ELLIE BELEW

*Ellie Belew.*

PO BOX 38, ENTERPRISE, OREGON 97828

Copyright Ellie Belew, 1997, 2003. All rights reserved. No part of this publication may be used or reproduced in any manner whatsoever without prior written permission of the author except in the case of brief quotations embodied in reviews.

ISBN: 0-918957-24-9 (paperback with CD)
ISBN: 0-918957-25-7 (paperback)
ISBN: 0-918957-26-5 (CD)

First Edition, 2003.

**Printed in the United States of America on acid-free paper.**

Grateful acknowledgement is made for permission to use lyrics from the following:

"Take Me Home, Country Roads" Words and Music by John Denver, Bill Danoff and Taffy Nivert © 1971; Renewed 1999 Cherry Lane Music Publishing Company, Inc. (ASCAP), Dreamworks Songs (ASCAP), Anna Kate Deutschendorf, Zachary Deutschendorf and Jesse Belle Denver for the U.S.A.. All rights for Dreamworks Songs, Anna Kate Deutschendorf and Zachary Deutschendorf administered by Cherry Lane Music Publishing Company, Inc. (ASCAP). All rights for Jesse Belle Denver administered by WB Music Corp. (ASCAP). All rights for the world excluding the U.S.A. controlled by Cherry Lane Music Publishing Co., Inc. (ASCAP) and Dreamworks Songs (ASCAP). International Copyright secured. All rights reserved. Used by permission.

"Fly Me to the Moon (In Other Words)" words and music by Bart Howard, TRO Copyright © 1954 (renewed) Hampshire House Publishing Corp., New York, NY. Used by permission.

"As Time Goes By" by Herman Hupfield, Copyright © 1931 (Renewed) Warner Bros. Inc. All rights reserved. Used by permission. Warner Bros. Publications U.S. Inc., Miami, FL 33014.

"I've Got You Under My Skin" by Cole Porter, Copyright © 1936 Chappell & Co., Copyright © Renewed, assigned to Robert H. Montgomery, Trustee of the Cole Porter Musical & Literary Property Trusts. Chappell & Co. owner of the Publication and Allied Rights throughout the world. All rights reserved. Used by permission. Warner Bros. Publications U.S. Inc., Miami, FL 33014.

"I Remember Loving You" by Utah Phillips, Luigi Del Pupo, and Tino Chumlevich, Copyright © On Strike Music, used by permission of Utah Phillips.

Creation of this work was made possible in part through a grant from Artist Trust.

While what appears in this book has direct relation to the author and her world, the connection to reality is more tenuous by far, and it would be a grievous error to confuse the two. This novel is a work of fiction.

Book cover design and photo by Justin Beckman (www.beckmandesign.com)
Consultant on typography: Maggie Hirsch

To those who believed, not so much in me, as with me.

To those who ate and drank and dreamed
and schemed and danced with me;
who laughed and cried and looked up and lifted.

To those who gave, forgetting their own gifts: I remember.

And to Doug, my dear one.

# PRELUDE

Imagine this: an odd-looking woman past her prime. She shows up for track and field, every practice. And somehow, is allowed. Training for the pole vault. Focused in a way that would scare the rest of them except she's old, think the young ones; female, think the males; a novice, think those with experience.

Run plant vault, that's what the coach tells them. Sprint down the tar. Plant the pole tip far ahead and keep running into it, tension building. Then vault. Arc up, riding the pole, testing the laws of physics in slow slow high motion.

This woman trains. She practices, craving the hovering altitude. A faint smell of old piss, or maybe vinegar.

Then comes a day. At a windblown track chill shadows hang like curtains on the spring afternoon. It is her turn to vault at the sparsely attended, strictly amateur track meet. Other members head to the team bus. She runs. She plants the pole solid into the pocket. She vaults. The pole falls from her hands as she crests the bar. And she keeps rising. I wouldn't call it flight exactly. More like a helium balloon cut loose.

Run. Plant. Fly.

Voladores. They play their flutes and drums from a rickety bit of scaffolding lashed to the peak of a tall pole, the bottom of the pole buried in the earth. Voladores: six in number, for the directions; men, to fly. They step off the tippy top of what is barely a platform. Each steps into the air and twirls downward, together they spin like a maypole.

Flutes and drums from below as they circle, round and round, down and down. The miracle? Their return to earth, sometimes with a bounce as the streamers go tight at their ankles.

Have you ever stepped off into pure air, knowing you don't have wings?

And is it flight, to take such a step? Do the birds and flying ones look down and wish and dream about those of us who are earthbound, those of us who crawl and walk and swim?

· · · · ·

1

# 001

Daddy owned the store. Angie knew her Daddy hadn't actually started it, but he had made it into what it was. Utilitarian. One set of gas pumps out front in the gravel, a woodpile that stretched all the way back along the shady side; a decent porch across its front, with benches and one rocking chair; plate glass windows facing out. Pay phone to the left of the door, the bulletin board on your right as you step inside. Summertime the screen door slams from opening until closing, wintertime the storm door whooshes, fanning blasts of cold air.

It was Daddy who first ruled this roost. Angie took over gradually, incrementally.

Everyone else went to the store almost daily. Wandered the aisles, had a cup of coffee, read a paper. Kids rushed in after school for candy or a pop or a comic book. In the evenings certain folks stopped by for a beer, and stayed until the lights inside were flashed on and off, at closing.

• • • • •

# 002

Angie could tell it was going to be an early winter from the chilly nights of rain that came for a week at the end of August. The days following, brilliant and clear and sometimes hot, didn't fool her for a minute.

By mid-September she wore a wool work shirt almost until lunch and let her grey hair grow longer. She'd fired up the woodstove a couple times already and it was probably about time to hang storm windows. Most mornings she took a break to watch the sun crawl its way clear of the ridge, each day a little later. Still early enough the streets were quiet, enough into fall first light was gold.

Staring from the porch was what she was doing when a young man Angie'd never seen before, in a pickup she didn't recognize, came ramming up to the pumps and tried to get gas. He looked toward the store when he realized the pumps were turned off. Angie had been too busy gawking to duck out of sight. So she flipped the power on to the island and cleared pump #1, then watched the sun mosey into what looked to be a sweet fall day. Only when he came up to the porch to pay did the young man realize the store was still closed. Dark-haired and dark-skinned, he fumbled with his money, embarrassed. Angie took what he offered to the nearest dollar, told him she didn't have change. He frowned but said thanks and shoved the rest of his money back into his pocket, then shoved himself into his truck and took off, leaving a puff of dust in a sunbeam, to settle.

Angie went inside and rang up his sale, made note of the forty-three cents she was short. Favors were one thing, the till another. If she hadn't been daydreaming on the porch she wouldn't have had to start the pumps. Not until seven a.m., when she unlocked everything and opened to the public. That was how Daddy did it.

The man's son came in the next day, after school. He waited until the other children made their purchases and went outside, let each one give him the once-over as they walked by. Eyes down, he stepped forward and set a loaf wrapped in tinfoil onto the counter. "For helping my Poppa yesterday," and he was gone.

Angie unwrapped it. She broke off a piece and it crumbled, still warm, as moist and sweet as Momma's banana bread but with something extra, it had to be hucks. When she closed that evening there wasn't more than a third of the loaf remaining. She left that on the kitchen table for Daddy.

• • • • •

3

# 003

Panchito, the solemn one. Francisco Alvarez Llamado.

He came into the store maybe a week later, with a list, and handed it to Angie without speaking or looking at her. She wanted to ask him where his mother was, but one look his way killed her question. She tried other small talk as she gathered the items together. "You're going to the all-day kindergarten, right?"

No answer.

She moved down the list, item by item. "Are you going to carry all this yourself?"

He just looked at the edge of the counter.

"You made any friends yet? Maybe the Nelson boys?" The twins had started school this fall too. This time she waited. Finally he shook his head.

"Yeah, well, they can be jerks. I didn't have so many friends myself, going to school. And I was born here." She double-checked the list. "That's everything."

He paid with two twenties from deep in his pocket and took the two bags out to a wagon he'd pulled up to the porch. She could tell it would be insulting for her to help. He left the gallon of milk for last and hauled it off the counter with a grunt. "Thank you."

When he came in with his mother the following week Angie was ready. "Say, there's going to be a party pretty soon. For everybody. For Halloween."

The woman was like her boy, quiet.

But Angie had practiced. "Here's a flyer. It's free. Please come." That part she hadn't practiced. She looked down, and the boy was studying her. "Please."

• • • • •

# 004

Pancho had heard the other kids talking; he'd taken in as much as he could without asking anyone for details. After Angie gave his mother the flyer, he nodded his head at school, yes he would be going to the Halloween party.

He got his mother to dress him like a ghost. They walked together to the school, to the gym. As he came out of the cold and cloudy night, practically tripping over his sheet, what hit him first?

A wave of warmth pungent with the scorched smell of jack-o'-lanterns. They were lined up the full length of the gym wall, maybe fifty flickering faces. Then the kids, roving groups of harmless fairies with gossamer wings and glittering wands, baby clowns with big red noses, old people with warts and huge pointy hats, he wasn't sure but he thought he recognized a few faces. There were spookier costumes too. Draculas with fangs that dripped blood, dead men come alive, monsters with green faces, there were hunchbacks who dragged their feet and made guttural sounds and panted.

Pancho was glad his sheet covered him except for his eyes. Loud and ominous laughter paused and then began again. One part of the gym was lit up, the bigger kids lurked in the darker corners and near the jack-o'-lanterns. Pancho reached through the sheet for Analisa's hand. She looked down and just as quickly he let go.

It was then Angie saw them and came over to say hello. Her antennae bobbing, she led them to the trick-or-treat lineup. Pancho held out his bag and said nothing as he passed the parents who were giving candy away. When he finished, Angie led them toward the apple bob before she noticed his sheet didn't have a mouth. But Pancho was already watching as another little boy tried and tried, dunking his entire head, until the timer went off. Booby prize of a little candy corn.

Pancho handed his bag to his mother and yanked his sheet aside. With his chin and his cheek he corralled the apple into the side of the barrel, he got hold of it his second bite and came up triumphant. He pulled the sheet back over his head before he accepted his prize of a rubber ball, and put that too in his bag. Then he looked to Angie to see where they would go next.

Angie glanced around the gym, wondering if that first smile of his was a rare occurrence or saved for victories.

It was then Eisy appeared. From behind his hockey mask he'd caught the scent of heightened interest in the bobbing corner, he had been informed Pancho won a prize. Feigning interest and brotherly assistance, he spoke to the short ghost. "Want to try another game?"

Later Angie would remember herself as distracted, would know Analisa had trusted her judgment. The two boys slipped away from the women toward the clothes-pins-in-the-milk-bottle. Eisy bent over, whispering advice to Pancho as they went. Good advice. Pancho won an extra big candy bar twice before the woman running the booth suggested he try something else. Pancho knew it was Eisy behind the mask, he'd watched him at school, and around. So Pancho's trust wasn't total, even that night.

Eisy led Pancho further. To the side of the haunted house, near where the recorded laughter howled in cycles, where they could hear live screams and giggles and shrieks from inside the fabric walls. Eisy showed him how to slip in. Because of course, no one was going to let a little kid go through all by himself. Or with Eisy. Eisy lifted the wall and before Pancho's eyes could adjust Eisy gave him a little push and there he was, in the dark with nobody nearby, no way of knowing how to get out. Then arms were reaching, grabbing at him and there was a scream, right in front of him. Pancho jumped back and tripped on his sheet. Something bumped into him and there was more screaming and some kicking and he moved away. He made no noise himself, hoping the darkness would keep him hidden, would save him from being caught by whatever was everywhere in the dark.

Pancho tried, he told Analisa later, he had tried to find some way out, but it was so dark and hands kept grabbing and his sheet was twisted around him. Once or twice the hands held on and he'd had to fight to get away. But he never made a sound.

Analisa had been a little nervous when she stopped helping at the apple bob and looked around and couldn't see him. She excused herself and went outside, on the steps, but Pancho wasn't there. She asked two or three of the bigger boys who were nearby, they checked the bathroom. She looked everywhere then for the boy with the Jason mask, but there were several and none would stop to talk to her. Finally she went to Angie. Angie did her own quick scan and did not see Pancho, and couldn't spot Eisy either, which concerned her more.

So she got some of the other mothers looking. When no one led Pancho forward and he did not come himself, she used the microphone. Then they turned up the lights and the search began.

Only when they were taking apart the haunted house did they find him. He was huddled in a corner of the spook room in his sheet. Arms around himself, big eyes looking, not saying a word.

Analisa went over to him. He would not let her pick him up but he also would not let go of her hand.

When everybody finally left them alone, when they were walking home, she had to ask. Hadn't he heard all the voices on the microphone calling him?

He shook his head. "Laughing. I just heard the laughing and the screaming."

She heard some running, late that night, in the streets. And some laughing. The fear that went with Halloween.

Pancho saw Eisy a day and a half later. That is, Pancho was running a stick against the rusting wire loop fence, ka-hop, jig, jig, ka-hop, when Eisy skidded up on his bicycle.

"I hear you got stuck in the haunted house."

Pancho held his stick like a dagger.

"You were supposed to follow the next person out."

Pancho kept the stick up on his side of the fence.

"Here." Eisy held out a small and worn stuffed animal. A tiger. And had to keep holding it out. "Fine. Take it or don't." He set it on the fencepost between them. "You're a brave little sucker Puncho." Eisy whipped his bike into the street with a hop, careening down the hill full-bore.

Pancho watched. Then he picked up the animal; he stroked it. Named it Bean.

• • • • •

# 005

---

From the doorway Eisy watched his father make a great pretense of reading the paper, studied his stoop-shoulders, grey hair combed straight back so you could see the troughs the comb left, biggish ears and nose sprouting more hair.

Eisy let him work his way to the next page, waited until Samuel's eyes were once again on the upper left-hand corner.

"I need six bucks."

"Don't have it."

"I saw Ma give you money this morning."

"That's for the phone bill."

"Ma pays that herself."

His father turned another page.

Eisy snapped his gum. "Six bucks." He tore a small strip off the cover of one of his mother's magazines, rolled it into a pellet, tossed it at the creased spine of the newspaper. No response. He lobbed the next paper wad just over the top of the page.

"Stop it, goddamn it."

Eisy tore four more strips and worked each into a tight ball, rolled each along his thigh. He pitched them in a series as fast as he could let them fly, all pinging the two-inch top center of the newspaper. "Six bucks."

"You're not getting any of it."

"I'll tell Ma you wouldn't give me money for school things."

The man let the paper fall into his lap, pages slipping apart. "What is it really for?"

"Won't give me money when I need it for school." Eisy blew as big a bubble as he dared, bit into it, and threw a pellet at his father's foot. "She'll be mad when I tell—"

"You little bastard. Why are you asking me on a Saturday if it's for school?"

"Four bucks and I won't say anything. Not about what you already bought at the liquor store either." Eisy took a quick look to confirm his father was digging into his shirt pocket for the bills. "It's for a field trip Da."

"A field trip of your own. I know you're lying Chipper."

Eisy grinned and snapped a little bubble as he grabbed the money from his father's hand.

"You may be full of it now, but you're doing wrong." Samuel's words hung with the smell of stale cigarette smoke, draped themselves like a shawl over the shoulders of his worn sweater as the back door slammed shut.

Samuel folded the remaining bills into fourths and put them back into his pocket. He shook himself a cigarette from the pack on the armrest of the chair and lit it, inhaling slowly and deeply as he watched the ash grow, as the red ember worked its way up. Sass 'em all Chipper.

•  •  •  •  •

# CUZ

Eisy's my cousin. Everybody seems to know him. I mean they know who he is and think they know what he's about. Usually they blame him for things, is my observation. People forget we're related because they don't see us together much.

We compare notes, mostly in private. Eisy's the one who taught me how to learn by watching, showed me some of the best locations. Following him around was how I learned to look for what most people would be ashamed of, if they knew anyone was watching. It definitely helps to be a kid, but you still have to develop your own style.

People pay a lot of attention to Eisy, that's part of his style. They're so busy paying attention they don't notice all sorts of other things until it's too late. Which is why they always watch him and pretend like they're not. I think they're scared of him.

He enjoys the shaky way they watch him, looking and not looking. I read somewhere people always touch their money when they see somebody they think might be a thief. When I told Eisy he laughed and said, "People go for whatever they're hiding, that's for sure." Eisy wants them to know he saw. He likes it when they feel uneasy.

My style is more to stay on the edge of invisible. Besides, I'm a girl, so it's easier to be ignored. Eisy started teaching me when I was really little. By the time I was seven or eight, I had permission to follow him around. When Eisy and his gang-du-jour settled on a plan, I was first to get picked on, first to be ditched. By the time I was nine I'd learned to go invisible right before they made a plan. That way I could decide for myself if I wanted to tag along.

I learned more than eavesdropping, hanging out with them. Like about love. The way one person starts being all tuned in to somebody else. I didn't know for a long time how little of it was physical. Or that a person can love just about any other person, place, or thing, if they put their mind to it. The physiology of mating, I couldn't believe it at first. I was confused, and made the big mistake of saying the word love out loud.

It took Rancid shoving a whole stack of crude pictures in my face to shut me up. I guess I was following him too closely at the time. After he showed me I kept a good distance. His nickname was about the way he acted, not because he smelled or was dirty. Even Eisy got enough of Rancid sometimes.

Rancid did achieve something that summer. He eliminated both my tailgating and my TV-glazed ignorance. About a year later my mom took some time and tried to explain. She used gentler terms and wanted me to believe it was all a tender *thing, but it was too late. Rancid's interpretation had demonstrated itself to be mostly accurate. Mom's version was nice to think about, but it just doesn't happen that way very often. At least not around Raventon. I didn't think of asking her about her own experiences, until much later.*

• • • • •

# 006

Angie's walks took her all over, they patched time and space together in ambling fashion. The history of Angie's walks went like this. Her mother took her from when she could be bundled, and even before. Daddy confirmed this. After, without Momma, walking was a way for Angie to be in between. Which was where she liked to be, not quite here and not quite there. Angie walked the places Momma had taken her, or sent her, and she walked to avoid these; she trekked long distances to get away, and then she trudged back.

The physicality of her walking—one foot, the other, one and the other, low-grade concentration, total osmosis of ongoing motion. On long hauls she suffered strained knees and tired ankles, blisters like orange sections, callouses as thick as wood, skinned knees and bruises, varicose veins and coral-like fans of minuscule and permanent rupturing, a crick in her gait. When it was hot she sweated, her temples pounded, her face throbbed. In the winter her hands went numb and she picked up a deep chill. One day she slogged, discontented and disconnected, on another she bounded with ever-increasing joy.

She always covered ground. The geography of Angie's walks was by habit away from Raventon, toward the river, up the ridge. Sometimes she went on overnight trips, occasionally she hauled gear further, to pinnacles and lakes with names she ignored, sometimes she roamed the hollows and saddles, backtracked the places of in-between.

Her homeland held her, she was accustomed to its worn roofs, worn trails, worn stories and recitations, even her boots were worn into a kind of comfort. The call and chatter of birds, the sound of each car as it went by were identifiable. Angie and the town dogs and the smallest of half-asleep children could place each motion around them with their eyes closed. As close to infinite as she could know, her web of wandering and earnest transport cradled her. Angie savored it.

Hence perambulation as a holy word.

Making the rounds was what Angie called her in-town walks. She stayed in town sometimes to fight off loneliness, sourness. She did it sometimes to get away from the house and the store and Daddy and all of what swirled around and through her.

Angie made the rounds to show to others and prove to herself she could be like other people. She prepared by poking through her mind until she had a list of half-excuses and plausible if not urgent errands, then she headed out.

Afternoons and dinnertime were best. She took advantage of any human encounter, and if the right situation presented itself, the whole afternoon or evening could dwindle away. No one ever came by the house. Ever since Momma. And no one stopped by the store just to visit. After Angie came back to Raventon, she'd just about gone mad before she'd thought of making the rounds. In the decades since, she'd gotten good enough there was almost always someone to bump into.

The first few years after the Llamados moved to town, she made the rounds most weekends. She put on clean clothes, found a library book that needed returning, maybe checked in on Toots to see if he was done with whatever tool he'd borrowed. Carefully, she would circle past Jorge and Analisa's. If they were home, they invited her in. Angie used her walks to keep her mind off the tune which whistled keen and low: none of them needed her, few of them wanted her around.

• • • • •

# 007

"¡Salud!"

"¡Salud!"

Angie had spent the afternoon going over the papers with Jorge and Analisa. Cantoni, Raventon's smalltime land baron, had done them no favors, but Jorge had been vehement. Angie could review the terms, but she was not invited when he and the old man signed. So in addition to hefty monthly payments and a big chunk of money down, Jorge had agreed to provide Cantoni with four cords of wood before November first. But to look at Jorge, gleaming—not just his eyes, his whole self—no matter how rickety the house was, no matter how ridiculous the payments, today Jorge had cut his best deal ever. Angie was proud she'd had anything to do with it, and lonely it had so little to do with her.

Analisa finished pouring Pancho juice and they all clinked glasses. "To our new house."

"But Mom, it's not new."

No lie, thought Angie. In three years of renting they'd made it feel homey, but it was run down, hanging together in the slow-settled way of Raventon. No amount of cleanliness and bright paint could cover up the drafts, the faint odor of dry rot in the corners, worn patterns in the linoleum.

"It's new for us to be owning it." Jorge leaned back and smiled.

"¡Salud!" They all clinked glasses again, everyone clinking everyone else, giggling; the little bit of juice and red wine gone almost instantly.

Analisa excused herself and returned from the kitchen carrying a cake, red and orange crepe flowers around the edge of the platter, one big candle in the middle. Pancho blew it out. Jorge served, topped each slice with a huge scoop of Neapolitan ice cream. When all had been reduced to smeary puddles of goo, cake crumbs floating, when even Pancho'd had enough, Angie said her goodbyes and stepped outside into a sullen cold the spring hadn't driven off.

She overheard Jorge as she came to the edge of the porch, stars popping out of the twilight sky. "She needs her time alone."

Walking home, Angie thought to herself she'd had most of her fifty-four years to be alone.

When Daddy heard her in the kitchen he repositioned the book in his lap as though he hadn't been dozing. Put it down again when she started directly up the stairs. "Dairyland called, said you hadn't placed the order yet."

She stopped and the stair creaked under her. "I have until tomorrow morning at four."

"You're cutting things too close, Angeline. It's not my business to ask where you've been. But the store is."

"My whole life, I have never neglected the store and you know it."

He looked toward her, but not as though he saw her. "I heard Cantoni sold to those Mexicans and that you pressured him."

"That's a lie." She could see his watery eyes behind his glasses, his face drawn back like a hawk's.

"I know you had your finger in the pot. And that you didn't get the Dairyland order in this afternoon."

"Good night, Daddy."

"If those people need help there's plenty of government money, you don't have to help too."

Angie went up the stairs. Later she dreamed: Momma bringing in a birthday cake with crepe flowers, Daddy smiling. But Momma never quite made it to the table and her cake kept getting bigger.

The alarm went off at three-thirty. The house big and still, not even a crackle from the woodstove. Angie walked to the store under a small half moon, wisps of fog drifting in from the river. She called Dairyland before she made coffee, and worked on accounts until noon. Regulars knew immediately to be quick with their orders, they could tell it wasn't a good day to bother her.

• • • • •

# CUZ

You didn't have to be a genius to know Raventon was a going-going-gone kind of a place, in its gone stages. I mean, if you wanted a job or anything like that, it was obvious. The chipplant was an abandoned and moldering hulk. The geezers who spent their days arguing on the bench in front of the post office had a lot of theories about how it caught fire and why it was never rebuilt, but for as long as I have lived it was history. When we had the chipplant Raventon made its money from logging, and before that mining, but from what we heard nobody anywhere was prospering in a mining town or a logging town anymore.

The spring before the Sim was a very long time coming. We got a big blast of beautiful blue sky and sunshine and the snow started melting and everybody lightened up. Then bam, cold winds and low clouds and a good bit of winter came back and sat on us to the tune of about three feet of new snow. So we were all feeling a little raw, woodpiles drawn down, blown-around garbage frozen in place, too much time inside and too many bills, something always breaking. The men who'd been waiting for it to get warm enough to look around for work were in nasty moods, low on cigarette money and sick of each other and themselves. That spring taunted us with a glorious taste, then took its own sweet time in actually arriving.

There was a bigger kind of tension floating around too, maybe from so many people leaving for wherever, for whatever work they could get. Maybe it was the way rich people were coming over and setting up fake-rancheros on our side of the mountains, replete with a horse for the kids and a satellite for the TV, all posted "No Trespassing." There was this feeling that we were getting to be second rate in our own home. More was changing than was staying the same; sometimes we liked to talk about it, sometimes we liked to pretend.

That spring people were desperate, a little or a lot. Sniffing around, watching to see if anybody had something going, watching their own backsides at the same time. Ripe for the picking, is what I think now.

• • • • •

# 008

Morse came back to stay at the beginning of June.

Terminally lanky, knobby to his roots, grey as she was around the edges was what Angie spotted instantly. He had slipped into the store while she was waiting on a tourist couple who wanted gas and ice and snacks. Eventually he came forward with a box of crackers, a cheap six-pack, and a tub of cheese spread. In keeping with his stretched-out ways he dug in the front pocket of his jeans to come up with crumpled bills and change.

"Know anybody who needs help on a job?"

Angie sighed. "What kind of work are you looking for now, Morse?"

He smiled. "Good work. Most anything that doesn't require extreme skill, terms of payment negotiable."

"Can't think of anything in particular." She folded over the top of his sack and creased it. "You could put up a card."

"Don't have a phone yet. If you hear of anything, would you keep me in mind?"

Despite herself, Angie nodded.

"You look as swell as ever, Ang." He took the sack and ambled out the door.

Morse came in fairly regularly after that. He started getting jobs Rosco Popper was too busy for, hauled and split firewood, finished off a roof, replaced a clogged sewer line. Demonstrated himself once again to be reasonably reliable and highly capable. He bought food from the store on a need-to-eat basis: JoJos and burritos and rotisserie chicken, an occasional burger plate. Mornings, a cup of coffee and two or three doughnuts.

Angie told herself she expected nothing. That the past was past, and long ago. Morse didn't seem to have a girlfriend, didn't talk about his time away, skittered away from anything that approached the topic of himself. What little he recounted seemed outrageous and a bit strained at the edges. Maybe she was jealous.

A couple evenings a week he came in after work and stuck around. Drank a fair number of beers through the course of a night. He'd sit at the counter and ask her questions, catching up on the details of the time he'd been gone. Some nights when it was slow, they touched on bigger topics. Why one kind of people hated another, what money could and couldn't buy, how it felt to be up first and all alone in a good place, best conditions for viewing moonrise over Raventon. They acclimated to each other's current-day selves; or maybe it was only Angie who needed to ease into the present.

She got to where she looked forward to their chats. Catching sight of Morse perked her up, put a little edge onto whatever she happened to be doing. Angie could tell when he'd done laundry from which of his flannel shirts he was wearing, noticed when he got a new pair of jeans. They developed a routine, a banter between them, a way of setting each other up for a smile or a laugh, against her pledges of good judgment and years of silent vows.

When the rains came cold and regular, draping melancholy mist over the ridge, when what Momma had called tea-weather kicked in, that was when Morse put some money down on the old Todanovich place. It was tucked up at the edge of town with a beautiful view, but not much in the way of recent upkeep, its porch attached out of habit.

Angie'd caught word from Rosco Popper. He knew the house had sold and was pleased to have figured out to whom. Morse never told her directly, he just came in the next Saturday with a list, bathroom cleanser and light bulbs and such. When she teased him about becoming a home owner, he only shrugged. Which she took to mean don't ask. Morse did laugh when she blurted she might lend him the store truck for moving. "Everything I own fits in the back of that beast," he'd said, pointing with his thumb to the bottomed-out Chev he'd arrived in.

Angie thought she was adjusted to Morse's presence, so it caught her like a gut punch when he told her.

"And I'll be working on Jorge's foundation come spring." Morse was counting off work possibilities on his fingers.

"I didn't know they were even thinking about a foundation." She'd been over there two nights before, as cozy as pie, and hadn't heard a word.

"Well, seems like they decided. Jorge's been talking to me for awhile. Then today he asked what I'd charge and when I thought I could start."

Angie wished there was a rub in Morse's voice, that he meant to hurt her. But when she looked it was the same old Morse, taking a sip from his schooner. In only a few months he'd become everybody's confidant.

"Gonna be a bitch of a job." He grinned. "First thing I'll have to dig out the whole back of the house."

Angie kept quiet and to herself the rest of the evening, played like she was a little tired, wanted to think she was maybe getting a cold. Nobody, including Morse, took any notice. All of them cleared out early, the next day being another working day and all.

· · · · ·

# 009

---

Heir to Raventon's only bank, Minor Haynes ran down Railroad Avenue with a speed both tremendous and tremulous. He took off running, respectable adulthood fluttering like his tie, down the street he'd known all his life, and he disappeared around the first corner.

Eisy'd been sitting on the bench beside the Frog's Ears when the lights went off inside the bank. Minor and three others stepped outside, talking while Minor locked up. Eisy caught only snatches, and couldn't sneak closer without giving himself away. "I think you'll find Raventon more than pleased at this opportunity." That was from the mucky-muck bank officer whose appearances in Raventon precisely coincided with the days Minor wore his best suit. That jerkface Koalnivic, vice principal and weekend real estate salesman, laughed in his hyena way. "As much as Raventon can stand to show it's pleased about anything." The foursome shook hands all around. "We've got ourselves a winner," the unknown man had said, and slapped Minor on the shoulder. Then he and jerkface and the visiting banker drove off together while Minor stood in front of his bank, waving.

It was then he took off, heels kicking air as he sprinted. Eisy stayed hunkered down on the bench as the pounding steps faded, ever so slightly embarrassed for Minor. He should have known better than to run around all excited the minute he thought he was alone.

"I wouldn't have guessed him such a sprinter."

Eisy nodded, repositioned himself on the bench and hoped he hadn't actually jumped. Morse struck a match with one hand and lit a cigarette.

"Well, carry on. I'd invite you inside but I believe your youth and reputation precede you. Arrivederci." Morse turned and reentered the Frog's Ears.

"Asta-la-pasta," muttered Eisy under his breath, but he had to admit Morse had style for an old fart.

Angie used the squeak of the Frog's Ears' swinging door to cover her own footsteps, and circled the back way home.

• • • • •

---

"Who cares?" Morse accepted the beer Angie floated down the counter.

"I just wondered if you ever thought about Todanovich, now that you live in his house."

"I'm not a sentimentalist."

"What do you mean?"

"I don't get off on brooding, don't much like mucking around in the past. I've given up on that." He slurped the foam off his beer.

"Those who don't know the past are doomed to repeat it."

"Takes one to know one, is all I'm saying."

"One what?"

Morse rolled his eyes. "Takes a person who spends large portions of time living in her memories to spend a lot of time thinking about someone else's past."

"So what if I do?" Angie could hear the tartness in her own voice.

"So you do." Morse recrossed his legs. "I don't care myself. Just don't try and drag me in. I have my hands full living in the present."

Fuck you, she thought. "Here today, gone tomorrow you mean."

"Gone quite shortly, I do believe." He laid two dollars on the bar, next to his unfinished beer. "And a pleasant time was had by all."

"Last call." She said it loudly, although the only others were Waldo and Samuel.

Morse glanced at the clock before he could stop himself and slapped Waldo on the back. "Sorry I shortened your evening." He bowed as he turned from the bar. "Captain-may-I? I'm not playing Angie."

"Neither am I." Her words were barely audible.

Waldo took his cue and followed Morse out the door. Samuel remained, tuned into his own world.

Angie remembered while she washed glasses, mopped, swept. All the games she and Morse had played in the schoolyard as kids. She knew she'd been insufferable as captain, just as she knew Morse had cheated and had taught all the other kids to cheat too. Here today, gone tomorrow. Hide-and-go-seek; when it was Morse's turn to hide he used to disappear entirely. When it was his turn to seek he'd send them off and then never look. King-of-the-hill had been his game.

• • • • •

# 011

Angie remembered:

All of them lined up near the back fence of the ball field. Mr. Huree with his whistle around his neck, supervising. Morse was one captain and Julie Smuthers was the other. Angie knew Julie wouldn't pick her, no matter what, not even if it meant Julie had to be a whole team by herself. But Morse would, he was Angie's best friend. She didn't think until later making Morse a captain must have been one of Mr. Huree's little tests, to see if he could get Morse to care about winning.

Julie of course picked her little pet first, Katie Koalnivic. Angie stuck her tongue out at Julie when Huree wasn't looking. Morse picked Bobby Nelson, the best athlete in the school. Angie got quieter as those waiting with her against the cyclone fence diminished. The two lines, one behind Morse and one behind Julie, got longer.

Angie was last pick, Morse's very last pick. He hadn't even actually chosen her; everyone ran to play after Julie made her last pick and Angie was forced to run to catch up.

The next few times Angie was a captain she ignored Morse, but the other captain always took him right away, he was too good to ever be left. If anyone other than Julie and Morse had been captains, Angie would have been picked quickly, she knew that. She also knew the look Julie had given her just before they had all run off to play. She just never knew why Morse had left her that day. Any more than she knew why Morse had come back to Raventon.

• • • • •

# MegaCorp
# Incorporated

████████████████████████████████████████

CONTACT: LUCINDA CHATTERS
(206) 448-6071

FOR IMMEDIATE RELEASE

## Simulator Site Chosen

(Seattle, WA) MegaCorp Incorporated has chosen Raventon, Washington, as the location for its first fully commercial Simulator®, A Family Experience®. Gleed Overholt, MegaCorp's CEO and President, confirmed the purchase of a site adjacent to this small central Washington town, and predicts the Simulator®'s doors will open to the public next summer. "As we enter a new century MegaCorp is leading the way in family-oriented entertainment. Our Simulator® is a visionary breakthrough," said Mr. Overholt.

The Raventon Simulator® is the flagship of a fleet of franchised destination entertainment complexes MegaCorp plans to have in operation within ten years. Founded in 1987, Seattle-based MegaCorp is the developer and manufacturer of customized virtual reality systems.

A press conference with Mr. Overholt is scheduled at MegaCorp's headquarters in Seattle, June 10th.

For further information contact:
Lucinda Chatters
Office of the President, MegaCorp Incorporated

# 012

---

"What part of a press release don't you understand?"

Harold Hastings, FutureLabs' lead on the Simulator, kept his pounding head down while Gleed Overholt fumed.

"Jesus Harry, you knew this was coming. We've settled with that kid's family, that's history. You yourself just said there hasn't been a single incident since."

"It's just—we haven't compiled enough data yet. The Lab's been running as many Sims as we can, but it will be another few weeks at least before we're sure it can't happen again."

Overholt pulled the press release out of Harold's hands. "Do you know how much these goddamn lab-Sims are costing us?"

Harold knew exactly: $215.37 per minute of operational time, not including staff. He deduced Overholt didn't want to hear the answer.

"This is out." Overholt rattled the paper. "So you and your little project group are going to do what's necessary to get the FCC approval without a hitch. Do you understand, Harry?"

"Yes sir, Mr. Overholt." Harold stood and backed out of the conference room, furiously scratching the palm of his hand.

The misfunction involving the test subject had been predictable, if anyone in the lab had properly considered potential outcomes. Sooner or later some Sim-junkie would find a way to get the Sim to kick into overdrive. This particular poor soul had either mixed two Sims concurrently or tapped into what had been stored in another junkie's feedback history. Whatever he had done, he had been unable to adequately respond to the stimulus he'd triggered. What was really pathetic was the lab had no real data, just the huge instantaneous jumps in the victim's biofeedback. Worse, his flipout had been the first documentation that any kind of combinational Simming had been going on.

Harold knew everybody in FutureLabs considered the Sim-junkies losers, happy to go through the Sim whenever they got a call. The staff used them like glorified lab rats, ran them through the Sim protocols, the Experience patterns, never asked them anything that wasn't on the clipboard questionnaire. They were paid accordingly in satin jackets and recreational Sims, with as little cash as possible.

The Sim-junkies got their nickname from their hunger for Simming. Those who most craved the Sim tended to seek out oblivion or horror. Lab techs had deprogrammed these possibilities as quickly as they were generated, had denied some of the most obviously demented individuals access to further Sims, and meticulously tracked the Experience choices each Sim-junkie made.

But no one had hypothesized an Experience strong enough to drive a junkie into psychosis. When all the junkies were extensively interviewed after the misfunction, their consistent response was best summarized by an interview Harold had conducted with an eighteen year old male subject. "The Sim's just a glorified video game, so what's the big deal? You got one nut case. I'm doing my goddamn job, I go through the cowboy Sims, the nature bullshit, whenever you want, as much as you want. I signed the waiver, right? And we both know you're making beaucoup bucks off me. So back off." Only when threatened with expulsion would any of the Sim-junkies admit what they had been messing with: ways to streamline Sims so they got more time in their own fantasies, time to find a way to play off each other's Experiences.

Overholt had performed immediate and remarkably effective damage control: he personally visited with both the victim's girlfriend and his parents and made what must have been a quite enormous and definitely most private cash settlements. Hence no CNN coverage, no magazine expose, not even a mention in the scientific community. And to Overholt's credit, he shut everything down until the lab had a chance to reprogram the Sim. Of course, the pressure to get back up and running had been tremendous. Harold was concerned the statistical potential was still present, and significant, even if there had been no reoccurrence of the malfunction.

So what choice did he have but to continue directing FutureLab's research? There was a correlation greater than coincidental that the Sim generated dangerous stimulation. But if he left, who would be there to document, and if possible, correct the problems? And as far as a commercial Sim went, Overholt might be right. Perhaps it wouldn't happen again. That was the overwhelming probability, after all.

• • • • •

# 013

Even after Thanksgiving there had been little snow in Raventon, and less that stuck, leaving a nasty crust of ice. Cars and people on foot, arms full of dishes and wrapped surprises, made their precarious way over this one December evening, toward a small house with a big porch and a wreath on its front door. A piñata, either a donkey or a dog, was strung up on a scaffold in the side yard, swaying in the half-light from the windows of the house, and inside the living room window you could see a Christmas tree.

Analisa was relieved when people started arriving. Angie had promised her everyone would come, and come they did. By seven-thirty it was standing room only, both Analisa and Jorge talking to people they had only waved to in the past.

Pancho passed trays of snacks for as long as his mother was watching, then faded into the periphery. The windows steamed over, the first round of food on the table was replaced with a second, and a third; women Analisa knew from church helped her clear, washing dishes periodically. About nine she nudged Jorge, some of the little ones were about to get packed off; it was piñata time. That got lots of people outside, shivering with or without their coats, packed into a circle. Jorge picked Beto to go first and retired to operate the ropes, shouting directions, bobbing and dipping the piñata, just beyond his contestant's wildest strokes. Beto was more than a few beers into his swing, and serious, so the spectators had to jump out of his way. "Time's up."

Next was a little girl. Jorge let the rope way out and one of her timid pops actually connected. The kids went wild. It was one of Analisa's church group members who finally smashed it. Teenagers dug in the snow for the last tiny bits of candy. Beto took a playful swing at Jorge. Then the little girl who had first hit it came up and asked if it would be all right to have the head of the piñata. She carried it off like a dolly as some people drifted inside, others gathered their children, called their goodbyes, and headed home.

• • • • •

# 014

Pancho stayed inside to study Angie's father. It was clear he was irritated, it was clear he did not want to be in their house. He had spent the evening in the best armchair, ate almost nothing and talked mostly to other old people. When most of the visitors went outside for the piñata Pancho made his move. "Don't you like us?"

The old man stared at him but didn't say a word.

"Why did you come?"

"It's a party. I was invited."

"Are you invited to other peoples' parties?"

"Not very often. You're their boy?"

Pancho ate a pretzel from the bowl on the table.

"Of course you are." Alexander Mettle took a pretzel for himself. "Do you have a good slingshot?"

Pancho studied the old man. Sagging neck, big ears, brown spots on his hands, his pants fit him funny. Pancho shook his head.

"Come into the store then, when my daughter isn't around. There's one that doesn't get much use."

"You didn't have to come to our party."

"I'd like it if you came and got the slingshot."

"I will pretty soon."

Then the old man surprised him. He held out his hand.

Pancho shook.

• • • • •

# 015

Jorge insisted upon walking Angie's father home. After they left, Angie accepted a refill of rum punch from Morse, and savored a sip as she leaned against the doorjamb and looked out over the dwindling party.

"They really fixed this place up inside." Morse leaned against the wall.

"Yeah, it has a good feel to it."

"My place is getting kind of homey too."

Angie snuck a glance. "Are you offering holiday tours?"

"Sure."

Angie laughed. "Well, book me for the deluxe version."

"You want to take a look? Since you're so interested in it historically, and everything."

Angie couldn't read Morse's steady smirk. "Actually, I would."

"Let's go then." He grabbed his coat and was on his way out the door.

Angie looked around, but nobody in particular was watching. She found her jacket and stepped outside. The lining of her jacket was icy in the time it took to work her arms inside and zip up. Morse was waiting halfway down the sidewalk, huffing cloudlets. The snow was like Styrofoam, rigid and crunchy where it wasn't ice. The cold carried every noise clearly: a car growling its way home down the hill, their footsteps. A dog banished to its porch let out a small growl as they squeaked by, unwilling to further expose himself to the elements.

"Colder than a witch's tit about covers it tonight," Morse contributed.

"Cold enough to freeze the piss off a pecker," Angie added.

They both laughed.

"Snot-freezing cold."

"Likely to shit a popsicle out here."

They kept it going all the way to Morse's place, even up the hill. After stomping her boots on his porch, Angie followed Morse into a room that was only marginally warmer. She stayed just inside the door, watching him start a fire in the woodstove, looking around when he was too busy to notice. The newspaper roared, the tinder began to crackle. Morse latched the firebox door and they both stepped close to the stove, to where it would eventually be warm.

"Mother-fucking cold."

"Father-humping bitter cold."

Morse excused himself, went into the next room and returned with two blankets. Both had seen better days. He offered her one and draped the other over his own shoulders. "I'll give you the guided tour once I can feel my fingers again. You know who I think about in this house, is Unc. He lived here too you know?"

Angie nodded.

"He only came to visit our family about three times I can remember." Morse added kindling to the fire. "Once at my granddad's funeral. Just the funeral, not any of the other stuff that was going on. Another time he came to our house, talked with my Dad for a while, near the end of some big family dinner. Why I don't know. It was right before he moved in with Todanovich. He stopped by again when my sister was born. Visited Mom while she was in the hospital and left her a big box of candy. She was too sick to eat it."

"He never came over for holidays?"

Morse cocked his head and studied her without answering.

They both adjusted their blankets. Morse left the small circle of heat to grab a teakettle and tea-makings from the kitchen end of the room. "Unc was broke, but I didn't even know that until quite a bit after he died, when my Dad groused about how he'd had to pay for Unc's funeral and everything."

Angie thought of all sorts of questions: What would your Dad think about you living here, in Todanovich's house? Did you came back so you could live in this house? Are you going to stay around this time?

The fire built to a steady purr, the water began to boil. Morse made two mugs of tea.

"So are you glad you got this place?"

Morse shrugged.

Angie had to smile. "You don't know."

"Nope. For now, I'm here."

She shook her head and bit her tongue. Typical Morse. Come back, move into this house, offer her a tour, and then he couldn't even admit he liked being here.

"Did you ever talk with Unc?" Morse poured a mug and handed it to her.

"A couple times. He was an old man." Angie didn't feel like telling him the little she could remember. Unc had been one of many old timers who liked to talk to Daddy. Crippled up, he'd moved pretty slow, always wore smooth black lace-up boots, either overalls or work pants that he sawed off at the ankle. He came into the store once or twice a week, paid for his purchases out of a coin purse with a metal snap at the top.

He'd moved in with Todanovich in the wintertime. The two of them switched to deliveries, and it was her job to haul everything to their back door. She couldn't remember him as especially friendly or mean. Todanovich died, then a few years later so did Unc. Both had been buried in the old city part of the cemetery. After that the house had stayed empty. Angie opened the woodstove door and gave the coals a poke, then added a log.

Morse raised his eyebrows and let them down when she was finished. "Come on. I'll show you around." Two bedrooms and a bathroom was pretty much it.

When they came back to the stove the front room was almost warm. "Have a chair." Morse gestured toward the lumpy couch. Angie sat, blanket still around her, surprised when Morse flopped himself down next to her.

"Do you think your uncle would be glad you're here now?"

"Don't have a clue. Why are you so protective of Jorge and Analisa?"

She put her mug next to the lamp. "Thanks for the tour and the tea." She folded the blanket and laid it on the couch.

Morse pulled himself up. "Before you go. Certain rules of hospitality."

She looked at him for some clue but didn't get one. "See you."

Morse walked with her to the door, opened it, and kissed her full on the mouth. "There's mistletoe in the air." He grinned. "Good night friend."

The door shut behind Angie as she hunched into her jacket. His mouth had tasted faintly of tea and smoke, and Morse.

She was most of the way home before she noticed it was beginning to snow, flakes falling as light as dreams.

• • • • •

# CUZ

I watched. I saw Angie and Morse leave the party together and considered my options. Anything interesting would take a little time to develop, so I stuck around until Pancho's mom told Eisy and me she thought it was time to head home. Eisy headed downtown, a little wobbly from his surreptitious sipping from the adult punchbowl. I walked two blocks toward my house, then doubled back. As I saw all the lights were on at Morse's, I knew it would be worth hanging around. I couldn't see much because of his curtains, but I did see them both walk past the front door, draped in blankets. That got me to hunker down near the corner of his porch. I was freezing, and trying to tell if it was beginning to snow or just so cold my breath was condensing, when the door opened and out came Tía Angie. Morse was right behind her, with a kiss. Lucky for me she was mightily preoccupied coming down the stairs. And luckier still, Morse didn't linger outside. Usually his radar spotted anybody nearby, he was sharper than everybody but maybe Eisy. So I had to figure his distraction into my overall observations of the situation.

I kept motionless, ducked down in his bushes, for what seemed like forever. I could even hear the first snowflakes hit the nylon of my jacket. When I was completely frozen and had no choice but to move, I tippy-toed a full block, then ran like the littlest piggy, all the way home.

• • • • •

# 016

Colder seeped colder. The cloudy sky stayed a low thing, mirroring the few lights still on around town. A few flakes at a time drifted down, not particularly big or well-shaped, not enough at first to cover the hood of a car, too cold to stick to tree branches or power lines. They fell in random fashion until the last lights went out, all except Angie's, left blazing while she stumbled into sleep.

Somewhere in that cold and quiet the temperature rose as the air thickened, a wall of falling snow. Each flake took its own sweet time. Individual objects lost their distinction. Animals outdoors took notice; mice and squirrels burrowed in closer to whatever kept the snow off, dogs and cats scratched mercilessly to be let in. Humans who crawled out of bed to pee or add a log to the fire took note of the deep snow, knew they would have to shovel when it was morning, and went back to the warmth of their beds. So much snow added a glow, a lightness with no color to it.

It didn't stop, not until an hour after the sun had officially and statistically risen. The store thermometer showed 18° Fahrenheit. The flakes made themselves fewer, but they got fancier, six-sided wonders adding their final fluff to the general whiteness. The snow stopped as approximately as it had begun, with a few lingering flakes.

Low grey clouds rose and turned a harder white. Bright enough it hurt to look around, a patch of blue over the ridge. Raggedy fringes of fir branches, the siding of buildings, the bark of trees, that was all that was not snow. Even the jays took some time to find their way out, then squawked, flitting from branch to branch, screeching in irritation as their every move dropped snow, mostly on themselves. The sun blasted suddenly brilliant on a world of diamond white.

The Christmas Storm, the Big Dump. Even as they climbed out of their beds for a first look, the humans of Raventon knew this was an epic snow.

•  •  •  •  •

# 017

At two, Angie ate in snatches, between customers. This constituted both her breakfast and lunch, and the way it was going, dinner too. She'd gotten the pumps and the woodpile plowed out just before ten with both generators up and running almost an hour before that. It had been chaos since she'd woken up, everybody and their brother coming by to see if they could help, jabbering about the snow and since they were there and it was warm and everything, maybe they would have a cup of coffee or a doughnut or a candy bar before they tunneled their way back to wherever they'd come from.

Lizzie Blacksoe was on the grill cranking out orders at record speed and volume, she'd brought over the unsolicited burger plate when she saw Angie would be inside for at least a few minutes. Every shovel and battery and pair of gloves, all the milk and bread and anything you could eat without cooking was already gone. The crowd was shifting from the curious into those stranded or needy, anybody with a shovel madly digging out, only to realize there was no place to go.

The door opened for the millionth time and yet another bundled figure made its way in, doing its part to keep the store at around forty-five degrees no matter how Angie stoked the stove. She recognized Morse's frosted eyebrows above the scarf and sighed through her mouthful. He made a great show of stomping and brushing off for the pretty much captive audience, dumping snow inside the store of course. Angie ducked behind the curtain into the backroom, telling herself she suddenly needed to get the orders together.

It had been no big deal, she told herself. If the kiss meant anything to Morse, that would be the surprise. She saw nothing that was worth the effort to move out front, took a deep breath and went back out, to her place at the counter.

Morse was there and waiting, with a smile. "Morning."

"Afternoon, actually." She took a bite from her burger and rang up a dusty deck of cards for one of the Nelson twins.

"Angie?"

"Yep." The last of the toilet paper and the ketchup went to Toots' daughter and her five kids. Angie straightened the bills and shut the till with her belly.

"I was wondering if I could use the plow for a bit. Thought I might help the boys get the road open."

"When have you ever run a plow?"

"Never. That's what makes this such a golden opportunity."

Angie took her plate to the sink. Everybody in the store was all ears. No one, no one but Angie ever drove the plow.

Morse waited at the counter, unfazed, small puddles forming at his elbows. "Dream on."

"I've been dreaming since last night."

Angie lined her face up with Morse's and looked.

He had a smile but it wasn't mocking. "OK, no plow. How about your big shovel?"

Angie put her head into her hand and rubbed her eyes and forehead and nodded.

Morse slapped the counter. "Thanks. I'll pay you for the candy bars later." He pocketed two, and blew her a kiss. "Thank you dahling."

Leaving even Cantoni smiling and shaking his head. Morse exited the store whistling, *"a kiss is still a kiss, a sigh is just a sigh..."*

• • • • •

# CUZ

The Simulator was coming, the Sim was coming, it was really coming to Raventon. Word spread like a virus over the telephone lines, over shared pitchers of beer, as we waited in the store and the post office. We all speculated aloud, pontificated and pretended we knew what it was, we dreamed and conjectured in silence. Construction would begin as soon as the snow melted. We recalculated our futures and our mortgages, and most of all we waited to see who would get hired.

The blunt and sometimes bitter way we got along, especially during the long chill of spring-might-never-come February and early March, combined with an actual and approved building permit, sprouted a fever of hope. Big cars, clean new cars came to town. They parked in front of a once empty storefront MegaCorp rented from Cantoni; its windows were tastefully screened to keep what went on inside from our prying eyes. So instead we kept careful tally of the arrivals and departures of the anointed: Minor Haynes and his-out-of-town bank bosses; Arnie Blacksoe, former manager of the defunct chipplant; other men who had demonstrated their commitment to work, who had their own heavy equipment and debts. We picked their brains, poked the most casual of observations from their wives and children, and prayed what was coming would be bountiful.

I did research. I found out everything I could on MegaCorp and the Sim, then passed the more amusing bits off as a school science project, none too well received. There had been a prototype, which received little mention and almost no press. I found only one picture, a cross between the old golden-arches style McDonald's and George Jetson's cartoon house. For some reason it reminded me of an abandoned spa we drove by once, a huge brick manse crumbling into the sagebrush amidst steaming pools of lily pads.

Information was rather skinny on the entire process of getting the Simulator into commercial production. They built this prototype, which seated twenty, hired test subjects, and ran them through. Technical papers indicated there were problems with Experience consistency, one person's dreams being another person's nightmares. Also, it became clear a certain small but definitive percentage of test subjects had seizures when Simming. So MegaCorp's own lawyers demanded user pre-profiling. There was quite a flurry of equipment failure as well. The FCC went along with MegaCorp's program throughout, changed a preliminary investigation into a cautionary report. Meantime and always MegaCorp worked with the Defense Department, gave away flight and battle Simulators, built specialized testing units to screen applicants. And *after a lot of lab work in a very short time, MegaCorp was ready to go commercial. They found just the site they needed too, right in their own backyard.*

*Location, location, location.*

*Our town. Raventon. Funny where demographics will get you, that analysis of little things. God being in the details, or maybe it is hell, all these little things and how they add up. A photo, a burning ember, a nuance; the clues to what will follow as clear as a newborn's face. But we cannot discern the future visage within the cherubic smile, we cannot foresee what we will know so well, what we later know by heart, and memory. Until it is too late.*

• • • • •

# 018

Staunch crocus, hardy daffodil, and steadfast tulip, all perform their long-awaited miracles. Grass gleams green, first dandelion, and spring is sprung. When there was more mud than snow even in the shadows Morse reviewed plans for Analisa and Jorge's new foundation. When cherry blossoms plastered the streets and the ground crumbled with wormy promise Morse started digging.

Days it rained steadily he stayed home with a heating pad on his back. He could have made almost triple money working on the Sim, but he had made a promise to Jorge months ago. Sim subcontractors were scrambling for bodies, and it got clearer by the workday the real money this summer would come from the Sim.

Instead Morse worked on the foundation every day, weather permitting. Analisa fixed him lunch. Pancho observed. He started out poking around the yard, then scooted closer, eventually squatting near enough to hand Morse tools as needed. Jorge helped when he could.

The two men spent most of a weekend in the damp-walled ditch Morse'd dug to stack cribbing, weaseled in between wooden beams and the edge of the house. Jorge told Morse he'd gotten offered a new job, one he could not refuse.

"No such thing." Morse winced as he freed his finger from behind a concrete block.

"Yeah, well... maybe not for you. But for me, a big improvement."

Turned out his landlord, Cantoni, had put in a good word for him. Cantoni suggested Jorge to Bobby Nelson, who had already talked his wife's family, the Koalnivics, into bidding on more Sim work than they could handle. So Jorge was hired on for the summer at least. "What could be better?" he grunted as he pumped on the jack in front of his face.

Morse shrugged and kept shoving at a four-by-four.

"Things are looking up my friend."

"That's because we got our faces underground. Are we plumb?"

Jorge laughed and nodded and spit out a bit of dirt.

As children on purring bicycles schemed tree fort additions and a new rope swing over the river, Analisa opened windows and clothes-pinned a load of clean laundry outside. Tía Angie came by with another hydraulic jack, commended the bracing already laid in, offered pointers on what should be done next, and forced herself to greet Morse civilly. The sound of Jorge's jack ratcheting seemed loud against Morse's barbed and brief response. Angie took the hint and made arrangements for another time with Analisa, then continued on her rounds.

Once both the back corners were level Morse called it quits for the day; they needed to give the house a chance to catch up anyway.

Analisa was taking laundry off the line when Jorge pinched her, tugging at her blouse and teasing until she laughed and came inside. Behind a quickly closed door they made love on a pile of sheets scented with wind and sun and soap, together they watched a lazy cloud drift past the branches of their pear tree.

Pancho wandered home at dusk. He and Jorge toured the back of the house, admiring the cribbing. Jorge dared his son to climb on it to the back door, and started to follow him. But in his rush his boot slipped and Jorge slammed onto a pyramid of excavated dirt.

Pancho snickered from the back doorway. When Jorge laughed, Pancho jumped down, pointing and laughing from just beyond Jorge's reach. Then he helped his father brush off the dirt, letting Jorge run his hand across the side of his head and for a moment Pancho ducked in closer to Jorge.

His son, his house, the woman he loves, his wife.

Currants blossom like blood; summer fulminates. All green things become greener against the damp soil. In the woods lurk the last avalanche lilies and the first trillium, lupine spurt silvery leaves and indigo flowers, balsam root blossom so thick the hillsides seem yellow; the world is green and haunting with its promise.

"What do you think we start a tribe" Jorge whispered to Analisa when they were finally in bed. She tensed. His arms remained around her, but she had retreated to the place inside herself where he was never allowed.

And he couldn't say anything more. He had no grand and particular plan. But he could feel good times ahead for them; she was wrong to think they'd used up their luck.

• • • • •

# 019

Jorge was enjoying a beer on his own porch, glorying in his first overtime bonus as Analisa finished getting dinner together. Pancho sat before him on the steps. Jorge, full of his own good cheer, called to him from the doorway. "Cisco, what you watching?"

Pancho didn't answer. His habit of looking down or away angered Jorge. "What's so special about the floor Frisco? What makes your plate more interesting than your mother's face?" Jorge mocked the boy when it was just the three of them, but nothing he said could elicit more than a flickering glance.

If Jorge hadn't been in the mood for talking, from drinking, he might have let it go. Instead, Analisa heard the irritation in his voice. The warning. "Son, I am talking to you."

Analisa went to the doorway in time to see Jorge step in front of Pancho, beer can in hand. He said something else to Pancho, she never heard exactly what; she saw their son shrug his shoulders and scoot almost imperceptibly away from Jorge along the stair.

As fast as spilt milk Jorge slapped Pancho. "When I ask you answer."

"I ain't looking at nothing." Pancho kept his eyes on the ground, focused close to his father's feet.

Some kind of pause completed itself and Pancho came inside, his amazing eyes still down.

Jorge pretended to study the view, looked out over town.

Analisa studied his back. Smelled dinner getting too hot and returned to the kitchen.

Pancho came to the table when she called him. He watched his plate, his food, the dishes she handed him. Jorge said as little as his son until they were finished, then laid aside his napkin. "I'm going out."

The screen door whooshed behind him.

"May I be excused please?"

"Panchito, you need to understand. Your father, he wants you to be proud, he's—" Speaking to the top of her son's head. "He wants to be close to you."

Pancho sat unmoving.

"Yes, after you clear."

He left Analisa at the empty table.

Jorge bought a six-pack from Angie and went down by the river. Water

38

twisted around tree roots, rocks on the bottom rattled slowly. Serpentine twirls of black-green water, smelling of marsh and fish, reflected twilight sky.

Jorge dreamed that night.

He was playing basketball and this game, he had to win. He kept getting passed the ball. He would stop dribbling for a minute to look around, to pass. But then he couldn't run anymore without traveling. And everybody was blocking him, nobody was open. He twisted and feinted, tried to keep the ball free until he could see what to do, but hands were reaching in from everywhere. He woke, sheets twisted around his sweaty arms and legs, and thought he heard the river, although it was way too far away.

• • • • •

# 020

---

Eisy'd seen it.

He'd been working his way up the hill to Pancho's, knowing better than to think he could get himself invited to dinner. Knowing from the clockwork of Pancho's life there was maybe a half hour before Pancho would get called in. Sure enough, Pancho was sitting on his front steps, zoned out. Eisy cut left immediately, between houses, pretty sure Pancho was too preoccupied to have noticed him. That was the tricky part about Pancho though, you never knew for sure what he was watching.

Eisy stashed his bike in the alley and crouched by the fence, trying to pick the precise bolt-from-the-blue maneuver he would attempt, all ready to pounce, when Pancho's dad came out the front door, behind Pancho. So Eisy paused for station identification, in case Pancho's dad was in one of his less than cheerful moods.

"What chu watchin'?" Beer in hand, friendly as pie, he walked around Pancho. "I'm talking to you."

Then he smacked Pancho.

Eisy scooted backward soundlessly, made sure he was behind adequate brush. Pancho's father said something more.

Pancho stayed where he was, head down, like nothing had happened. His mom was in the doorway; she must have seen it too, but all she did was stand there.

Eisy didn't dare move. Pancho's mom went inside, Pancho followed her. A little bit later Pancho's dad, with his beer, went inside too. Eisy stayed where he was for a good long time before he snuck to his bike.

And he never so much as mentioned anything he'd seen to Pancho. He studied Pancho's face the next morning, but couldn't see any mark he was sure of. So why? Pancho hadn't been trying to provoke his dad. His father must have known how Pancho was; everybody else did. The worst was Pancho's mom, her just watching. Go figure, was what Eisy thought.

• • • • •

# 021

One week later it was Analisa who proposed the specifics. Jorge knew as soon as she spoke it was as powerful as their wedding vows had ever been. The agreement: they would no longer demand from each other the full terms of marriage. "We need to undo our marriage. Between ourselves." The church would not be involved, nor would Pancho. Anything more than household responsibilities would have to be specifically negotiated.

Out of the endlessly murky braid and twist of their love and their desire and the history of what they together had been through and borne, the agreement stood out like a skyscraper in the middle of a field.

Jorge was at first relieved for anything with some truth between them; he came to resent it for being true. He loved Analisa for her quietly bullheaded and desperate way of knowing so well what she needed, he hated her knowledge of the part of him that brought this decision about.

Soon the agreement took on the same muddiness as everything else between them. But the-words-spoken-between-them had given Analisa some strength and she surprised even herself with her suggestion. "We need to do something that will make it clear."

"How do you mean?" Jorge knew everything but the exact mechanics of her suggestion.

"One thing we could do is melt our rings. Or throw them away."

"But I want to be married to you."

Now Analisa waited.

In some soap opera he would have said "Is this what you really want?" and she would have broken down and everything would have been good between them just in time for a commercial. But in this life, the only life they knew, Jorge felt like a spider trapped in the sink, sides too slippery, too steep. He could never quite climb out, didn't have the right words ready. Didn't even know the words that might help if he had the courage to say them out loud.

Analisa waited a little longer. "Let's put them away then." And slid hers off.

Down came the splash, and washed the spider out.

• • • • •

41

# 022

When Analisa was sixteen she tried hard when her teachers asked. She had plans for herself after high school, probably a job at first, until the right boy came along, which he hadn't. Then married, with a nice house, and children, but not too soon. Analisa and her girlfriends had been practicing, pining away after imaginary boys.

It scared her, how much she wanted sex. And how little the boys showed respect, how they played one girl against another, then came strutting after someone new. Her family was strict, she was wary. She was sixteen, some of her girlfriends were practically married. Two dropped out of school with babies. Meantime the teachers made it clear: nothing was going to change for any of them, they didn't need to bother dreaming. With a lot of work they could maybe avoid fieldwork, but look at their brothers and sisters, their undone homework, listen to them talking Spanish all the time.

Then Jorge entered her world. Cocky. He was older by two years. Not very big but wiry, half Anglo, always preening. In front of the whole giggling group of girls, in broad daylight, he got her best friend to kiss him. A week later he asked Analisa for a date. Her girlfriend said she didn't care, then wouldn't talk to Analisa for a month. Jorge was rude when Analisa only let him kiss and touch a little. Made fun of her for being so cold. "Are you saving yourself?"

She tried to counter. "You aren't exactly the lifeboat I'm looking for, as far as saving goes." She wept when she got home, wept quietly because there were big ears in the house.

Analisa couldn't help it, she still watched for him all the time. Not because she liked him. He was watching her too. Because at the next football game, while everybody was hanging around the concession stand, he spoke to her politely. "How you doing?"

She couldn't think of anything clever, not so quickly, so she shrugged. She and her girlfriends started the walk home, then he came up to her, asked if she'd like a ride.

He chewed his lip, rubbed his chin with his shoulder. "I won't bug you. I just want to give you a ride."

Her heart, it was pounding.

He drove her straight home, reached across, opened her door. "You want to maybe go to a movie, tomorrow?"

He still hit on her when they were alone, but he stopped when she gave him the signal. He was going to graduate in the spring, he had serious thoughts. They spent more time together. One night, after they drove around, they found themselves hot and wordless; she was scared but he had protection.

When he dropped her off she was positive everybody could tell, but how? If she said anything, even to her best friend, she would be a slut, that was all she knew for sure.

Jorge barely talked to her the rest of that long week and she went crazy, nuts; he was going to go around bragging, and she had been thinking this was love? Then he came by for her, on Friday. Told her his feelings had scared him bad. Her feelings frightened her just as much, but she never said a word.

• • • • •

# 023

Just like they had all warned her.

It had been two months no matter how Analisa counted. She never thought she'd be wishing for her period, hoping all the time for cramps, looking forward to tampons. A month ago she'd told herself she just wasn't counting right, she couldn't remember. But ever since she'd been waiting. It had been six weeks, and more. Eight weeks she could be sure of.

• • • • •

# 024

The wedding, the wedding, the wedding. Analisa thought she would throw up if she heard another word about it. And here was Jorge on the arbor swing beside her, acting like they'd never sat together before.

"How are you feeling, Ana?"

"Swell." How was she feeling? They were getting married, she was going to have a baby, there didn't seem to be many other plans. But there would be no tears, not in front of anyone. She was fine because this was what she had wanted, to marry. Till death do us part. The words were already laid out and waiting, all she had to do was say them.

"Ana? Are you still getting sick?"

"Not so much." And what if she was? She'd learned to muffle the sound of her puking. No one at home was curious.

Now it was her turn to ask, back and forth, like some stupid card game. "How is work?"

"OK I guess." He took her hand out of her lap, stroked her fingers gently. "Are you happy about what we're doing?"

Analisa laughed. She cut if off before it took flight, because none of this was funny. It was because they messed around, because she was going to have a baby. "Don't I seem happy?" Better not to think if Jorge would be here right now if there weren't a wiggle of life growing inside her.

"Not to me. Ana, you have to let me know if this is a good thing." His hands held onto hers tight, his face drawn, he shifted around so they could see each other, even when she ducked her head down, down further. "I'm scared. Do you hate me?"

No tears, no matter what. And she should answer right away. "I'm not sure, Jorge." He put his arms around her and she let him, but she wouldn't look him in the face, especially not the eyes.

She felt a drop. He was crying. In the arbor, engaged, to be married.

Jorge paid for their rings using every penny he had and a hundred dollars he'd borrowed from his father. Once she looked at the jewelry store display she'd wanted these as much as any, as plain as they were. She'd wanted nothing that could be seen upon her as a sign.

They had worn them privately before they gave them to each other in the church. That had been her idea too. After they were married, she read aloud to him how a movie star said wearing nothing but a wedding ring was the sexiest. Jorge blushed.

Do you? And do you? They both said yes.

· · · · ·

# 025

Analisa said some more about the agreement. They would put the rings in her jewelry box, then see.

It was like a death. They both mourned. Some kind of joy they had only gotten a little taste of was being buried in the back of that velvet box, and neither of them had a way to get it back.

• • • • •

# CUZ

Slats of wood, lettered and numbered, were laced with day-glo plastic that fluttered in the breeze; our hearts fluttered with opportunity as surveyors pegged the seventy-five acres across the river, site of the Sim-forthcoming.

Seventy-five acres with an option on two hundred more, MegaCorp's supervisors hired locals for clearing and grading. The sound of chainsaws and the smoke of slashpiles returned to Raventon, floated across the river in the first balmy breeze. Then came other sounds, in snatches: bulldozers' and graders' throaty grumbling, huge dump trucks and the raucous rattling of their spewed loads of gravel. We all biked over after school to watch. Those of us who could linger avoided the last workers and climbed piles of slash, shimmied over the newly graded roadbeds, scrambled into the operator seats of the big machines, and dared each other to push buttons, to pull levers.

It was past spring but not yet summer, a time to suspend the darkness of doubt and previous misfortune, throw caution to the sweet and alluring breezes. Infectious vigor, addictive optimism, dare we dream? A round for everyone, first paychecks popped open like the buds of leafy trees. We had learned in and of this place, that this fervor could not last, we had learned to celebrate when we could.

Spring hatched into summer, cracked into feverish heat. An outside crew had been hired for the big construction, but there was plenty of work for those of our men willing and able. Work and pay, one thing to be done and another, show up with tools and hustle.

Nailguns rat-a-tat-tatting replaced the more solitary rapping of the piliated. The river was no longer out of the way, it was even a bit of an obstacle, with Raventon on this side, and the Sim-to-be on the other. The shake and bang of bridge traffic was a commonplace chorus, dawn to dusk, truck axle by truck axle; the binary chatter of the internet came to town then and was deafening.

We fell asleep exhausted, thrilled for the next day to come. Our parents dreamt mythic dreams: Boeing and Nike and Microsoft had started in small ways, with funny ideas, just across the mountains; Raventon was only a mountain pass away from such possibility. We children dreamt of big houses and computer games and fancy tennis shoes. We had been waiting, it seemed, all our lives.

• • • • •

---

Eisy, Cuz, Rancid, and Pancho were eating their recent candy purchases as they came around the corner of the path to the chipplant, thinking they might smash the empty bottles that always appeared, or scratch graffiti onto the remaining wall, or come up with something better to do once they were there.

A woman they had never seen before was sitting on one of the creosoted logs in the parking lot. Her brownish-purple hair fluffed when the wind gusted. She was sideways to them and oblivious, studying the ridge, then doing something on a big sketchpad on her lap.

Cuz was ready to step right up and take a look. Rancid wanted to sneak up close and pitch pinecones. Eisy commanded them to shut up before they were discovered, while Pancho finished his candy bar and pointed.

A man had appeared from around the side of the chipplant.

Eisy led the foursome as they ducked behind the nearest rise.

The man stood near the woman as she continued to draw, looking up the ridge with her, then strolled the service road around the other side of the hulk of a building.

The woman was too old to be a student, had fancy hiking boots but old jeans, and looked like she could sit and draw for the rest of her life.

"Bor-ing." Rancid kicked his heel into the ground, scraping a trough the width of his shoe.

"Shut up." Eisy was about to issue another command, for what he wasn't sure, when the woman flipped her sketchpad closed and jammed it into a backpack at her feet. "Rudy?" She stood, stretched, and followed the service road out of sight. The back of her jacket had a black Cat-in-the-Hat outlined in little white buttons on a big red square.

"Post-punksta." Rancid got up, hitched his pants, and headed toward her unattended pack, Cuz on his heels. Pancho moved to the top of the knoll; Eisy surveyed the situation and flopped down beside him, listening to the graders grind and beep from across the river.

The couple reappeared before Rancid was actually poking through her pack. They had been holding hands but let go when they saw Rancid and Cuz. Cuz just kept walking on the road, right on past, like she was on some crowded boardwalk. Rancid's head bounced around from the couple to the pack to Eisy, then he scooted to catch up with Cuz as she traipsed past the chipplant and into the woods.

The man and woman turned to watch them, spotted Eisy and Pancho, and the woman laughed as she swung her pack over one shoulder. Rudy kicked at rubble, hands in his pockets, not quite ready to leave.

"He's more than irritated."

Pancho nodded at Eisy's commentary. "I would have liked to see her picture."

Dorth stared at her painting of Raventon: narrow steep-roofed houses and sheds cramped together against a bowled hillside of dark woods, in the right foreground the funky general store. Spots of color—red metal roofs, blossoming wild rose, dandelions by the gas pumps, the glint off a puddle. A slight cant toward the center of the canvas in the buildings, to the dirt roads between them, in the trees along the top of the ridgeline. The oil paints were thick and mostly dark, her brushstrokes slightly choppy, the sun a Van Gogh ball cockeyed in the sky. It needed something, but what? It was too close to cute as it was, too close to finished for anything but the right detail.

She tried to remember what she'd glimpsed that had made her want to stop in the first place. She grabbed her sketchbook and flipped through sketches from that car trip and others she and Rudy had taken. She stared at a pastel's grey sky. Fir brooding rich green, smatterings of pale and water-striped sandstone in another, one monolithic pine trunk sucking golden light into its scaled bark. She and Rudy had picnicked on a lobe of that sandstone a little way up the hills behind town.

So many times she'd watched small towns out the window, rambled through tiny stores wherever they stopped, made small talk with waitresses and gas station attendants, then wandered until Rudy got bored with her halting explorations. Looking at this painting, she felt like she felt when they had to get into the car and drive home.

Dorth heard Rudy pull up between the garage and the house and swore. She tossed the sketchbook down, knew it was her own fault she was quitting for the day. Sunlight and heat and the smells from the garden blinded and baffled her as she stepped out of the garage-studio; the world was always shocking after several hours in a windowless room.

Rudy gave her a kiss and followed her into the house, dropped his briefcase, and hung up his jacket.

"You don't happen to have any ideas about dinner, do you?" Dorth's legs ached, her eyes burned.

Rudy plopped into the good chair. "Not really. What about a pizza?" All he wanted was to flip on the news and decompress.

"We had that last night." Dorth dropped onto the couch and kept talking, autopilot, so much nothing even as she spewed it forth. She cut herself off when Rudy did his uh-huh, uh-huh routine in response.

She shut up and he flipped on the news. All the maybes and why-nots and not-quites of the show she had to have up in less than a week were bogging her down.

Because something of what she was trying for would disappear if she hung her new work too soon. And because this same new work came closer to what would sell, had that quality of titillation, of the "raw" that kept the gallery crowd talking. And Dorth knew she would be sorry if she let this talk start before she was solid as a rock inside, before she had moved to the next place in her painting.

• • • • •

---

Two of Dorth's new paintings went into her show, neither of them the portrait of Raventon. Her first interview was with the yuppie weekly three days before the opening. The reporter, having arrived exactly on time, was waiting for Dorth at the gallery, and seemed incredibly young. Her outfit alone was worth the appointment, patent-leather storm boots, a black silk skirt slit to the hip, faux waif makeup and hair. She whipped out some little module of a computer in addition to her tape recorder. Clariche, the gallery owner, made introductions, and the interview rolled.

It was all Dorth could do to remember she was the subject as the young woman asked pointed questions about influences and intention and what she called the somber tonality of Dorth's work. Then she packed away her equipment, made some off-hand remarks about the Seattle art scene to Clariche, and left. Her review ran within a week, with a small photo of one painting, muddy and inarticulate in newsprint reproduction.

The second and final interview was little more than a sound bite for public radio. Dorth wished she were more glib; it was over before she'd said much. Come see it for yourself was all she had really wanted to say; let me know what you see.

Her show closed at the end of the month. She'd sold four and had several offers on one new painting, clearly labeled "not for sale." It was a self-portrait with none of her body parts connected, each of them doing responsible things while her heart just hung there, near the middle, **Disjointed**.

After the show Dorth went to work with a vengeance. Clariche said she might be able to move one more of the older paintings, but also said in the same breath (and she was the breathless sort) if Dorth had any more new work, well then, please bring it in. As though painting were target practice: load up your easel and aim for the bullseye. Dorth thought it was more like trying to be in the right place at the right time, ready to make your move, hoping what you were hunting chose to cooperate, and that you were prepared to take a clean shot.

At least Dorth had cash from what sold. Minus, of course, Clariche's commission. She also had news she'd been selected for a small solo exhibit at the big art fair in Spokane, come September.

Dorth decided she wanted to paint the woman she thought of as Such-a-One, a patroness of the arts. A portrait of the real woman. There was a so-called rustic artist who painted huge canvasses with little cartoons all around the main figure, each tiny scene an incident in the figure's life. Dorth wanted to somehow get the little pictures incorporated into the main portrait. Such-a-One was the perfect subject because she was so smooth in her vicious ways. Another painter called her the viper; human would be a better animal category for her sly and insidiously selfish ways. The treachery Dorth observed was mostly between Such-A-One and other women, but that didn't mean there wasn't an active sexual allure to her. Such-a-One didn't quite have the animal hypnotism of a big snake but the analogy—seamless and lithe motion, attracting and enticing, slithering until the instantaneous and venomous strike—this rang true.

So Dorth revealed herself, to herself, as equally insidious. She called Such-a-One and asked her to come over and pose. Dorth made the necessary remarks, extending a general invitation to "sit." Then cleared her studio of all new work. On the agreed upon day Such-a-One's pose was selected for its ease, its psuedo-simplicity.

Dorth adjusted the space heater and did several quick studies in charcoal. One was of the woman's actual features and gestures, the way she repositioned herself, the way she lifted her head. Then a gouache, non-figurative, trying to capture the aura that radiated from Such-a-One's well-modulated voice and fluid hand motions, a lurking power that contradicted her new-speak of sensitivity. And Such-a-One kept talking, nonstop, until they called it a session.

Dorth paid. Not in dollars, that would have been beyond crass, and Such-a-One had class. She paid with her small talk during the session, she paid in having asked the favor. But more than anything, she paid when Such-a-One looked around the studio. And paid again when the grand dame chattered and gossiped about their morning together.

• • • • •

# CUZ

By late April security on the Sim-site became ever-present. Even with Eisy leading us, we were run off no matter when we tried to explore. A crew of twenty electricians came over from Seattle almost before the roof was on, and they stayed, long after the HVAC techs and the sheetrockers and even the carpet installers had come and gone. Every possible bit of room around Raventon was rented. Nights, downtown was filled with men I'd never seen before. Cantoni raised our rent May first, and my mom knew she had to pay whatever he charged, and on time.

Practically everybody put in applications at the Sim, each and every one was kept on file. About the time they laid sod, calls went out. Many were interviewed, a very few hired. Word on the street was there would be a skeleton crew for starters. But those chosen few, after their meetings and trainings, walked out of the Sim office with a bounce in their step and a knowing look in their eye. Not much they could tell the rest of us, what with so much of their training confidential.

Don was one of the first hired. He lived two houses down from us, had a leg he kind of swung in front of him when he walked. My mom said he got it logging. He used to spend every nice day futzing with his garden, or washing his faded truck. Suddenly, come seven forty-five a.m. every single weekday, you could set your clock as Don cranked that old beast up and headed down to the MegaCorp office.

A fever blister of anticipation swelled in Raventon when the Sim's parking lot was paved. Every car that went by slowed to watch the installation of the huge and illuminated gateway arching over the two-lane entrance to the almost-Sim, the drum beat of opening day pounding in all our veins.

• • • • •

# 028

---

"Ladies and gentlemen, esteemed members of the Board of MegaCorp—" Harold Hastings' complexion above his tight shirt collar was a deep ruby red. "I have been asked to explain to you a small problem we recently documented with the Simulator. I must stress the importance of the statistical rarity of the event I am about to describe.

"There is a pattern of Simulator stimuli which seems to affect a negligible percentage of the population, far less than one percent. But it does not fit with anything in our projections, so we thought—it seems wise to bring it to your attention."

The tremulousness of his words voiced Harold's best attempt to control his own frustration and appear earnest instead, a facade he hoped would be the professional equivalent of a dog rolling over and showing its belly. His intention was to in some way lessen the traditional response inflicted upon the bearer of bad news. Which Gleed Overholt, CEO, had ordered him to present today.

"Lights please." Lights dimmed in MegaCorp's small amphitheater. The first visual was a pie chart: the total number of individuals undergoing Simulation, the number of individuals in each demographic category having reported any negative response. Harold talked the audience through the 3-D columns that followed. "Our database contains biofeedback from every individual Experience, including heart rate, levels and locations of perspiration, breathing rate and volume—" he double-clicked on his own computer screen and one bar of the graph expanded to refill the screen.

"In this projection, note the small percentage of commercial users, .09 percent, who will have more than three Experiences. Of this one-in-approximately-eleven-hundred individuals, there will be an even smaller percentage who Sim extensively. It is this group that may be vulnerable. Or rather, we have taken note of a certain type of Experience that could occur when an individual undergoes numerous and frequent Simulations.

"Let me call your attention to something else. With all the feedback we receive from each Experience, we never know what exactly the individual makes of his or her package of stimuli. There is no way we can. FutureLabs has conducted post-Experience interviews. And this data is indeed interesting, but it only reveals what people choose to divulge. So we have never been able to precisely correlate stimuli to perceived Experience. Ahem." Harold had sweated out the armpits of his shirt, his undershirt stuck to his spine.

"The long and short of it is, within the group of Sim test subjects—there is a statistically almost insignificant group, what some in the Lab call the 'Sim-groupies'—" a few snickers and some shifting among the Board members. "They seem to seek collective or collaborative Simulations And furthermore, there is a statistical possibility they may use, together, what I would call a feedback loop. Which can slightly, and I must stress the word slightly, alter the Simulator's stimulation patterns." The audience was more than restive, they were talking to each other loudly over their armrests. Harold picked up the pace.

"We first became aware of this situation when we had a very unfortunate Experience, clinically speaking. Most of you are aware of what I am referring to. A young man—" a table of pertinent data filled the screen, "went into psychosis during his thirty-fifth Experience. I must also note that he has not, to date, fully recovered. As best we can deduce from anecdotal information, he was aware of a potential for a group Simulation, and seemed to have been attempting it during his final Experience. I stress again the limits of our ability to precisely document any individual's perception of an Experience." Not wanting to dwell on this, or that the entire research team had been clueless until someone thought to threaten the lab-junkies with no more Sims, cold turkey. That was when they found out group Sims even existed.

"I would like to once again call your attention to the demographics of these, uh—Simulator-groupies. They are all young males, ages eighteen to twenty-eight. To make sure there is no avoidable probability of such an occurrence, we have imposed a limit on the number of Simulations for all users, and a lower limit for those who fit this profile. As we prepare to put the Raventon Simulator online, we feel confident this matter has been fully addressed.

"So rumors regarding—" and here Harold, panting, very carefully avoided use of the word addiction "a potential 'thirst' for Simulating are just that. Rumor."

The auditorium was in as close to an uproar as Harold wanted to witness. He had grossly overestimated the rationality of his audience. "Lights please." And like a captain before his mutinying men, he squared his shoulders and prepared to walk the gangplank. "Questions?"

• • • • •

# 029

Raventon had been scrubbed until it was raw behind the ears. Polished and painted and spit-shined, it was a gleaming picture of Americana to behold, beholden, flags well-weathered from frequent porch flappings, petunias and geraniums everywhere. Even the weeds along the alleys were in full flower. A perfect Saturday morning, replete with a gentle breeze that would lift the released balloons above the ridge. Opening Day for the Raventon Simulator.

Downtown was where the celebration began. Not quite on time, of course. Kevin Koalnivic, assistant principal, had spent the previous week issuing edicts that kept fidgeting little kids lined up by grade and the high school band right behind them, ready to march.

The convertibles at the very front started their engines, last year's prom royalty in one, Mrs. Madeline Evangeline Haynes, Heritage Queen, in the other. Headlights on, Popper at the wheel, the fire engine sirens howled, tissue paper streamers flew as those in the parade threw them back to bystanders. Everyone in Raventon had some reason to be present although it was not always clear who was to march and who was to stay in one place and applaud.

Waterqueen spied on the parade as it crossed the bridge. She crouched out of sight and shivered, and wished there was no Sim, although she loved parades. When everyone else had paraded or strolled or driven on, she crept down to the bank of the river and lifted its water in handfuls, watching the pattern its silvery cords made as they returned to the river, and she wished again.

The first ponderous speeches began before the last stragglers arrived. The crowd jockeyed for position around the base of the Sim entrance, out-of-towners no match for the locals. Quite a crowd was gathered: representatives of MegaCorp (Investors in Your Future), developer and builder of the Simulator, dogs, the few who had come just for the parade, and the many who had come to Sim. All stood. And discreetly or indiscreetly, they waited.

The mayor strutted forward, freshly shaved, profusely after-shaved, ungrammatical and full of himself, and gave a few remarks lasting almost one-half hour. Men from out of town in suits and silk ties smiled and chuckled but could not quite follow what-all he was saying. Speech after speech was duly delivered, endless handshakes exchanged. The crowd applauded as Gleed Overholt sauntered forward with a pair of gold-plated shears and presented them to the mayor. Glinting blades snipped and the long gold and scarlet ribbon was finally parted, dispersing doubt like so many dandelion seeds.

The rush was on. Where were the free hot dogs? The free T-shirts and baseball caps? Where was the line to go inside? Free, today only, step right up with the Opening Day Admission Pass you have just been given. Experience first person the wonders, the mystifying totality, the indescribably amazing Simulator. Safe for the whole family (free child care for children under ten), yet something even your teenagers will get excited about.

The sparkling glass doors swung open. Into the Simulator ascended the picture-book families, seniors, and youth groups who'd come mostly from Seattle, mixed with locals of a far more random nature. Each had signed a liability waiver, a publicity release, had been quick to fill out the user profile. All were a slight bit strained as they entered the magnificent, the awesome, the magenta and hot-pink orifice of the Simulator.

Local kids ate free ice cream and pop until they were sick, more than a few of their parents consumed even greater amounts. Those who had passes grew more expansive in their observations as those who weren't sure if they wanted to go in listened, considering their options.

An hour later the cries of the two Nelson boys went up. The first participants had made it to the glass-enclosed room that offered refreshments and souvenirs. Almost on cue the high school band dug in on a new and grinding serenade. It was only then the carefully orchestrated day fell a little flat. Those emerging were paler, subdued, they stood somewhat huddled in their family groups. Slightly distracted and a little breathless, they sought out the eyes of others who had just completed the maiden voyage with them, flashed peculiar sorts of smiles, almost grimaces, as camera crews shot footage for the evening news.

The sky was a pale taffy blue as the long line made its way into the Simulator and eventually trickled out. Out-of-towners retreated to their minivans. Locals made excuses and went home. Spotlights roamed that starry night in complement to suddenly permanent neon:

## THE SIMULATOR: A FAMILY EXPERIENCE.

The next morning the town crew had the street sweeper out on Raventon's dusty streets first thing, lowering its brushes only where there was actual pavement. The sprayer truck followed closely. Steam lifted from Raventon's streets, leaving a scent like the beginning of a hard rain, as local dogs sprawled once more at their accustomed intersections, snoozing.

• • • • •

# 030

Waterqueen watched Raventon day and night; she watched over Raventon. She peered out when her neighbors mowed their lawns, raked their leaves, shoveled their walks, and especially when they set their sprinklers; she observed so carefully she knew what went into their grocery bags regularly and what was a treat. She memorized each detail as batch after batch of neighborhood children grew from toddlers to teenagers. She was saturated with Raventon's smallest actions, steeped in its most delicate nuances.

Her neighbors sometimes noticed slight motion at her windows when an unfamiliar truck parked nearby, or when crows treed a hawk. In the winter her sidewalk had a narrow footpath chiseled out of the snow, steady smoke came from her chimney. Each evening lights went on and off behind her yellowed shades. But as much as Waterqueen scrutinized Raventon, very small children were the only ones who noticed her presence. Gossip filled this void: an unrequited love, a fear of people, a grotesque and unspecified physical defect.

Older kids tried occasionally to make a game of her mystery, daring each other to go after the plums on her backyard tree, to run up the porch and knock even once on the door, to swing on her front gate. But then there would be a flutter of curtain and even the oldest boys would hesitate, would suggest some other game, or maybe run.

She was watching that day.

Eisy'd come by for Pancho mid-morning, given him a buck on his handlebars, and zoomed down the hill. She watched the empty street after them, rubbed a pain in her elbow, and she frowned, studying the back-curved wisps of cloud drifting over the ridge. She couldn't see but she knew Eisy and Pancho were headed to the park, where other young ones met them.

Eisy, full of thirteen-year-old daring, was itching for action once they got to the park. He threw rocks from the creek at the much-abused restroom wall while he considered the possibilities. His legion kept their distance, wary of his indecision.

Rancid had the idea. "Let's go in the green house."

Cuz felt a twang in her gut, a little stab of iciness. Nobody had lived in the green house for a long time. It wasn't that she thought it was haunted, but it was creepy, and they weren't the only ones who'd poked around inside, you could tell by the gross things that got left behind, by the spray-painted pictures and words.

Thwack. Eisy pitched the last of his rocks hard and hit the edge of the restroom's metal roofing. "What are we going to do there?"

"We could try and get in the attic. Come on." Rancid pretended he was ready to go but everyone knew he was waiting on Eisy, who was watching Pancho for the slightest signal. Once Pancho committed he never backed down, but Pancho could just as easily drift into his silent world.

Pancho rocked his head sideways, back and forth. Looked at Eisy and gave him the ghost of a smile.

Eisy took charge. "OK, let's do it. But everybody's got to arrive separate. Hide near the back."

"See you in a little." Rancid slouched his baggy shorts and was on his way.

"What if we get caught?" It was Sharon's brother who asked.

"Don't come if you're chicken." Eisy flipped his bike up from where it balanced on its handlebars and seat. "You coming?"

So he knew Cuz didn't want to. "I'm not sure." She tried to think of a decent reason.

"She's the one who's chicken." Roger Koalnivic hadn't moved his fat butt from the picnic table.

"Am not." Cuz knew she was doomed.

"Scaredy-cat. Scaredy-cat girl."

"Better than being a tub-of-lard."

"Come on." Eisy offered Pancho a ride.

Leaving Cuz, who kicked the leg of the table and then ran before Roger could get up and come after her.

Only Eisy, Pancho, Cuz, and Rancid showed.

They crawled one-by-one through the broken basement window. Rancid led the way up the stairs, pushed open the door at the top so it creaked in a long slow whine. Even Eisy jumped when Rancid lurched out at them from around the corner of the living room.

"Asshole." Eisy shoved Rancid close to a petrified mess on the floor.

"Let's go upstairs" Pancho spoke to the floor.

They never had. Last time the trapdoor at the top of the built-in ladder was jammed. They'd thumped at it with part of an old chair until they heard a sudden rustling. Each of them had climbed over the other to get out. Rancid had run straight out the front door, in broad daylight, not that anyone outside had seemed to notice. They'd figured out later it must have been bats, Cuz had seen some come out a window as she left.

The bats stirred and flew this time, but Eisy kept banging the trapdoor until it bumped open. Pancho started climbing right away, which meant the three of them, all older, had to follow.

The only light came from some broken slats in the vents at each end of the attic and one scum-covered dormer window. As their eyes adjusted they noticed a few boxes, a trunk with its contents strewn across the dirty floor. Cuz walked over and pushed aside mice-chewed bits of cloth and paper with her sneaker. The entire attic reeked of batshit.

"Bor-ing." Rancid kicked at a hanger.

Pancho pointed out the window. "Wanna see me climb that?"

The knot in Cuz's belly returned. She pushed in between Rancid and Eisy to see for herself a rusty flagpole mounted dead center above the window. It splayed out a good fifteen feet.

All it took was Eisy's laugh and Rancid's silence. They could only shove the window partway open so Pancho had to squeeze. As he wiggled, one piece of the window sill broke off and fell, bouncing on the sidewalk below.

"Hey Punch, maybe you shouldn't." It was Eisy who was uneasy.

Cuz didn't even want to watch as Pancho scooted his butt onto what was left of the sill. "Hey—I know. Let's go downstairs and see if those jars in the kitchen are still growing."

Pancho's fingers were white around the bottom edge of the window as he swung his legs out.

"You go." Rancid dismissed her without taking his eyes off Pancho.

"Guys, this is scary. How's he going to get back once he gets on the pole?" Cuz couldn't shut up.

"Punch?" Eisy tapped on the glass beside Pancho's ear. "You win. Come on back."

Instead Pancho squirmed, worked one foot under himself and stood, smearing dirt from the window onto his T-shirt. He shifted his hands from the bottom of the window to the sides of its outside trim. Unsmiling, his eyes shining.

"Pancho—"

He ignored the three packed together against the window, elbowing each other. At first Pancho couldn't quite reach the base of the flagpole with his free hand. He took all the time in the world to stretch. Then his fingertips brushed it. But he still couldn't get his hand around it. Pancho lowered his arm, both hands clutched the sides of the window frame as he repositioned his feet on the sill.

With a grimy grin through the window, but not at them, he let go. Arms out from his sides, tippy-toed, he wavered, swayed out from the glass—

—and caught himself.

"Jesus. Give it a rest." Eisy's voice was too loud and slightly squeaky.

Pancho steadied himself. Then jumped.

Cuz turned away from the window and snagged a big splinter in her hand as she tripped down the ladder, then tore through the living room and out the front door. Pancho was hanging from his knees and his hands, shimmying himself out to the end of the pole. He let loose with one hand and waved to her.

"Pancho, you quit it. Right now." Cuz was screaming.

He let go with his other hand, swinging upside down from his crisscrossed legs. "*Fly me to the moon—*" grinning.

"You're crazy. Come in." Even Rancid was yelling.

Pancho swung and caught the pole with his hands once more, dropped his legs, let his feet dangle.

Pancho waved again, with one hand, this time toward Waterqueen's house. Then he let go.

He was falling and Cuz couldn't catch him. He hit the dirt beside the sidewalk in a roll, round and round, still grinning. Eisy and Rancid rushed outside. Pancho sat on the ground, holding his left hand at a funny angle, and wouldn't let them come near. Cuz raced home, weeping. Rancid was gone. Eisy told Pancho not to worry, not to worry a bit, and raced on his bike for help.

Waterqueen watched the others run, she came close to Pancho then, followed the edge of the overgrown lilacs and plum that skirted the green house. She came close enough Pancho could hear her as she sang. "*Fly me to the moon, and let me play among the stars...*" They sang together until she backed away, the aid car siren howling its approach.

Pancho had a twisted ankle and a broken wrist, that was all.

• • • • •

# 031

Narrow white clouds ribboned the sky day after day. Heat made even the ridgeline shimmer, up close the trees were dusty, underbrush ragged, water-striped sandstone gone dry.

Angie was a little ragged too, as she did her best to ignore the barb in Cynthia Arpeggio's voice and finished bagging her neighbor's purchases.

"—So I shouldn't call it courting?" Cynthia batted her eyelashes, seventy-five if she was a day, scented hanky at her cuff. "It's just you and Morse make such a, ahem, cute couple." Cynthia drew her lips together, the habit of a smile curling them slightly. "We just assumed..." She had perfected an inquisitive, hanging intonation implying she only wanted to be sure. That is when her biggest smile came, when she was sure.

"I think the proper expression would be 'get a life,' Miss Arpeggio." Angie crimped her own mouth into a smile.

"Well. Do say hello to your father for me."

"Certainly." Angie grabbed the two bags of groceries and followed the shorter, sprier Cynthia, to her ancient sedan. "Give my best to your sister." Angie stood clear as the boat-like car backed out in stately fashion.

Morse—he loved Angie, but not all of her. Especially not that night when he swung by the store, as usual, for a beer and a little bullshit. No matter what he said, she snapped at him. So he decided to ask directly. "I grant you it's hot, but what in the hell is knotting your knickers tonight?"

She scowled, and got angrier when she saw Samuel grin into his beer. "This is Mr. Sunshine asking?"

"Yeah. For purposes of discussion, consider me Comrade Cheerful."

Angie turned her back on Morse to wring out the dishcloths she had soaking.

"Ang? Did something happen?"

"Not in your rainbow world."

Morse sipped some of his beer. "It's not about your father is it?"

"What do you care?"

"Jeez. Is he OK?"

"He's fine. Not as fine as you, of course. But just fine." She glared at Samuel. "You going to nurse that all night?"

Samuel shrugged and took a drink.

"I stopped by Jorge's, and things there seemed about the same." Morse was getting concerned.

"So now you're a social worker?"

Morse let out a deep sigh. "You are as sour as old milk tonight. Let me know if there's something I can do. See ya Sammy."

Samuel gave Morse a raised hand in salute, then gestured to Angie he wanted another beer.

Angie, our once fair maiden, our poor Angeline was attempting to drown her ghosts before they dared return. And so, skittering, she tried to cultivate within herself a disagreeable, a discardable approach to love. She fostered a vision of herself as immutable, not unlovable, the better to bypass her own desire. Because when her anger was spent she knew too well her loneliness would abound.

• • • • •

# CUZ

---

I say the word "dream" and what image hovers—someone in a prone position, eyes closed, rapid eye movement, and such? With this I have lost you.

Or perhaps you think conceptually, of something akin to an aspiration, a wish, a yearning for the unrequited? With this you take a more fantastic fall, demonstrating the clipped wings of semantics.

I was a child, and I had the dreams of a child: asleep or awake, on Santa's lap or counting the dots on the classroom ceiling tiles, my dreaming was fluid. I dreamed I could keep up with Eisy in all things, I dreamed of a bicycle of my own, I dreamed of ice cream and my mother's kisses, I dreamed of spacewalking and no mosquitoes by the river. I chose to step tenderly around those darker dreams: endlessly falling unto I knew not what, monsters with infinite patience who knew I was only holding my breath.

Now some of my memories are like dreams, and some dreams too much like memories, all of it together like a flavor my tongue cannot quite recall. I was a child and I dreamed much and wished for more, and could not fathom the distance to this, my now current self. I did not know then that a dream come true can no longer be a dream, but takes on the flesh and bone, the complexion and landscape of its immediate surroundings. Can a dream be true?

And what is the proper word, the precise name for the catch basin where those pendulous droplets of hope tenaciously cling?

• • • • •

# 032

The Spokane show was a huge disappointment to Dorth. Start to finish, soup to nuts, succorless.

She had presumed it would be in the part of Spokane she liked, near the old newspaper building with its plate glass windows and dark wood and brass, walking distance from the Spokane River. *CAPTURED! Images of the Northwest* was instead far from downtown, in a hotel complex that had been built after the once-in-a-lifetime World's Fair, and reeked of some forgotten concept of modern. Dorth peered at art and other humans and ate fresh-thawed banquet-style meals under hideous light in low-ceilinged conference rooms that should have been bulldozed long ago.

Lacking heart was how Dorth would have described the event if there had been anybody to tell. In a way, it was a good test of her painting. Unfortunately, the whole gathering had little to do with anyone's art. It was about reactions to a new century, and how images "capture" reality; some of the deadest horses around. And, under a heavy patina of gossip, it was about money.

In addition to Dorth's, there were shows by an animator, a sculptor, and juried work. The animator was only around for one day. He was off to NYC, Art Mecca, for something really big. So everyone and their brother drooled on him while he was present, then got out their knives the moment he left. The sculptor was an older woman, originally from France, who used huge boulders and rooms full of sand. When Dorth sidled up to her and complimented her at the first cocktail hour, she looked bored, with her high cheekbones and a dancer's way of moving. Dorth took it a step further and asked if the woman had seen Dorth's show, and was told she had promise.

It was all a matter of nerves. Dorth had drilled herself: stay accessible, casual, tune in to the current line of bullshit, keep one ear perked at all times for any mention of grants or honorariums or calls for work. Ignore the ever-stronger urge to stay in her rundown hotel room. Don't even think about wandering into Spokane proper.

On day three, during the endless closing remarks, Dorth supervised the repacking of her paintings, looked over the paperwork, and signed the shipping order. She left Spokane in a sulk, with a full tank of gas, and headed generally west, committed to a meandering route.

Maybe it had been the unremitting shabbiness of her hotel room that had spoiled her phone call to Rudy the night before. She'd been too dispirited to even mention she'd sold a painting. "Dreary" was what Rudy'd said after the fifth or sixth long stretch of silence and sighs. Dorth had nothing to add. After another long pause they'd said their good nights and now she was driving.

• • • • •

# 033

Dorth drove two-lane blacktop from crisp mid-morning to late afternoon, clutching at ambient yet slightly removed humanity: drifting radio stations, snatches of earlier conversations, stale french fries. Above all, she held on to the steering wheel. Near Wenatchee the scenery was promising, jagged granite, cascades of scarlet huckleberry bushes, a touch of fresh snow up high. But all of this was more splendid in passing than anything she could enjoy from one place, no matter where she pulled over. So, bone-tired and discombobulated, sorely in need of a non-automotive break, she drove on, picking the most circuitous route at every opportunity.

She pulled into Raventon about dark. Through her eyes that night it was a dingy, half-dead town. The quaint appeal she remembered must have been some artistic hallucination she had while painting. She parked in front of the post office and considered her options.

The name and half-lit neon of the Frog's Ears settled it. She ordered a cold Rainier from a stool at the end of the bar, out of range of its mirror. Conversation around her, such as it was, resumed. By not much after ten her lack of sleep, food, and plenty of beer anchored a shroud loosely, but entirely, around her, allowing only a limited constellation of faces and events to poke through.

Dorth's first impression of Morse was of a hunkering vulture who chose the barstool next to her. He had a bony asymmetrical nose, watery green eyes under oversprouting eyebrows, and an Adam's apple that randomly chugged up and down his neck as he spoke or swallowed. He nodded her way as he hunkered onto his stool, bullshitting with the bartender, but she could tell he was watching her. As she nurtured her oblivion, this aberration of a man disturbed her.

Temperatures outside had meanwhile dipped into what might be called in other places unseasonably cold. In Raventon, weather was always seasonable.

A persistent voice, a tenacious tenor, followed Dorth as she blundered from barstool to car, querying whether or not she would attempt driving. Unsure whether she was holding court within her skull or with some phantasmic party just outside, she limited her reply to a very softly spoken "where the hell would I be going?"

The voice continued its dogmatic probing. Even in her stupor she came to associate it with Morse's oddly cheerful face.

When her eyes rolled open she was surrounded and smothered by floors too far from ceilings and huge walls that stretched between. When she finished the first round of retching, she came to realize she had made it to the porch of a house or shed of which she had no previous knowledge, that it was colder than shit outside, and that she was one sorry dog. With less than nothing left in her to spew onto the frost-wilted vegetation, she retraced her steps inside, shivering. If any amount of sunlight had not been painful it would have been a cheerful, threadbare sort of place.

When the late fall sun had mercifully moved to a more oblique angle, the face from the Frog's Ears reappeared, bearing saltines and a little ginger ale. Her stomach swayed, then took hold of a few crackers. When she peered through some kind of kaleidoscope that seemed to hang like a screen before her, that same face and its attached hands offered small comforts: more crackers, a damp washcloth to wipe the dried mess off her face. It sifted into her stultified brain that she was definitely not dreaming all this from the back of the car.

This caused her great worry because as low as she had aspired, she did not cotton to the idea she had initiated and perhaps consummated some sort of new, apparently intimate, relationship during her inebriation. "Who the fuck are you?"

In hangover, Dorth hovered on this question.

What she was asking of Morse, then and ever-after, was most basic. Because about the time a person passes thirty, this particular question gains resonance. Use of the word fuck is rhetorical, and a perspective slightly beyond blushing or flinching is attained, having bared one's ass and self more than a few times. So when she raised this question, it was not to make conversation, but from a real desire to know.

Morse smiled. "Your worst dream come true." Refilled her glass of ginger ale. "And you—who are you?"

Dorth attempted further thought. If he didn't already know her name she wasn't sure she wanted him to.

"Identity isn't such a simple question, is it?" With the same unrelenting smile he got up from his crouch. "Help yourself to whatever. I'm off to the races." Dorth was left with a new packet of crackers and most of a quart of pop.

He left. Dorth did her best to apply her spinning brain to the considerations necessary for her own departure, tried once and then twice to get her body to move. The results were messy, and drove her back into her blanketed corner. Finally, she abandoned all hope and slept, with small tremors of hands and head and heart. She saw Chagall paintings and stained glass, men and women lifted off their feet and floating, making a circle in the sky. They were astronauts, the earth a beautiful balloon without a string. Amidst such ethereal strangeness and motion without gravity or sound, Dorth awoke. The child-like wonder of so much beauty suddenly far from such a wretch as she.

All she wanted was to be gone before this man returned. By sheer willpower she was. Disheartened by the distance from the porch to her car, and the intensity of all light and motion, she contained her dry heaves until she had landed on the front seat, car door still open like a broken wing. Dorth studied the dirt and pine needles between her knees, spit, sipped air and swallowed. The keys were in the ignition.

She maintained wavering balance and drove onward, to a road she and Rudy had followed once, to a trailhead; pulled over at the first wide spot in the road, crawled into the backseat and slept.

• • • • •

# CUZ

Once upon a time, there was a little girl. Me. There was my cousin Eisy, older in every way. And a slightly younger boy, Pancho. Each with our own mommies and daddies, in three non-intersecting sets. It all gets more complicated thereafter.

I am Cuz, short for cousin, the name a gift from Eisy. Also short for "because": the cause of it all, the answer to what we ask from the time we are three- and four-year-olds, repeating why and why to anyone who might answer. Hoping then and ever-after we might receive explanation for what is inexplicable: Why is the sky blue? Why do birds fly? Why did my dad stay away? Why did Eisy and the others die?

Cuz. An insufficient answer then and now.

The long and short of it is, I pull the strings in this selective reenactment, this modest puppet show. It's only fair. Not that it was fair, what happened. Not that life is fair. Not that a puny one such as me would know fair if it kicked me upside the head.

My qualifications? I know the limits of my own recollection, know myself to be no better than a scratched CD, playing endless snatches of melodies never recorded; know I will lose and misread the wandering track of cause and effect. Why? Because those faded footprints are as complicated and bitter as DNA, that acid spiral of information, thin as a human hair and five miles long.

Remember, then, it is not for me to explain, but to illustrate. All my words running, like water, through your fingers.

• • • • •

# 034

Harold Hastings nursed his second vermouth; he gathered his nerve. He had left FutureLabs early specifically to be here, to do this thing. So he reached into his pocket for the photograph in question, and engaged the bartender in conversation.

The Seattle bartender took one look at the picture Harold held out, and suddenly had a lot of glass polishing to do. "Why are you looking for him?"

Harold flushed an even pink. "I used to work for him." He studied Fred's likeness once more. A sallow-faced little man with a nose like a leprechaun and wispy hair more or less parted, smiled a crooked smile back at him from within his ill-fitting suit and tie. Fred Mossback, inventor extraordinaire. "I'm afraid Fred might not be doing too well these days."

The bartender put down his glass and cloth and studied Harold. "No lie. Unless he won the lottery and used it to get some serious help—" the bartender tapped his own temple. "Not good. He hasn't been around here for quite some time. You sure you're a friend?"

Harold's mouth was twisted as his head nodded.

"Wacko Fred. I'm betting he isn't that much past forty. But he isn't a survivor, if you know what I mean. He ended up drinking his fucking brains out while he made himself at home here. But we're talking years ago. Like I don't think I've heard about him and I definitely haven't seen him for probably five years at least."

Harold put the photograph back in its glassine envelope, and then into his jacket pocket. "Fred has been out of sight for some time."

"Before he stopped showing up he used to mutter something about his mother, how she worked here, but I chalked that up with the bugs on the ceiling, kind of a d.t.'s thing.

"He took good care of himself. He always wore one of those tight little suits and shined shoes and the classic pencil holder routine. So I could believe he was an engineer or something?"

Harold nodded and the bartender racked wine glasses and continued.

"Fred always drank with a mission. Even when he still had some kind of a job. And he ran his whole operation out of the front pocket of his pants. Paid cash for everything out of that one big wad. If he hadn't been such a nice guy and kind of small, so some of the regulars felt protective, they would have found him in the alley right off. Maybe that's where he ended up...?"

Harold kept looking at his vermouth.

"From the beginning he talked to anybody who would listen. Used to irritate a lot of people, until he learned to cool it with the big words and the scientific mumbo-jumbo."

"Fred was one of the best, scientifically speaking."

"Yeah, well." The bartender freshened Harold's drink without asking. "The longer he hung around here, the weirder his stories got. That's how he managed to keep drinking after he ran out money. People used to cover him. Sometimes they'd request a story they'd already heard, sometimes they paid to see if they could get a new one. But he, his stories, after awhile what he was talking about was so totally unbelievable nobody would pay. People learned not to even ask questions. But I gotta tell you, when he was together, he had the greatest stories. Really knew how to make you think.

"I'm not saying he wasn't a drunk. But the things Wacko Fred talked about, if he liked you, were wild. His version of his own undoing was about the strangest, from what we all pieced together. You want another one?"

Harold pushed his tumbler toward the bartender.

"He said it started when he went and bought himself a TV. He always made it a big part of the story, that he got his TV in February. The dreariest month, he called it. He'd watched TV before that, he just hadn't owned one; is what he said. The story was about what he saw on that television, all by himself. According to Fred, being drunk hindered seeing these special things. I never knew him when he didn't knock 'em back, so I couldn't say, about that part."

Harold shook his head.

"Visions. That's what the other bartender called them. Hallucinations, probably. Wacko Fred was always worth the price of a drink or two, just for the weirdness of what he was willing to say with a straight face.

"Hey, you OK? Jesus... just get the hell out and don't get sick in here. Please. I don't want your fucking money, just get out."

• • • • •

# 035

What had Fred seen?

There was a night Fred dug into his second chicken pot pie as a picture grew, with micro-dot clarity, out of the slight crinkling hum of his new TV screen. The man's face on the screen was speaking of used cars, smiling while prices flashed across his chest. His suit jacket was a shade of electric green that adjusting the color-contrast dial couldn't help. Then the screen changed to a map of California with an arrow the same size pointing pointing pointing, to where the good deals were.

Fred took another forkful of his dinner and pushed a button on his remote, touring channels until he came to a man and woman standing behind a couch, both of them with crossed arms, scowling, while their teenage child (who looked to be about twenty) sat flipping through a magazine, making comments so funny a laugh track made it seem the walls surrounding them could not stop laughing. Their three-way conversation paused until this laughing stopped, all of them smiling while they waited, although the man and the woman seemed to attempt to stay mad. Fred pushed a remote button and the screen changed again and again. A dragonfly lifted a housefly off a flowering daisy and bit its head off, wings purring, a reverent woman's voice spoke about the balance of nature.

Click. Muzak with a solid blue screen and a constantly trailing band of numbers and abbreviations. Click. The fundamentalist whose name Fred could never remember twitched each time he said the word "God," stretching it into two syllables somehow; Fred listened through two more twitches, then held the button down. On another station a young Johnny Carson was taking his golf swing, standing in front of the curtains and making faces while an equally young Ed McMahon led the audience in guffaws.

Fred eased farther back in his chair as Johnny strolled to his desk, drumming his pencil as he introduced a woman who looked vaguely familiar. She started singing under a spotlight; Fred's eyelids slid closer, closer, closed.

He dozed, his partially open mouth cottony from the chicken pie, the secondhand rainbow of TV colors bathing his unfocused dreams, the jingle from a game show playing into his brain. It was music that made him open his eyes. A man in a grey suit with a tense and constant smile stood to one side of a stage, three buxom blonds in parallel poses stood to the other, all nodding, as an unseen audience clapped.

Then came commercials. Pizza, hamburgers, a special offer on a set of records that included the sound track from every musical Fred had ever heard. He clicked the sound down to a murmur and kept working through channels. He watched a Western until the shootout was done, two cop shows, some kind of painful family dilemma (until the soundtrack crescedoed as a woman walked down a dark hallway and he knew there would be violence). Then Fred was back to Johnny Carson. The singer was sitting down, ducking her head as she spoke. Her dress reminded Fred of the one his mother had worn at his brother's wedding. She was wearing a string of pearls like his mother's, too. The camera zoomed in on her face. She looked too much like his mother. Fred leaned closer to the set, and still the singer looked like his mother. The camera panned to the band, to Johnny Carson, it passed over the woman briefly and Fred tried to focus completely, unable to believe two different people could look so much alike. Johnny and Ed were laughing at the woman, making jokes at her expense, and she was embarrassed, then the camera switched to the band.

Fred was frantic, he wanted the control in his hand to allow him to control the camera, he wanted a clear view of the woman. He punched the volume button but he couldn't hear clearly what any of them were saying. Johnny called the woman by name. Fred's mother's name.

Fred tried to change the channel, but those buttons didn't work; he tried to turn off the set but he couldn't. He tried messing with the antenna, he was ready to rip the back off the set, but at the same time he didn't want to take his eyes from the TV screen for more than a second, he wanted to see that this was not his mother. There was a commercial for dog food and a new guest. His mother had moved down the couch, toward Ed McMahon, and was rarely even visible. There were more commercials. Another show came on and nothing made sense to Fred although he stared at his TV screen, almost unblinking, until it was time for work the next morning.

• • • • •

# 036

---

Harold's assistant gave him the word. Resignation. Overholt was requesting Harold quit, and that he put in writing, effective immediately. Harold had some sense this might be coming. And since Harold could not provide Overholt with the statistical assurance requested, he gave his boss the next best thing: his signature, Harold Hopstead Hastings, at the bottom of the letter Overholt's secretary had drafted.

And then, as he packed the few personal items he had in his assigned desk and workspace at FutureLabs, Harold brooded. "The thing no one wanted to acknowledge was the true source of the Simulator. How FutureLabs got the concept, the initial concept.

"Fred Mossback was how. He was lead tech when I started in at FutureLabs. Only two years older than me, a real whiz kid. He'd graduated from a second-rate technical college in New York but he set the pace in the lab, averaging something like six viable patents a year. And he set the tone. Fred thought it was great MegaCorp got rights on all patents automatically, future rights, related developments, everything that came out of the lab. I asked him once why. He said he didn't have time to run a lab, he just wanted to work. All MegaCorp had to do was mention the Amazing Mossback and whatever wonderkid they were interviewing signed.

"Fred and I were never friends, never anything like friends, but then I don't know that Fred was ever really close with anyone. Fred and I were accustomed to each other after sixteen years. I considered him sort of the last remnant of the fifties-style engineer: Mr. Sliderule until a calculator came along with sufficient memory and graphics display. Anything that didn't interest him was a distraction, he lived by rote, the better to put all his thought into his work. For as long as I knew him he ate the same thing for lunch every day: tuna fish on rye, with a dill pickle. But he had new concepts, new questions practically by the hour.

"Then Fred started to change. He had never been a particularly healthy-looking individual, but instead of being skinny he got scrawny. He had always been hyper-focused on his own work, but suddenly he stopped generating New Ideas. That's what we called them, even though it was pretty corny. Fred had established the system, and it was a design engineer's dream: once every couple weeks everyone working in the lab—we're talking petri dish preppers up through Fred—would meet for coffee and doughnuts, first thing.

"There was a huge blackboard and the idea was to fill it with possibilities, things-to-be-invented, questions. What would happen if a particular chemical were chilled and recrystallized with another? Make a list of habitual objects and how they usually break. There was no common thread, some of the New Ideas were hypothetical soap operas, some were Tom-Swiftian solutions that generated their own problems, it was never about answers. It was fun. Individuals who were irritated by these sessions never stuck around for long. FutureLabs paid for the doughnuts, the coffee, lunches if we were on a roll, as well as our paychecks and most any kind of gizmo or supply anyone requested. Because this method worked. Someone could spend years analyzing how and why; I think it was Fred.

"So it was big news around the water cooler when he stopped attending New Ideas. There had been other times he might skip one, maybe two consecutive meetings, but only when he was working on something big, or when he was stuck. He'd come to the next session and explode with ideas. This was different. Even if he came, he just sat there. For months.

"No one knew what to do. Fred taught you to keep some distance. When he was in the middle of something and you in any way disturbed him he could bite your head off before you knew it. So why did I go into his office and ask? I remember I needed his signature on my vacation request, but anyone who had been around the lab for more than a few days knew better than to walk into Fred's den unbidden. He took my form and signed it without a word. It could have been a check for a million dollars, he would have signed anything. That was sufficiently chilling, but worse, his office was immaculate. He had not been working on anything. I was at the door, on my way out, when he spoke.

"'My TV.'

"I turned, thinking there would be more forthcoming. He spun around in his chair and looked at me. Every time I'd spoken with him prior to that—for some sixteen years—his eyes were like probes: azure grey, almost over-focused. When he looked at me that day in his office, they looked as though he had cataracts, they had a cloudy quality. He rubbed his eyes, his forehead, his temples. The man was pitiful. He spoke almost in a whisper.

"'I think I may have cracked.'

"He continued to stare at me. What could I say? Everyone has some fear of insanity. That day Fred seemed to fit the bill. All I wanted right then was to get away from him. What I said was inane. 'Sorry to hear that.'

"Fred grabbed his jacket and was out the door ahead of me. 'Let's go.' That was more the old Fred's way. I thought he meant somewhere in the lab, or on the grounds. He'd taken me out to watch a cow being milked once, so I wasn't totally surprised when we got into one of the lab cars. Fred drove.

"He talked me through the concept of the Simulator. You had to know Fred to comprehend how meticulous he could be. With words, with symbols, with tools. Precise. But that afternoon he had a great deal of trouble telling me what had happened. He was frustrated with the different implications of his own words, the 'it appeared to me' vs. 'this happened' vs. 'my impression was.' He wanted me to find the error in his logic. The problem was, if his observations were even approximately correct, then everything else did logically follow. What I couldn't independently verify were his observations. They were just plain cuckoo.

"He knew this. He knew no one would believe him. He didn't totally believe what he'd seen himself.

"He had already done prodigious research on deja vu, hallucination, kinesthesia, engrams, and such. He had purchased a number of TVs and had attempted to duplicate his experience. He took me to his place to watch TV with him and see what I concluded. I admit it, I went along because I was curious.

"We agreed I would do nothing but observe the whole situation, including Fred and his behaviors, no matter what my own thoughts and immediate responses or hypotheses might be. He had been trying to isolate the critical element, what made his experience different, and he didn't have a clue. He was desperate for independent verification but he also knew the whole thing was way too out-there for almost anyone whose methodology he trusted.

"I had watched Fred in action on a thousand other projects. Projects that each started as totally harebrained ideas. So I went with him to his apartment. The first and last time I was ever there. I monitored his brain waves, his EKG, the works. This monitoring system, combined with variable sensory stimuli, became the Simulator. FutureLabs used everything Fred physiologically generated, his patterned 'inducers' or 'enhancers,' then gradually altered the TV show phenomenon into a more richly sensual process. I translated. Fred would say, 'I saw my mother' and I would present the question, 'What if you could see your mother, or someone from your past?'

"Naming it the Simulator was what really did Fred in. He always referred to it as his TV-dreaming. By that time he was spending all his time on anthropological research: vision quests, rituals for altering perceptions, and such. The joke around the lab was that he'd entered his Timothy Leary stage. But even after he'd undergone shock therapy he could never quite bring himself to view his experience as non-real.

"Fred had always gone along with whatever Marketing suggested for brand names. But this time, with the name Simulator, he said they violated the concept. He asked if they could wait until he came back with some alternatives. The entire situation became extremely embarrassing. The majority of the individuals involved in the Sim's development had been trying to humor Fred. It was clear the general paradigm of the Simulator had been modeled from the extremely striking experiences of a mentally ill individual. When Fred started pushing his agenda, he lost whatever sympathy there had been. I myself disbelieved him. The easiest and most obvious analysis to this day is that Fred went off the deep end. And now I am the one insisting FutureLabs is blurring the distinction between perception and objective reality.

"Fred blamed me personally for the way everybody turned on him. I lost my temper. I pointed out to him his experiences had never been duplicated objectively, that what they paralleled most closely were the patterns of psychosis. I told him it was admirable that even in his reduced state he contributed to developments at the lab, but sooner or later he would have to admit the fact: he was a sick man and could not rely upon his own perceptions.

"Fred was put on temporary leave, then they pulled his access to the lab. It was as though he died. In absentia, everyone spoke of him in the sweetest and most glowing terms. The one thing no one but no one would discuss was, what had happened to him? Was he OK? I heard stories. One of the janitorial staff told me she'd seen Fred, and gave me the name of the bar. It took me almost six years to start to look for him. Now that I am, it comes as no surprise Overholt is furious. Because Overholt is not a patient man." Harold took a last look around his office, then carried his small box of personal effects, under security escort, out of FutureLabs.

• • • • •

# CUZ

*And now an interesting question, Dear Reader.*

*Could you use the Simulator to see God? What about Jesus? Jesus begs the question because he was a historical personage, so allow me to refine my question. Could anyone use the Simulator to see Jesus as the Son of God?*

*Let's say a truly devout Christian goes into the Simulator. His or her goal, her quest, her single desire and fervent wish, is to see Jesus. And let's assume this individual is adept in Simming, can easily and successfully navigate through the options and menus with plenty of time and energy to spare.*

*She "sees" or Experiences Jesus. And, for purposes of our discussion, does it matter one whit whether we're talking kinesthetic physio-light patterning and alpha-wave harmonies or an animated sacred-bleeding-heart-of-the-Aforementioned? Jesus is seen.*

*What one might conclude from this Experience is where we'll get to serious squabbling, I suspect. For example, if Jesus spoke, are we all going to add his words to our Bibles? And if you heard about this Experience, if it belonged to your auntie, or your parish priest, or even if it appeared in a grocery store tabloid, mightn't you just give it a try, next time you're in the Simulator? Wouldn't you try to see God? And then what? Some see God, others don't. Are the results dictated by technical proficiency in Experiencing or by the divine?*

*Ongoing Experiences might corroborate the visionary's, it's possible they might contradict the first visionary's Experience. In other Sims God might state Jesus is not His Son, or provide scientific proof there is no God. A certain lack of consistency is to be expected. The original vision and the visionary are sure to be challenged, condemned, disclaimed, doubted. The one who has seen God will have triggered a full spectrum, a rainbow of additional burning-bush visions. Rumors will circulate, leading us back to our basic inquiry, no different than that of the shroud of Turin, identical to the consideration of any sign of God, Christian or other.*

*To move the discussion right along, let's say you yourself, in the total privacy of your own whatever, have an Experience, and know conclusively you have seen God. Be it God-the-Aforementioned-Son, God-as-a-Big-Pine-Tree, God-as-the-Fish-That-Got-Away, God-as-the-Big-Bang-Theory-Made-Imminent, or perhaps God-as-a-Wave-of-Forgiveness-for-the-dark-parts-of-your-heart. The details are important only to you, I'm afraid, although I will concede the divine may exist in these details. My supposition: you are personally convinced you have witnessed the Big-Picture, the Prime-Mover, the Call-It-What-You-Will.*

*And then? The hall lights come up, they unstrap you, you make your way past the concession stand.*

*Do you blow the whole Experience off, a bit of undigested porridge and all that? Do you buy the authorized Simulator Memory Pack including photos, and keep it as a memento, next to the pictures from your last vacation to the Grand Canyon? Do you construct a shrine? Visit your chosen place of worship more frequently? Or do you shake your head and smile at the wonders of technology, concede it has outstripped your own ability to discern reality, and take your doctor's prescription while you think it over? Perhaps you walk around the corner and go back into the Sim for another Experience?*

*I am not saying I have had such an Experience. Nor have I come across anyone who ever mentioned Experiencing anything exactly like this. But if you are a person of spirit and/or intellect and/or heart, well....*

*I guess I'm asking you.*

*And I want to know something else. What if you don't experience anything when you go seeking God?*

• • • • •

# 037

Angie was in kindergarten when Daddy came home from one of his buying trips with an idea that couldn't wait. He returned just in time for dinner, and didn't say much at first. He was watching Angie. "Daughter, do you know where I went?"

"Away." She ate quickly. Daddy had said he'd brought home a special treat for dessert.

"True enough." He tilted back on his chair, studying her as she continued to eat. "But where is away, precisely?"

"Everywhere but here is away, my love." Momma stood and put his plate on top of hers. "Somewhere and nowhere and over there are away, from here."

"I'm done too." Angie stacked her plate on top. "And in between places Daddy. There's different amounts of away."

"I should have known I lived in a den of philosophers." He smoothed the tablecloth with his palms. "What I'm wondering, little brainchild, is whether you have knowledge of the away to which I most recently traveled?"

"Do I know where you went?"

"Exactly."

"Seattle?"

"Maybe."

"Portland?"

"You're guessing."

Momma returned from the kitchen bearing in one hand a white unfrosted cake, in the other a small bowl of huckleberries. "Timbuktu."

"And you're leading the witness. Did you know this cake is named for you? Or did we name her after the cake?" Daddy winked as Momma smiled.

Angie looked from her father to her mother and back again. "This cake is named Angeline?"

"Angelfood dearie." Momma handed her the first slice, huckleberry juice staining the cake a dark purple. "The food of angels."

And it was. Soft as air and sweet and then it was gone, the hucks soaking in like syrup on waffles. Angie asked for another piece as she finished her first.

"I did in fact go both to Seattle and Portland on this trip. But the larger question, the reason I ask if you know where I have been, angelic-eater-of-angel-food, is to determine how far from here, how far away, you have been."

Angie had to think. "Wenatchee. I went with Momma, when she saw the dentist."

Daddy and Momma looked at each other. "I believe you are correct."

Momma poured herself and then Daddy more coffee. "What kind of trip are you planning for us?"

"Are we going on a trip?"

Would you like to?" He finished his first slice of cake.

"Where?"

"She's a born traveler. Already discerning."

"Where, Daddy?"

"That's what we are all going to decide."

Momma smiled and shook her head.

Daddy had gone on buying trips for the store since before Angie could remember. Momma said she had gone along with Daddy after they were married, before Angie was born, to all sorts of places, depending more on Daddy's whims than on what the store needed. Angie asked a couple times, but Momma said no, she didn't miss going. Momma said she much preferred staying home with her girl while Daddy traveled. Traveling lonesome was Momma's name for his trips.

Their first trip as a threesome was to Seattle for a weekend. By eight a.m. Daddy was waiting by the car, Angie was running in and out the front door.

"You've got a sweater, my dearie-do?"

"Yes. Momm-aaa, come on." Angie followed her words up the stairway and into her parents' room.

Momma gave the room a final look and picked up the small suitcase by the door. "I guess I'm as ready as I'll be."

Angie ran to the stairs and rode down them on her butt, ka-bump, ka-bump, beating Momma to the bottom.

Daddy reached inside the car and grabbed his camera as Momma closed the front door. "For posterity, miladies." He ushered them together on the front steps, in their matching dresses, checkered blue and white. Angie clung behind Momma's hip and made faces and Momma had her hand along the side of Angie's face. Momma had been looking down at her and was lifting her smile to Daddy, to the camera, one eyebrow slightly arched.

After that trip they went to Seattle regularly, for what Momma called cultural activities: to see a play, or pictures in a museum, or to eat in a fancy restaurant, or hear the symphony. Almost every trip they rode the ferries.

Then Momma decided she would stay home. "I travel enough in my mind. You two go farther if you like" was her answer when Daddy tried to get her to reconsider. Momma loved to help them plan though. She spent hours picking out where they would stay and what they would see. And she and Angie took plenty of walks together, around Raventon.

Angie and Daddy visited all sorts of places in the next year. On their trips to

Seattle they stayed in a hotel where you could leave the windows open and hear the ferries and the seagulls. In Portland Momma found them a hotel with dark wood and chandeliers, where the carpet had elaborate patterns Daddy called paisley. Angie tried to color a picture of it for Momma. And Daddy always seemed to know somebody no matter where they went.

"Raventon probably seems pretty good-sized to you, but it's a small and narrow place. The world is generally not much wider, but it is somewhat larger. It has plenty to fill those eyes and ears of yours." Then Daddy would give her a wink. He always said "business required" the buying trips, but sometimes the only things they brought back were dirty laundry and a memento, something they picked out for Momma, together. Like the wooden mermaid with wings they'd found in a curio shop in Seattle. Momma hung it over the kitchen sink the minute she unwrapped it, hung it so it twirled.

She had been helping plan a big trip, the biggest ever for Angie, Denver and New Orleans and Chicago, all on a train. Momma ordered special tickets for a room on the train that had foldout beds. That was just before.

After, neither Angie nor Daddy went on overnight trips, not for pleasure, and not for the store.

• • • • •

# 038

Alexander Mettle watched his little girl squat as he ate his sandwich, watched her pudgy fingers patiently work a twig around the opening of an anthill while the ants tried to rebuild. Alexander chewed slowly and swallowed.

When he moved his feet to stretch Angie spoke without looking up. "Daddy—"

She dropped the stick. "Is Momma gone for good?"

He had no words and so said nothing.

They did their looking then, father and daughter. Her eyes into his.

It was Momma who had made a game out of looking. With Momma, it was like peekaboo. Her hands and fingers opened and closed, moved to one side and then the other, and Angie tried to get a clear look. Finally she would grab Momma's hands, clutch her fingers together. "Peekaboo, PEEKaboo."

Momma would laugh, her eyelids fluttering, "I see YOU, peekaBOO." They played this forever, way after Angie was big enough to know lots of other games.

With Daddy it was a different and serious game. It started with Angie following his one moving finger with her eyes, without moving her head. Sooner or later he would point to his own eyes. The game then was to look into each other and not laugh or look away or blink. Momma would watch, she made faces, said things, tried to distract them. "You two are a perfect match." When one of them finally did blink it came as a shock, as though someone had suddenly waved a hand in front of her face while she was reading. Looking into Daddy, Daddy looking into her, Angie thought it was like they had gone somewhere. Daddy could stop Angie's crying if he got her to play. And no matter how sad she was, she couldn't help but play. Neither of them ever played it with anyone else, not even Momma. It was Daddy's way of holding her, sort of. Because he had never been much for touching, even before. Momma was the one with hugs. Daddy and Angie did their looking, and that was all the answer there was.

• • • • •

# 039

From the time Angie was little, once Daddy left for the store there was no more playing with her food, no more padding around in the footed pajamas with the long zipper, it was time to get busy. Momma would send her off to dress herself, and there would begin the allure of stuffed drawers. Pants and shorts; ones she liked the pockets of, ones that felt cozy or cool, the ones made of green corduroy, the ones that were her favorite but just too tight. Then she had to pick a top. All these possibilities made Angie, from her earliest days, more than slightly partial to the layered look.

By the time she remembered she would need underpants and an undershirt and socks to complete the clothing figure laid out on the floor, by the time she was actually ready to put on these clothes, by then Momma would have stopped calling. If Angie was not dressed by then, she lost autonomy. Only wails and weeping could win back the smallest of her garment selections when Momma had to come upstairs and help.

But if Angie managed all the intricacies of dressing herself quickly, then she could stage her entrance into the kitchen. Angie could remember more than once, but not predictably, being scooped up in Momma's still sudsy hands for a hug and a spin as Momma's fingers smoothed some detail—a collar, a short sleeve, the ribbon in her hair, smiling and smoothing and smelling of dish soap and coffee breath and sometimes a faded whiff of perfume, dancing around the kitchen table.

When Daddy was late coming home, Angie and Momma ate dinner in the kitchen. Soup and homemade muffins were what Angie liked best. Sometimes ice cream for dessert. Then Momma would read to her from the fat books, stories that lasted for weeks, stories of animals, stories about places Momma called exotic.

Kisses: this part of remembering caused a sudden soreness in Angie's heart, a need to swallow several times and maybe go and do something else.

First thing in the morning, very last thing at night. Smells of her mother, smells of outside, smells of furniture polish and laundry. If Momma and Daddy were going out, a last goodbye kiss while Angie sniffed perfume and hair spray and the sachets Momma hung with her best dresses. Some mornings Angie would look in the mirror and find the soft smudged butterfly of her mother's kiss, an echo of the lip-sticked peck she had begged from Momma in trade for promises to be good.

There were kisses in darkness too: Daddy's whiskery cheeks smelling of cigarettes and drink and faintly of his aftershave, his skin cold; then Momma's whispery kiss, some of the wilder smells of Daddy mixed in.

Momma had her special days, when all-of-a-sudden they had to pack a lunch and be gone. Momma picked where: the farthest corner of the backyard, the broken-down cabin across the county road, the best was a walk away from Raventon, to some place neither knew was their destination until they arrived. Momma took Angie out to greet the first snow and the first spring puddle; they walked all the way to the top of the ridge on days the gusting wind was frightening, when the trees moaned and chattered.

All the time Momma talked. She asked, read, yelled, patiently explained, and somewhere trickling through all her words was the melody of her voice. "Angeline, would you bring me the desk scissors? My angel of the coloring book—of the finished lunch plate—of the matching socks—"

And then.

Into the aid car. At the hospital. Gone. Daddy never answered any of Angie's questions with words. He cried too, and tried his best to hug her. Momma gone and others, there were others, they would talk about Momma being an angel. But Angie was the angel, Momma's angel. Momma was gone.

• • • • •

# 040

After, Daddy sat outside for hours, just sat. Angie learned how to move quietly so the house stayed silent except when the lilac scratched low along the house, or a curtain dragged across some windowsill.

Sometimes Angie moved extra quietly, thinking she might surprise Momma's spirit somewhere. But the only times Angie felt a snatch of Momma nearby came when she was distracted: playing in the living room with the box of soldiers and dolls, or reading in her room, she would suddenly feel Momma passing by to look in on her. But Momma never was. And even though Angie tried to stretch these feelings, even though she tried to set things up so it would seem like Momma was right around the corner, Angie was alone. By fall, when the time between school and dark was a tantalizing sliver of sunlight, by then Angie had to study a picture to get Momma's face right. It scared her, how far away Momma already was.

So she moved quietly to match the silence all around her, to blend in. Daddy kept sitting outside even when it was dark by the time he came home. During the summer some of the men had wandered by, talked a little, left long spaces in between. By fall Daddy was by himself.

Angie thought maybe he was waiting for Momma too.

In the books Angie read, a neighbor woman would have come and scolded Daddy and cooked for them and gradually it would have been the three of them, and the woman would have made them turn on more lights around the house. Or Angie would have found a secret special friend, and that would have made Daddy stay inside, and maybe smile. Instead, when the rains came, Daddy quit with his porch sitting and hired Luce to fix them dinners week nights.

Luce came, and she cooked, and she would talk with Angie if Angie lurked around until it was impossible not to. But mostly Luce made meatloaf or tuna casserole or spaghetti hotdish and left it in the oven with a note about how to heat it, and left. Daddy said it was all right to read at the table and sometimes they both did. Other times only Angie did. Both of them were careful to leave little things, scissors and socks that needed mending and a grocery list Momma had made, they left these where they were.

By springtime Angie felt like she was going deaf. The house drank up all of what was inside her, and more. When it got spicy outside and the birds were back, the weather made her itch to do something. Her birthday was coming, and still Daddy sat. Luce came and cooked and left and didn't care if Angie was there or helped or talked or not.

One afternoon Angie came home from school and she shouted at the empty house. She yelled jump rope rhymes, the alphabet, the name of every kid in her class. The house absorbed all of her noise and had quiet to spare. Outside, the yard was scraggly and bitter-looking most places, but in the corner by the shed there were flowers. She picked some and decided she would put them in a vase like Momma used to. She put them in the special vase, the china one by the front door. Then Angie remembered there was a yellow table cloth Momma used for special occasions and she went upstairs into the linen closet where there were all sorts of pretty things. She took them and the yellow cloth and she decorated. She made chains of paper rings and a crown for Daddy and one for herself and put out all sorts of silverware and fancy dishes from the big wood cabinet.

Luce arrived and stuck her head in and told Angie she shouldn't be standing on the back of the couch to hang things. Angie ignored her, pretended Luce was complimenting her work. Luce made some mean comments, went back into the kitchen, finished cooking, and left like she always did.

When Angie heard Daddy on the porch she started lighting all the candles.

Daddy stopped in the doorway.

"It's a party, Daddy. A spring party."

He didn't say a word.

That was when she wept. Nothing would ever stop the silence from creeping into her and drinking her up.

Daddy picked her up and kissed her. He had some tears too but he was trying to smile the smile he only gave Momma and her. "It is a party Angel."

He carried her around while he admired the decorations. When he saw the crowns he put the right one on each of them. He even put one flower behind his ear and turned on some music, twirling her around in time. They ate with all the candles lit, from the fanciest plates, then together they went to the store and picked out a cake and a carton of ice cream. Daddy kept different music playing the whole night. Even when she took her bath.

"Thank you for inviting me to the party." Daddy stood by her bed, his mouth doing everything but smile.

"You're welcome."

He tucked her in and turned off the light. He sat at the foot of her bed, where she could keep her legs up next to him. That was how she fell asleep.

In the morning one of the flowers was on her pillow, looking kind of mashed and wilted. Daddy was making breakfast when she came down, and he was wearing his crown.

• • • • •

# 041

It was the Dairyland delivery man's first day, and he was running late. Raventon had a big order, then three small stops and he'd be on his way back to Seattle. The dispatcher's directions warned him the turn-off for the store didn't look like much, so he was in low gear when he spotted the rutted drive. Even with the directions right in front of him he thought twice about taking the gloomy, muddy lane. Tree branches closed in around the truck, he could hear a few of them scraping. Then he came out to a turn-around behind a big and worn-down house. The rest of town, including the store, was on a slight grade behind it. He paused beside the house, noticed a faint set of tracks, and followed the cardinal rule of truck drivers: take command of the situation, and do it before anybody can tell you to stop.

By the time he pulled in front of the store, quite a few people were on its porch. He set the brake, grabbed the delivery book. "Took the overland route today?" said one cracker and everybody else laughed too.

He ignored them and made his way past, straight to the counter at the very rear of the store. A young girl was sitting on a stool behind it, next to a huge brass cash register. "Is the manager around?"

"Yup."

He paused. The girl didn't even look up from her magazine.

"Well, could you go get him?"

"I'm the manager." She looked up from her reading. "What did you want?"

"I'm looking for A. Mettle."

"You from Dairyland?"

"Uh, yes I am."

"You're late."

"Why don't you just go and get Mr. Mettle, girlie."

"I am A. Mettle."

He looked around the store. A few people had drifted in from the porch, they weren't even pretending to do anything but watch. He made eye contact with a woman near the cooler. "Where do I go to find somebody to check my stuff in?"

"She told you right" the woman said, nodding at the girl.

He turned back to the counter. "Fine then. But I do need the signature of A. Mettle when you're done."

The girl jutted her chin out. "Please hand truck everything in the back way, things that don't need refrigeration separated out."

He did as he'd been told, slamming the cartons and cases, then returned to the counter and shoved the clipboard her way. "I need the signature of the person who placed this order, right here." He pointed to the blank line. "And I talked to him once on the phone to tell him when I'd be here. So you run and get him little lady."

She took the clipboard and slid off her stool and went back to the storeroom. He followed her and watched as she methodically checked off every item on the packing list and handed his clipboard to him. Then she pulled out a checkbook and wrote one to Dairyland in clear grade school cursive, signed it "A. Mettle, Junior."

"Junior." He spat the word out. "I'll get this cleared up before the next delivery."

"Don't you want me to sign your packing slip so you know we got everything?"

He held the clipboard out and she signed it the same way.

They told the story all around Raventon and, for a joke, called her Junior to her face. Angie, as usual, didn't respond one way or another when anyone could see. So Julie Smuthers started calling her Junior, and kept calling her that. Some of the adults did too. It stuck; shorter than Angeline, and she was her Daddy's Junior, when it came to the store.

• • • • •

# 042

Angie and Daddy worked hard in the store, after Momma. Other people thought it was for the money, she knew. And Daddy did cling more to the dollars, over time. But every part of running the store was a challenge. Each supplier would second-guess Daddy's careful choices, substitute one brand for another, slip in a different grade or package size, inch a price upward. Customers paid no attention to entire shelves of goods and then the minute Daddy finally discontinued an item someone would walk in and want six or seven each.

Pricing reminded Angeline of conducting music. In the fall there were school clothes and stationery supplies, Thanksgiving and Christmas time had specialty foods and spices, in the summer picnic items and anything cold. From October to April cold cure-alls and small personal comfort items inched their way out, money was tight and you had to watch certain people's checks carefully. Around late April or early May the cheap bright things near the register, sunglasses, and gardening supplies would take off.

The cleverness came in making all the changes, none of them too suddenly. Daddy gradually got rid of the more fanciful stock, sticking with what immediately and reliably moved. It was the store itself Daddy poured his attention into. The store didn't run itself is what Daddy said about a million times. The store did make money, but that wasn't why either of them worked. When Angie was in there by herself, when all of it was quiet and dark and in order, she could smell the coffee corner and the feed and oiled hardware. The wood counter was worn down and kept shiny with lemon oil, there were smooth spots on the floor, the door to the backroom creaked in a certain pitch. It was the store, all of what came and went and who bought it, carton by carton, pound by pound, day by day. Money was what kept it going, that was all.

• • • • •

# 043

When Angie was sixteen, a month after she'd gotten her driver's license, she told Daddy she wanted to try making the next run to Seattle by herself. The next Thursday she had a thermos of tea, the travel notebook with the order sheets, the checkbook, maps, and the jitters, even though she knew every stop by heart. Angie'd filled the truck with diesel the night before, after she and Daddy finished loading it with empty pallets and the few returns. In the morning they added four five-gallon buckets of huckleberries, bought off local pickers.

"See you later Daddy."

"You look good in the truck Angel. Have fun." He stood with his hand raised and unmoving while she put all her attention into cranking the steering wheel hard to clear the driveway in one swing. Double-clutching, she was on her way.

She'd taken the big truck out solo a few times, but this was the first time she'd driven it alone all the way to Seattle. When she got up to the Pass she had to pee. As she gunned it back onto the highway feeling much relieved, she saw Morse.

He was standing on the shoulder, one thumb out, the other hitched into a belt loop of his jeans, grinning. She slowed down easy, thinking of the hucks in back, popped open the passenger door, and waited.

"Where ya headed?" As if she didn't know. As if her whole body didn't feel a spurt of heat and nervousness.

"Seattle, same as you." He climbed into the cab, slammed the door, and leaned into his seat.

Angie made sure her shifting was smooth as glass, working the truck up to cruising speed before she looked Morse's way. When they caught each other's eyes they both laughed.

Fall colors zoomed by, tires whining. As they came flying down the last of the foothills Seattle stretched before them. They'd decided to do the store run together, then lock up the truck and knock around until Angie needed to head back.

Morse stayed on the loading dock of the produce house when Angie cut the deal on the hucks. He didn't say a word until they were on their way to the next stop. "So how much of that huck money is profit?"

Angie hadn't thought to go inside the warehouse to settle. Daddy'd never said anything one way or another about telling anyone wholesale vs. retail, but he was discreet himself and now she understood why.

Morse put both feet up on the dash and lit a cigarette. "Wouldn't want to pay an undo amount to the kiddies who picked them, that's for sure."

Angie concentrated on driving.

Morse stayed in the cab. Angie calmed herself with double-checking paperwork at each stop, made sure she loaded the truck so nothing could shift around. It was mid-afternoon when she got permission to back the truck up tight to one of the loading doors at the last stop, promising it would be gone by three a.m., which made even Morse snicker.

They headed on foot to the waterfront. Morse showed her how to ride the ferry out and back, as many times as they wanted, for one fare. Angie bought a bag of popcorn the second time the boat left the city dock.

They talked of a thousand things, of nothing. She watched the wind scatter Morse's hair and the way he rubbed his thumb when he was thinking. What he took note of she had no inkling. A part of her started worrying about the truck when it started to get dark and Morse did notice that. "Well. See you back home."

"I can wait awhile if you want a ride."

"Naw. You better get back to your Daddy's store with your Daddy's truck." When he saw her face go red and lose its smile he shrugged. "Thanks for the ride. And the popcorn." Morse headed down the street, skinny, bouncing a little. But at the first corner he turned and did a weird little jump that made the people around him stare. Angie laughed and Morse waved back, then she was on her own.

• • • • •

# 044

It was close to nine when Angie backed in to the loading dock of the store. Daddy tried to make it seem like it was natural he would be right there waiting, but he'd closed the store early and he never just sat around in back.

Together they unloaded. She gave him the paperwork, the price sheet and ordering deadlines for Thanksgiving turkeys; told him when he asked what she'd gotten for the hucks, avoiding the memory of Morse.

Daddy said almost nothing but he looked shrunken in his sweater and the glasses he'd started wearing. Angie felt bad, but it wasn't like they'd ever discussed when she might get back. Besides, Daddy always let her do as she liked. So instead of explaining she waited him out in a way she never had before, until she defeated the questions Daddy couldn't quite ask.

They checked everything in, put the perishables in the cooler, looked around the backroom once more, and locked up before walking in silence, side by side, back to the house.

• • • • •

# 045

Meeting Morse on the Seattle run became a spontaneous habit. They had eaten their usual clam strips at Ivar's and had been strolling the waterfront after dark when he grabbed her arm. "Come on. I got something I want to show you." He ran.

Angie followed him under the viaduct, between its massive concrete legs, stumbled over old bottles and newspapers and who knew what until he stopped so suddenly she ran into him. They laughed, even though she'd bitten her lip hard.

"Now you got to stay right here no matter what, OK?" She felt the warmth of his breath along her cheek.

"What's going to happen?"

"Promise?"

"Are you staying too?"

"Yep."

"OK then." She heard the train coming, a whistle from near the produce houses. "There's a train coming." The tracks were right in front of them.

Morse looked at her as though she had already stepped back. The train got louder, its headlight cast channels of light and dark that pivoted off each concrete pillar. Louder and closer and brighter, she kept telling herself it had to stay on the tracks, it had to. The train was—the engine rushed past with a roaring sucked-down whistle. Its light was gone and she almost fell forward into all of the rest of the train: car after rattling car, squeaking wheels grating past not two feet in front of them. Her head throbbed, car after car, she forgot there would ever be an end until the caboose went by. The train receded into a fading clatter, other small sounds filled in.

When Morse took his hand off her shoulder was when she noticed it had been there at all. "Intimations of immortality."

"You got that right."

There wasn't much they could have done to add to the thrill; the thrill added to everything else they did that night. All the time Angie remembered Morse's hand on her shoulder, his breath on her cheek.

They wandered downtown, looked in store windows, ran across streets in front of cars. Angie was getting cold, she was tired. "I'm thinking I'll head back. You want a ride?" Only once, during a storm, had he ever accepted her offer of return.

"Naw."

"Well. See you then."

"Yep." He kissed her quick, his lips on hers and then he was headed elsewhere.

Dazed, she drove home.

• • • • •

# 046

"Daddy?"

He laid down his pen and leaned back in his chair.

"I want to go away."

Angie had his full attention. "I'm going away, by myself."

His face didn't change but behind his glasses his eyes did.

"I want to get away from what I've always known. Especially the store. For awhile anyway."

"There's no way of getting away from all of that, Angel."

She sat down on the couch and picked up a magazine, flipped through its color photographs of expensive clothing and cars and perfumes against backgrounds of places she had never been. Her father came from around his desk and sat next to her. "Is there a particular place you want to go?"

"That's the part I'm not sure of."

"I see."

She tossed the magazine onto the coffee table.

Her father rested his head against the back of the couch, eyes closed. "Did I ever tell you how I decided to marry your mother?"

Angie shook her head.

"It wasn't here. I went away. I made a point of going away for a time. Morse's father ran the store. Your mother and I, we'd spent quite a bit of time together, before I left. To make a long story short, I wrote your Momma a letter and she wrote back."

They both sat where they were for some time.

"Are you lonely?"

She took a good look at him, the flock of wrinkles at the corners of his eyes and mouth, his hair thinner and not so black somehow. When she didn't answer he opened his eyes.

They started to do a little of their looking, then Angie looked away.

"I am, Daddy. I don't belong here. I feel like I'm missing everything, but I don't know what."

He gave her a crooked version of his old smile, from before. Coaxed her hair behind her ear. "Fly away, fly away home." Then he scooted forward, bent into himself, and put both hands around her face. "You belong here and everywhere, just like your Momma. But if you need to go away, we'll figure out how."

"Daddy."

"If I could help you find your way I would Angel." He stood and left the room.

By the end of the week Angie had decided she would take the car and head north, into Canada. Touring was Daddy's word for it. He got her maps and would have given her more money if she hadn't refused. The morning she was to leave she was near tears and ecstatic. "I love you."

"I know you do."

Then it was time to start the car. He knocked on her window. She rolled it down. "Write sometime."

She nodded and backed out and put it in gear; Daddy waved and she waved back and he nodded and stood where he was, holding his one hand up the way he did long after she was out of sight.

• • • • •

# 047

Alexander Mettle spoke first. "Thanks for coming Morse."

"Uh... that's OK."

The kitchen was smaller and dingier than he remembered.

"Please. Make yourself at home."

Morse followed Angie's father to a chair at the kitchen table.

"I should offer you something. There's cookies or I could make a sandwich?"

"I'm fine." Morse stretched his legs under the table. It had been a long time since he'd been inside the house.

Daddy sat down beside him, folded and unfolded his hands.

Morse put his hands in his lap and listened to the ticking of the hallway clock.

"I have a large favor to ask of you."

"Ask and I'll let you know if I can do it."

"Yes. Well that's pretty much what I thought you would say. The first favor will be to hear me out. Because we are friends of some sort. Eh Morse?"

"I guess. Yeah." Morse was worried now. Because Alexander Mettle never asked; he offered, he suggested; almost everybody did as they were told. Morse watched the winged mermaid over the sink slowly rotate. He had thought this was going to be about a job, some kind of work Daddy needed done.

"I would like to make you a financial gift."

Morse was on his feet, clenching the top of his chair. Even in the faint light he could see the pleading in Daddy's face. "We might be some kind of friends, but what you—I'm leaving."

"Would you keep me company while I have a beer?"

Morse couldn't sort out what was happening. If this had to do with Angie—wouldn't she write him directly, or call, if she was pregnant or something? "Say what you're wanting to say."

"You're right." Daddy had the nerve to look right into Morse.

Morse barely had enough to look back.

"I'd offer to make you partner in the store, but I know that wouldn't be to your liking. At least for now. What I'd like to do is help you along. I know you have some ideas—

"You would be doing me a favor. And no one, not even Angie, will ever ever know." Daddy let out a big sigh. "I guess since you haven't hit me or walked out we'll continue to be some kind of acquaintances either way."

Morse had to laugh. "I wouldn't hit you." Then he realized what was happening. "But you leave me alone."

"A beer?" Daddy rummaged through the refrigerator. "I know you don't want anything, especially from me. But you are young and I am not. So I think you should grant me the privilege." Daddy put a bottle of beer in front of each of them. "I set up an account in your name, not through this pissant bank." He gestured toward downtown with his beer. "I put $7,000 in it."

Morse chugged his beer. Fucker. Mettle did this kind of shit to Angie her whole live-long life. "You're making assumptions that could end our acquaintance. You—you think—"

"Hear me out. This is money that would be sitting in some bank anyway. Now it's in Citizen's Bank in Seattle, the downtown branch. What I am asking of you, as a huge favor, is that you let it stay in your name. And that maybe, maybe someday you use it." Daddy finished his beer. It was the fastest Morse had ever seen him drink. "I may have done something very stupid. You tell me."

"You got another beer?"

Daddy nodded toward the refrigerator.

Morse used the time it took him to crack the beer and return to the table, to think. Angie's father always used his money. Morse thought he had stayed clear but he should have known it was a matter of time. Money and the store, he moved his bottle in circles on the table. What he didn't know was why, and why now.

Daddy spoke very softly. "Even when you were a little boy you took charge of how things would be. Admirably, I think. Until now I have known better than pry. But since Angie's left I've—Morse, I feel old. I know how small my universe is. I knit it this tight myself, stitch by stitch. You are like a son to me, and not because of Angie. Because of your own father.

"So I am asking a favor from you. Let me feel like my own—Let me offer encouragement. Please."

Morse finished his beer.

"You're asking too much, Alexander Mettle." Morse took his two empty bottles to the sink. "Too much even for a friend."

· · · · ·

# 048

All his life dreaming, sometimes Morse felt like that. Time slowed down around him, rich colors, everything extra-savory. When he was little he used to think there was some message about to be revealed, just to him. He'd learned to know better. But when daytime events seemed like dreaming, when life as it happened had the floating quality of dreams, it was hard to remind himself it was nothing, nothing special.

One of the first times he could remember daytime-dreaming was when he was maybe ten. Unc took him along, the way he sometimes did; they were going for firewood with some other men. Unc just told him they were going, and what to bring: a jacket, gloves, and some water. They took Unc's truck and met the other men in the woods. Morse's job was to carry or roll or push or drag the cut rounds to the trucks, and to make sure he didn't get flattened by a falling tree. By the time everybody had a load, the day and the woods were looking especially beautiful, the air full of fall-fetid, rotting-after-the-frost smells, but of ripe grass too. Morse's jeans had ripped out. His arms ached inside and were chewed up on the outside. The men stacked the wood into their trucks, razzing each other.

The best part came at the end. Morse was allowed a few sips of beer while they all laughed and drank around him. He rode home squeezed in the middle of the cab, smelling man-sweat and pine-pitch and bar oil. Everything had soft-edges, like he wasn't quite there, like he was watching his life live itself.

All his life? In a way he had been dreaming.

What Daddy had already done made Morse realize he'd been focused on one thing while what really mattered was happening elsewhere. Which is the way Angie had always made him feel. Especially when she'd announced she was leaving.

For the last year, since they'd become lovers, they'd kept to themselves. Other people made for complications. They still met in Seattle. They went on long hikes. It had been a good feeling, doing things together, like they'd finally figured out how to be. Morse had learned to stay clear of day-to-day Raventon; he hitched back and forth from Seattle jobs, ripe and ready and full of himself and what he could do. He never once thought they had made a pledge to each other. He thought Ang wanted to be wilder, and was sort of using him to get free.

So when she told him she was going to leave he thought, fine. Good. Stopped himself every time a twang of jealousy started to swell up inside. Pretended it didn't matter her Daddy set her up the instant she wanted to be on her way.

Then she was gone. And Morse, being nineteen, cut off at the quick any little nagging part of him that truly missed her. He'd managed pretty well until Mettle had him over. Morse knew they were talking about Angie. It felt like somebody'd kicked the bottom of his feet while he was sleeping; there wasn't even time to think about falling, you just the hit ground.

Hit the ground running was what Morse tried to do. Because he couldn't say it ever brought him much good, that feeling, of dreaming.

• • • • •

# CUZ

---

Lots of babies are born out of that thing called love. There was a year with a big moon time of month, or maybe a silver sliver hung crooked and high. A vintage year? I'm not the one to say.

Girl baby, out of two comes one. Words float together into the strange language of adults, the painfully clear statements of children, mirrors within mirrors within mirrors, smaller and smaller exact images, of what?

My dad. My mom was washing dishes when I gathered my courage and cornered her.

"Your father? He's like the day the buds pop out in spring. That wild time when it's blustering snow and blasting sunshine—you—your pizzazz. That's from him."

"Do you, do you know who my father is?" That got her to turn around and stare right at me.

"Of course I know who he is."

But why, why wouldn't she tell me? Dishes sloshing, silverware clinking, the light in the room reflected like a golden star above her head. I asked that night. "Who Mom? Please tell me."

I received the hollow answer of time. Older, and older still, that is when, then I would understand.

Touchstones, talismans, that which you cling to. Hold them tight, tell yourself what you must.

I'll tell you who I picked. After long and serious deliberation, the envelope please.

I knew she was talking about Morse. I picked him that night. I had put extra effort into watching him, listening to him. I'd taken careful note of his attitude toward me in particular. Granted, he was nice to all of Raventon's kids. Once he bought an ice cream cone for everybody who happened to be hanging around the store. Tía Angie grumbled as she scooped the tenth, the eleventh cone.

"That's right, Angie, I am the fairy godmother." Morse pirouetted for us then, teetering too close to the steps, but he didn't fall. His brown hair was going grey, the tails of his ratty shirt and his smart mouth flapped as usual. But he said something extra to me that day. "And you, my little pretty, I would grant three wishes." And bowed, just for me.

There was another afternoon, it was in the spring. I was running around the school and then the post office, running a huge repeating figure eight, I couldn't tell

104

you why. Maybe I was pretending to be an insect, maybe it was a too-hot day. Morse made one of his impossibly sudden appearances on the bench in front of the P.O. as I came zooming past.

"Your endless revolutions are going to change the rotation of the earth" was what he said.

"I don't weigh enough."

He laughed. He has one of the best laughs ever, when you catch him off guard. "I think you hold your own on the cosmic scale. Maybe not a heavyweight but a serious contender. I'd say you're a chip off the old block." Then Morse winked at me.

I took off in sheer explosive joy. Twelve years old, I sprinted for miles, everywhere and anywhere but near the post office.

Is he my dad?

Have you never noticed the gyroing stabilization of our actions, our very lives? We spin on the tiny head of a pin, the tiny footprint we call home. Spinning creates a balance, we could call it love.

So I ran, I sprinted, I spun like an Olympic figure skater, tucked in tight to myself for speed; I zeroed in on Raventon. And when the time came for flight—I hit the wall of memory like there was no tomorrow.

• • • • •

# 049

---

When Dorth came home from the Spokane conference she went to her books and read about color theory. November rains drummed on the roof of her studio as she practiced with pigments, tried to document the precise shift from one color to another, knowing the entire spectrum to be fluid.

Dorth concentrated and was left exactly where she'd started. What separated red from yellow, dark from light? Could she paint the exact distinction between an eye with a twinkle and one without? Between a twinkle of habitual good humor and that of malice?

The portrait of Such-a-One had turned out well in this respect. So well the woman herself had hemmed and hawed and visited the painting several times before deciding she wouldn't buy it for her own collection. Her tongue had flickered, she'd hesitated, her hand had come up to caress her throat and then she had laughed, saying "it would just be a little too, you know... vain." As though vanity had ever slowed her in the past.

Change: there had to be a way to document the not-quite noticeable shifts of emotion, of expression, of reality, of light. Time passing worked its magic, like the tendrils of a vine or the roots of a weed, there was a slow-twisting way one thing become inseparable from another. Like dawn coming, or dusk; like growing old. Was change a thing throbbing to get out or a trap slowly closing?

Dorth watched raindrops chase each other down the windows and lost her own edge.

She made two plaster masks of her face. She tried to paint one the exact colors she saw looking into a mirror in full light. She painted the other the colors she saw when she closed her eyes and imagined her face. She cast the back of her head twice, and joined one to each of the masks she had painted.

She mounted the head painted in the colors she saw with her eyes closed into the center of a piece of plywood, so you could only see one profile at a time. She painted one side of the plywood with a series of micro scenes of the city: skyscrapers at night, people waiting at a bus stop, storefronts and a school just letting out. The other side of the plywood she left blank. She wanted to somehow paint it so that profile looked like a cloud, like it could shift any moment into a million other shapes, as though it had only a momentary integrity.

The head whose face was painted in the actual colors of her flesh, she set on a narrow white pedestal. Over the course of a week she coated it again and again with resin, remembering a mask her grandparents had of translucent plastic, and how it blurred features, making everyone who wore it look like a mannequin. She wished she could rig a bubble machine inside the mouth. Instead she glued fragments of mirror for the eyes.

What was separate and what was not?

• • • • •

# 050

On a Saturday in early December, Dorth took off by herself, driving. At first she thought her only goal was to cruise, to take a break from the familiar and all too dreary. But as she headed east, when she hit the first feathery fishtails of snow just before the Pass, she admitted to herself where she was headed. With the heater on high she began the east-side descent, snow and iridescent sunlight beckoning.

Under a bank of low grey clouds, Raventon looked hard-bitten, buildings weathered, trees bare, not all its streets plowed. She got a cup of hot chocolate to go at the store, and was coming back down the steps of the porch when she heard an all too familiar voice.

"So you lived to tell about it, huh?"

It was the vulture-man from her drinking escapade.

"Near as I can tell." She blushed instantly. "Um, thanks for putting me up." Praying her lack of memory of anything beyond a corner to crawl into was a true and complete representation of what had taken place.

He leaned out the window of his pickup with a smile that came close to a smirk but didn't quite cross over. "You're welcome."

"I might be staying here for awhile."

His eyebrows went up. "I'll see you around then." And drove off.

What part of her was thinking of staying?

Dorth studied the pay phone, hesitated, then punched digits.

"Hello?"

"Hiya Rudy."

"Dorth? You OK?"

"Yah."

He could stretch a pause too.

"Rood, I'm—I'm, uh, going to set up a new place to work." Her words sounded untrue even as she said them. "I'm thinking—I drove up to Raventon and I want to try working here."

"When were you thinking of making the shift?" His voice sounded as though he'd swallowed half of it.

It made her choke too. "The end of next week."

Ninety-five miles of telephone wire dipped, drooped, and sagged between them.

"I was thinking I'd come home and load up some stuff."

"Some stuff or everything?"

"I'm not exactly sure."

There was more silence. Eventually they both said goodbye. Only goodbye.

Dorth spent some of the afternoon calling numbers off the store's bulletin board. She tromped icy streets, trying to imagine how she could make any of the few places she looked at habitable. Knowing she would, but she didn't want to think about why.

Another thing she knew, and Rudy knew too—he was not going to be part of this. He could have made arrangements somehow, if she had in any way included him in her decision.

Her heart, even to her, it was an icy heart. As she drove to Seattle she worried, about the snow, the sleet, the tires on the car, pretended it was the weather bothering her.

• • • • •

# 051

Packing was far worse than Dorth had imagined. The sheer volume of objects overwhelming, and that was only the physical part of the difficulty. She focused on her studio, but the more she took down, the more what was left had its own associations; whether she hauled everything with her or not, she did not want to leave any part of herself or her work exposed.

After two days she knew there was no way she was going to be ready by the next weekend. So on the third day, when she and Rudy passed each other in the kitchen, as they avoided eating dinner simultaneously, let alone together, she told him. "It's going to take me an extra couple days."

He nodded and went out for the rest of the evening.

Dorth packed things from the house when Rudy was gone, which was most of the time. She set aside her pillow, two towels, a washcloth, and a couple of the extra blankets. Books and furniture were more than she could deal with so she didn't even consider them. Kitchen stuff was dicey. Dorth packed only what was necessary and without sentimental value, as though she were going on a long car-camp. She made a list of what she hoped to pick up later: whisk, cutting board, cast iron skillet, steamer, chair, couch, bed. Hauled what she'd packed into the studio.

By the following Tuesday afternoon she was exhausted. Her former studio was piled with a disturbing number of cartons, stacks of wrapped canvasses, odds and ends. Dorth called a guy who had his number on a card at the laundromat. The only catch was, he couldn't haul anything for another week. She tried Hertz and Avis and Rent-a-Wreck and realized she'd have to wait; he was too much cheaper. She sighed and left the house on foot.

Rudy didn't come home until fairly late. It seemed like he must have already eaten. The tininess of the house made their avoidance of each other ridiculous; Dorth sleeping in the living room made everything crowded.

She opened the refrigerator, took a beer and held out another to Rudy. He ignored her at first, then took it and wandered off to the only free chair in the living room. Dorth followed him as far as the doorway. "I'm not going to be out of here until Saturday. That's as early as I can get a truck."

Rudy took a sip of beer and grabbed a magazine she'd watched him read the night before.

"Rood?"

He turned magazine pages.

She wanted to go and hold him and say nothing. She wanted to be gone and leave him be.

"I'm sorry, Rudy."

He turned the pages back to front, head down.

"I'm sorry to be hanging around." She stayed in the doorway watching him. Finally she went out to the garage, taking the rest of a six-pack with her.

When she came back into the house it was after midnight. Rudy was crashed out in the chair. She went over and turned out the light behind him. And could not help but stroke his head, its curve so familiar, and feel his short coarse hair; could not help but trace the side of his face the way she had a million times before. He shifted but didn't move away. She kept her hand against his cheek, trying to drink in through this touch his gentleness. His hand came up to hers and held on.

Faint smell of soap and sweat, she worked her face into the crook of his neck from behind, eyes closed. Rudy leaned his head closer and her arms came around him.

Eventually she let go; he kept hold of her hand and led her to the bedroom. She could not look at him, even in the dark.

They came close together and they kissed. The first kiss in a long long time. Dorth hid her face in Rudy's neck, where shadows met darkness. He ran his hands down her back and they pulled each other closer and kissed again and didn't stop. Her body and all its parts knew the way.

Rudy felt like if he let her go for one second he might hurt her, but for now he wanted her close, he wanted her hands to rub the fur of his chest, he wanted her in the cave of his arms.

They kissed and this was not the love of golden trumpets or of silky butterflies. This was a love as broken-in as an old pair of jeans, a love worked between them until its rhythm had been curved into their bed, into their bones. Delicate like the tendril of a pea in a gentle breath of breeze; driving like the first pounding rain of a thunderstorm. Fondness and original passion and a touch of lust. What shattered them both was the new feeling that opened and closed and folded around them until they were beyond their usual ridiculous positions, the parameters of beloved habit, romping and craving in some new place where the only order was in their jagged breaths, humming; bigger than either of them.

They remembered they were separate amidst bedclothes and scattered curly hairs and liquids and flesh. Found themselves returned, distant from all the looks that had no place between them and their bitter sometime-silences. They curled together and kissed again, falling closer to sleep. Dorth reached for Rudy, and this was all he desired, her love for him as he loved her; he relaxed and welcomed her into his arms, his sleep.

The mystery of love.

It kept them close for the next day, through most of what was not right between them. Gave them some glimmer of a way around, if they chose to pursue it. If they both wanted it. Caught off-balance from the cruel ways they had made into habits between them, they were tender with each other, careful, cradling some resonation of a long-before and a brand-new.

• • • • •

# 052

---

Since it wasn't actually raining when he stepped outside, Rudy decided he could spare twenty minutes and walk back to his office. Maybe then he'd feel better. So he started walking, picking the last of a Chinese lunch from his teeth. Lots of holiday shoppers were out and about, especially near Pioneer Square, a few of them pointing at a brick building. Rudy would have avoided the performance if he'd known. He'd pretty much avoided everything to do with art since Dorth had moved out.

Then came the first eerie trumpeting. Swelling high, a globe of sound filled the street not because it was particularly loud, but because it grew and flared out and melted back until it wasn't anymore. A pause, all the other city-sounds louder. Then again; the call. As this bowl of sound was poured around the crowd, figures appeared along the roof line of the brick building, one of them with a conch shell, blowing. Rudy watched two figures step to the center of the two sides of the roof he could see.

Human but not. Bare of feature, powdered white, naked except for a loin cloth. Anonymous. Without any exact moment of motion or stillness the standing figures curled into themselves and rolled over the edges of the roof. Each became a mirage of a fetus floating against the suddenly unbelievably square brick walls. Perhaps there was a flicker of red at the fingernails? The conch blew like some sea-breath as the figures, curled egg-shapes, were lowered, floated head first down the sides of the building, embryonic. The inverse of time-lapse photography: real-time action took forever as Rudy watched. The conch blew, sound expanding slower than a sleeper's breath, and then it contracted into a silence that held sound.

It was as if Rudy were asleep; it made him think of Dorth; it did a thing to time. The figures were lowered, one on each side of the building, in perfect symmetry. Each opened like a flower coming into blossom, still not really human, more like a soul or a spirit, like a child being born and growing.

The conch blew in and out, like ocean waves.

Then, like the touch of red paint he had seen—instant and sudden and wrong—one figure falls. Screams and gasps and yelling. One figure has fallen to the pavement and is bleeding but makes no motion, did not move during the fall. The other figure curls inward, inch downward, the conch breath continues like a huge chamber, absorbing even the approaching sirens. The living figure Rudy can still see is lowered, withdrawing into a smaller self like an aging larva, recurling to the fetal, somehow wizened.

Rudy stood back from the growing crowd and the ambulances and a fire

truck as the broken rope swayed against the blank brick wall; all those present strug-
gling between the ritual and the dying man.

Rudy walked. He didn't stop when the rain began. He made his way through
the shoppers and the people asking for handouts and the red lights and the green lights
and the puddles and the passers-by. He walked up Queen Anne Hill until he came to
the old style streetlights, continued to the park overlooking downtown. Sheets of rain
blew the dark water of Elliot Bay silver, ferries with their tiny golden lights chopped
across, undeterred. For him there was an empty house and his own heart and the one
who did not fall and the one who did, to a real death.

He should have been in his cubicle shuffling papers and filling out forms so
some tiny fraction of all the people who came to him for help would get food stamps
or temporary housing or a doctor to look at them.

Instead Rudy took another look at the neon and the holiday lights and all the
cars filling the streets below him, all the buildings with the lights from all the offices
like his, and he began the walk back downtown. Drenched, he wept.

• • • • •

# CUZ

When the final bell rang Friday afternoon, signaling Christmas break, we exploded into the late grey afternoon, backpacks overflowing with the miscellaneous papers, candy canes, and half-destroyed ornaments only our mothers would appreciate. It was snowing, we were free and we kicked snowdrifts, shoved each other and laughed when anyone fell. Eisy and Rancid and Pancho and I and just about everybody else scrambled to the big sliding hill as fast as we could get our sleds. It was Rancid's idea to leave the madding crowd for the ridge.

We each took another couple of runs to think about it, then started the trudge, Eisy in the lead. Once we got into the woods the snow on the trail was more slippery than deep. Sounds were muffled, except for our huffing and puffing and the plow as it worked it way through town. After about ten minutes of climbing we took a short test run, and it was fast. So we retraced our steps and kept going most of the way to the top. It was getting dark, that thick grey where you can see if you really look, but you can feel the real nighttime is just about there. I was nervous, and had been, ever since that little bit of a practice slide; the snow was fast because it was ice underneath. Chances were approximately one hundred percent I would be the last one down, which meant the trail would be even slicker.

Rancid ended our climb when he hopped onto his sled, gone before Pancho could get ahead of him, yelling the dirtiest words he knew as he disappeared into the trees. Pancho flashed me one of his beautiful smiles and took off after Rancid, his plastic sled whistling. Eisy got settled on his turbo sled, replete with steering bars, one foot on each side. "Do you want my sled?"

"No way." It would only go faster and leave me with no excuse for my lackluster performance.

"We'll wait at the traverse till you catch up. Give me a push." Eisy took off, his voice expanding into a mock-scream as he peered around his feet like an Olympic bobsledder.

I pulled my hat down, checked the cuffs of my mittens, and started. The scary part of coming down the ridge was always the trees. Sure there was a trail, but the faster you went, the less likely you were to stay on it.

Whaling, sailing, I tried to brake with my feet, which only spun me around or jammed my legs suddenly and painfully into incidental branch and rock. I tried scraping one hand, then the other, or both, and my sled flew out from under me. Eventually I developed a style of dragging something at all times, and periodically bailing, never quite slamming into a tree. I came around a corner and there they all were, I had no choice but to ditch.

Before I had come to a stop Rancid was laughing. "You need training wheels."

I wiped the snow from my face and didn't bother answering.

"You gotta at least try." Even Eisy was not impressed by my performance; they must have waited a long time.

"Are you ready yet? Or are you going to spend the night here?"

Without so much as rolling over I took a mittenful of snow from my side and ate it.

"How do you know I didn't pee there?" Rancid kicked snow at me.

"Come on." Eisy yanked his sled into position. I lay where I was. Their screams disappeared down the trail. A nuthatch resumed pecking nearby. It was dark enough I could barely see the snow clumped on the unwavering branches above me. A slow chill crept in. I lay there until it was as dark as it was going to get, my eyes able to see snow and not-snow, nothing more. I took my own very sweet time then, down the rest of the run. The snow was so smooth, the darkness cloaked me, I went just a little faster than I dared, and did not lose it once. Just me and the ridge, all the way down, joy beyond desiring. When I walked out of the woods onto the deadend street, a shadow moved and Pancho joined me. We said not one word as we hauled our sleds to where our paths parted, and I think he smiled, as I did, when we each turned to go home.

• • • • •

# 053

Pancho came bolting into the kitchen just as Angie was tucking herself in at Analisa's shining kitchen table, her Saturday afternoon cup of tea on the way.

"Can I go tubing with Eisy?"

"Where?"

"Up at the Pass. I got some money."

"I don't know, Chico."

"Tía told me I would like it." He pointed at Angie, who nodded, shrugging at Analisa at the same time.

"Don't use your finger to point. And be back before your Dad gets home."

Pancho nodded and disappeared down the hall.

"Be careful."

"Don't worry, Mom." And Pancho was outside and running, zipping his jacket as he went.

"I thought he'd already been there when he asked."

"It's all right. I'm glad for once he wants to go somewhere, even with that Eisy. And he's made you into an auntie."

Angie blushed.

"No no. It's a good thing. Like the quiet we have now, Tía Angie."

Angie loved the way it sounded when Pancho said Tía, she liked the softness of it when Analisa and Jorge used it to tease her into staying longer, to have a little more of whatever they were passing around. But when others began to use it Angie heard in this newest nickname other resonations she liked far less: old maid, single for life. Knew her heft, her height, her blunt ways made it easy to mock. Tía Dolores, sad-auntie, was what Analisa called her when she noticed Angie feeling low.

But gradually the name Tía came to complement and sometimes replace Angie, and the occasional Junior. Not because everyone knew what it meant, but because Angie answered to it, and she did so because of Pancho.

• • • • •

# 054

---

Winter took hold. So as a luxury, to relax, Angie used odd bits of time to drive between places. She planned detours. When she had errands that took her down the valley, she would stay as close to the river as she could; on the way back she zig-zagged, always avoiding the highway. None of her meandering was exactly exploration, which is what made her disorientation so unnerving.

It was as though she couldn't quite fit places together. She never actually got lost. But somewhere the assumed, her habitual knowledge of every rock and bush and who had how many hairs sprouting from which mole, somehow this broke down. Everywhere and everything grew more complicated.

It was like the tortoise and the hare, in order to get to what she remembered, she first had to get halfway. And to get halfway, she had to get part of that way. Angie spent more and more time taking the back ways, she studied more and more closely the faces around her. Always knowing that with one stomp on the gas she could be anywhere she was headed; that with one questioning eyebrow she could get somebody else to fill in the key detail that slipped her own mind.

If she had mentioned this to anyone, she might have said her navigational skills, and perhaps her mental powers, were crumbling. But she never spoke a word. Meanwhile, Daddy hovered, hemming her in with questions: Where was she going and when would she be home? Why did it take so long to do so few errands? Who had come into the store to buy what? Who had she talked to at the post office? He nursed a cup of tea nearby while she did the dishes, sat across from her at the kitchen table when she finally ate dinner.

One night as she was finishing he tapped the table. "I've got something for you, Angeline."

"Yeah what?" She knew everything that was in the house. Her feet ached, the dusty mermaid twirled. Daddy shuffled his way into the hallway, his slow steps returned.

A bit of candied ginger was what Daddy offered her. She loved its smell and the Chinese jars it came in, a remembrance of travelers like Marco Polo, of the exotic and the faraway. Daddy had told her that when he was little, a single tangerine had been like that. He found it in the toe of his Christmas stocking, ate it section by section for two days, then put the rind under his pillow to keep its scent.

Angie took the ginger and couldn't help but smile at Daddy as he took a piece himself. She closed her eyes and let the chair dig into a knot in her back and chewed the ginger. She measured her own sense of getting older by the way she sometimes enjoyed rehashing old stories. Remembering-when gave her a kind of strength, when it wasn't like a cage. What started as a memory spiraled into a series of bad times, the inexcusable things she'd done rose up around her like metal bars. She could scratch around trying to make excuses, but her only real hope was when a good memory came inside the cage with her, and she could daisy-chain her way out. That night, Angie knew the cage was close so she didn't follow anything the candy brought to mind.

She sucked the last bit of hot ginger from her teeth, licked the last sugar crystal from her lip. That's when she first thought of having the party.

• • • • •

# 055

Angie dropped off the last invitation and came sweeping home, feeling pretty damn good. Daddy was in his easy chair in the living room. It was time to make the announcement.

"Hey Daddy, I got a surprise for you."

He put the book he was reading down in his lap and waited.

"We're going to have a party."

"We are?"

"Yep." Angie studied his face. "We're gonna have a rip-roaring birthday party."

"For whom?"

Angie's stomach began a downward lurch. "For you."

He sat up in his chair. "Did I ever say I wanted a party?"

"Daddy, you're going to be ninety years old."

"I'm well aware of that. But this party you have on your mind. I don't want a party." He raised his book.

"I already gave out invitations."

"Well you didn't invite me until now."

"It's just going to be friends. I thought—"

He kept his book up.

She studied Daddy's gnarled fingers against the covers of his book, his almost wornout slippers. Fifty-five years old, she ran to her room, closed the door, and then she was trapped.

She sat on the edge of her bed with her eyes closed and rubbed her forehead, rubbed until it burned.

She remembered long ago, how she and Morse used to bicker and argue and try and puzzle out the difference between being alone and being lonely. "Back when the world was new, and I believe you loved me too, back when the world was new..."

Back when they were new anyway; naked loving so strong the other kinds of bare-to-the-bone sharing seemed part of a whole new world opening, as though all the colors and smells of the regular same-old same-old world had cranked up a notch.

She heard Daddy turn off his reading lamp downstairs, listened to him begin his step-by-step climb up the stairs.

She remembered the way the house had come close to swallowing her, how when she got that quiet at bay, she thought she could lick anything.

She took a look at the picture of Momma. Stood up and walked to the dresser and took a good look. The two of them in their matching dresses, Momma's love so casual in the way her hand brushed Angie's face. And in her own face Angie saw a laugh bubbling out. Both of them looking over to Daddy, behind the camera.

When Angie remembered it was a party she'd invented then to fill up the quiet, she could not believe how nakedly she had repeated her seven-year-old self. A one-trick pony; and Daddy knew, and this time he didn't need her trick. He had own way of holding on, he let the clock tick on by, did his morning things, and then his lunchtime things, all the way until it was time to get up again.

Angie turned and looked into the mirror. She tried to see in it what she had gotten used to thinking of as herself: her wrists, her smiles, her spark, her strength; a modest attractiveness she had never considered any kind of real beauty. But looking back at her was a big bullish woman with salt and pepper hair sticking out where it wasn't pulled back severely, breasts sagging, brutish hands crossed, skin that hung along her upper arms, a mouth that looked more ready to grimace than to smile.

• • • • •

# 056

Analisa and Jorge and Pancho were the first to arrive, and despite what they had promised Angie, they brought a plate of Analisa's cookies and Pancho brought a present for Daddy, who opened it on the spot. And Alexander Mettle, who never wore a tie of any kind, for anything, put this silver bolo tie around his neck and beamed. "Downright elegant, don't you think?"

Pancho nodded in solemn agreement. There was a knock on the door. Minor Haynes the banker stood there in his navy camel's hair, escorting his dear mother, Madeline Evangeline. Samuel shrugged his way in behind them, shook Alexander's hand and teased him about being so goddamn ancient. With that the party was off and running.

Angie double-checked that everyone knew to help themselves to the food, found a place for coats, and laughed to herself when she saw Minor had already cornered Cantoni's wayward nephew. Poor Piso needed a big loan and everybody knew it, so he was doomed to listen Minor's monologues. The door opened again and in came Morse.

Angie made her way over, giving him a half-wave high sign.

"Quite the shebang."

"That's right. The social event of the season."

Morse slipped out of his jacket and turned. "You know Dorth, don't you? I figured this was a perfect introduction to our dear community."

"Hi." Angie's former grin locked around her words. "Excuse me."

Morse cocked his head toward Dorth. "Did you two have a little run-in?"

"I don't think so. Maybe I shouldn't have come."

"Nuts. Half the people who'll be here didn't get personal invites. Come on, let's get some food."

Minor Haynes finished with Piso and worked his way over to the guest of honor. When he shook Daddy's hand it looked as though he expected somebody to snap a picture for the newspaper. Daddy eventually got his hand free.

"You know, sir, you really should be considering some kind of estate planning. After all, none of us lives forever."

"Isn't that a blessing."

"Excuse me?" And when Daddy didn't answer, "I would recommend an irrevocable trust. That sounds like a mouthful I know, but what it means, in simple terms—"

"I don't recall asking you, and it's my observation trust is always revocable.

Excuse me, I need to use the bathroom." Which left Minor to find a new victim.

Trust. Angie slammed a tray of cold cuts down on the table harder than she'd intended, then lured herself into some kind of outward calm. Dorth was an easy twenty years younger than Morse. Or herself. Mooncalf. Despite herself Angie was always too ready for Morse.

Dorth kept close behind Morse, filled her plate from the huge well-worn cherry table in the dining room. "Thanks for bringing me along."

"Yeah right." Morse reassembled his food into a serious sandwich and took a bite.

"I've been meaning to ask you about your name. I thought it was Morris at first."

"You may be thinking too much."

"Maybe." Dorth didn't know if she was getting into something personal or if Morse was goofing around. "Have you and Tía known each other all your lives?"

"Tía." He smiled and shook his head. "'All Our Lives,' isn't that a soap opera?" and took his plate into the living room.

"Have you met my father?" Angie appeared in her best imitation of Joan Crawford as Ice Woman.

Dorth finished chewing what was in her mouth. "Not formally. I'm sorry if I intruded. Morse made it sound like this was an open house."

"Morse likes to make events his own. Sorry I can't offer you a drink, but please, enjoy yourself."

"That's OK." No one was drinking. Dorth set her plate down on the edge of the table. "Thanks for having me here."

Angie watched Dorth say something to Daddy and leave. Then realized Morse had been watching her. She turned to clear Dorth's plate but Merta had discreetly taken it over, refilling it and one pocket of her house dress with more goodies. Several kids were poking each other and pointing, snickering. "Do any of you think you'll live to be ninety?" Angie's voice was louder than she'd intended. The kids looked at her, made a grab for the last of Analisa's cookies, and dispersed.

"Of course they will." Cantoni smeared his watery laugh around the dining room. "Why, your father made it, and I'm not far behind. And we were both just as greedy as those little rug rats.

"Piso, come here." His nephew came as quickly as a well-trained dog. "How many times have I told you about what a great man Angie's father is? How he provides the retail, and me, ha, I've been the one to buy and sell the houses." He turned to Angie. "I am so happy your father invited me here to celebrate—"

"You can be sure I wasn't the one who made the list of invitations Raso." Daddy helped himself to more cake.

Eisy noticed both Angie and her father were in the dining room. "Well, do you want to check out the house or not?"

Cuz took a look around. "I guess."

"Come on then." Eisy led the way up the stairs.

"You two there. Where are you going?" Madeline Evangeline Haynes called faintly after them. Seventy-three and doe-like as the last night-shadows in the morning, she startled just as easily. She had come to Raventon when Minor returned to reorganize the Company bank. Madeline was not of Raventon, and never would be.

"They need to use the bathroom." Pancho was at her elbow, arms crossed before him.

"Whose child are you?"

"He's my son."

Madeline peered at Pancho and his father through her thick glasses. "You're the ones who bought Cantoni's little house. My son says you are reliable in your payments. My name is Mrs. Haynes. Senior."

Jorge looked at her extended hand, then shook it.

"I'm Mr. Llamado." She was surprised at the softness of his grasp. "And this is Mr. Llamado, Junior." Jorge pushed Pancho slightly. Only those who watched her closely ever saw the possible sadness flickering in her. Pancho caught this and held his hand out. She stretched her neck to get a better look in a way that reminded him of a heron.

"My pleasure" said Pancho as they shook.

Meantime Samuel had worked up an audience, telling tales about Daddy. Even though he was only five years older than Angie, he was one of the few who knew Daddy well. "Who else could teach me how to fish? Daddy-o here, he showed me a trick. It only works lake fishing. You get yourself a little mouse, a cute little baby, and a piece of bark, about this big—" he held his hands about a foot apart. "Isn't that right?"

Daddy was shaking his head. "I can't believe you, telling people this is my idea—"

"Such modesty. But he was indeed the one who passed this technique along to me. So you hook that cute little mouse good, and float the bark out there, with the little critter on it. That's the tricky part. But damn if the biggest fish in the lake won't come up and bite—" he slapped his hands together and a few people jumped. "Just like that. Tells you something about the true personality of a fish, I'd say."

"Not to mention your own, you liar." Daddy was laughing.

"And then there's the time he got me to buy two dozen golf balls in the dead of winter."

Angie knew this one, and headed for the kitchen in time to spot Cuz as she came down the stairs. "Where have you been?"

Cuz was furious at herself. "I thought there was another bathroom."

"I guess you noticed there isn't?"

Cuz nodded, kept her head down, and went looking for her coat. Eisy waited at the top of the landing, just out of sight, until he hoped the coast was clear, then found his own jacket and took off.

The party reduced itself. Analisa beat Angie to the kitchen and was done with most of the dishes by the time Angie found her and made her go home. Daddy recorded his final cribbage score against Morse while Angie stayed in the kitchen.

"Not such a bad party." Daddy looked tired as he stood in the doorway. "Thank you."

Angie nodded.

"I think I'm going to turn in."

"Good night."

"Night, Angel."

When Angie heard his bedroom door shut upstairs, she left the rest of the mess and went for a walk, avoiding downtown. She latched the wrought-iron gate of the cemetery behind herself and made her way up the short bit of hill to Momma's grave, smiling as she remembered the story about fishing with a mouse. Daddy used to have all sorts of wild ideas.

Ninety years old. When she'd looked around the party she only saw a few people who knew Daddy as something other than a fossilized old man. Angie scuffed the snow to the side of Momma's plot. Momma would be eighty-five, if. More if than Angie could imagine.

• • • • •

# CUZ

Angie is the one who provided most of what we needed when we needed it. Even when what we needed was very little, and also very hard to come by.

If you pulled in to the store and saw Tía Angie working, you might think she was not so smart, perhaps even a little backward. Awkward looking, rough speaking, she was always busy, wiping down the counter, dust-mopping, working the register, cleaning the bathrooms, sweeping the porch. You could leave thinking she was nothing special. But if you stuck around, as you kept coming by, you'd start to count on her, like you count on your mom when you're a little kid, or the sun coming up, or the cold of winter. Tía was part of the days going round. She gave as good as she got and then offered the critical speck of comfort.

I think she always knew the world was no bigger than herself, the rest of us, the squawk of a crow, the sun on a rock. What went on inside, when her heart turned inward? If you watched carefully you could see, she had sorrows. I learned from her it was all right to live with ghosts. On the outside, to people who are so busy in their own lives they forget to look around, she served: mostly what they needed, sometimes what they wanted, rarely what they deserved.

She was our auntie. That's why the name stuck.

• • • • •

# 057

Dorth slept restlessly. Gusts of spring wind moved down from the ridge, rattled and scraped branches, then creaked and sifted through the house. She got up early and moody, built a small fire, watched the robins and sparrows poke the yard for grubs and old seed. Nursing her second mug of coffee she couldn't help thinking of Rudy. Once she started thinking it wasn't long before she grabbed her jacket and headed down to the pay phone.

"Hey Rudy."

"Dorth. Morning."

"How are you?"

"OK. Waking up."

Dorth tried to enjoy the slice of March sunlight she was basking in under the sullen, shifting sky. "I just thought I'd call."

"Yeah."

She could hear him moving around, he must have still been in bed. "Sorry I called so early."

"That's OK, I had to get up anyway."

"Hey Rood?"

"Yes?"

"What would you think about coming up to visit? This weekend?" Dorth switched the phone to her other ear.

"What would I think?" His voice had changed completely. "Is something wrong? Did something happen?"

"No."

"What are you asking me then?"

"I'm asking you to come visit."

"One day you phoned in and announced you were out of here. Came home, packed what you liked. Left."

Dorth picked at the paint on the wall of the store.

"You left me, Dorth. Why would I come visit?"

Dorth knew herself to be ridiculous, and also close to tears. "Because you want to see me, I guess." Pinched herself hard enough to hurt. "That's what I'm asking."

"Shit. I'll call you—I mean, can you call back, tonight?"

Dorth took a deep breath and let it out. "Yeah, I can. When?"

"Let me think." And Rudy took some time. "Maybe after eight or so?" He sounded defeated.

"Sure. Or you can say no now."

"I need time. I've been trying to think, since you took off. I'm not so sure I want to be around you right now."

"Maybe if I could show you what's—why I'm here—"

"Assuming I want to know."

Dorth stuck her fingernail into the side of her thumb.

"Or want to try. You—" Rudy's voice dropped. "You haven't wanted to know what's going on with me, as a far as I can tell."

Silence.

"So if you're really serious, maybe you should come down here. But I gotta say. I don't exactly trust you. Not with this kind of back-and-forth shit."

"What if you came just for a day then? The weather's been perfect and it looks like it's going to continue for a little—"

He was quiet when she stopped.

"Dorth?"

"Yeah?"

"What is it you are asking me? Really?"

"I want to show you— I... I want to try and make things right between us. So I'm asking—I'm asking a lot."

A big sigh. "Yes. You are." The flatness of his voice made Dorth feel flat too.

"Forget it. I'll give you a call when I can see my way to coming down. Rudy." Dorth cleared her throat, trying to get her voice straight. "I was thinking this would be a start. No obligation."

"You call and all of a sudden I'm supposed to drop everything—"

"I love you. That's what I'm trying to communicate. I'm sorry I fucked up. But I can't just come back and have everything be the same."

Rudy was silent.

"So I'll call you tonight?"

"Um, yeah."

"I love you, Rudy."

"OK."

"Bye."

Dorth hung up, wiped her tears, and blew her nose. The sunlight tart on the last melting piles of snow, on the touch of green along the edge of the parking lot. Her heart felt like lead.

"You aren't hung over again are you?" Morse slammed his truck door.

"No."

"Well you look terrible."

"Thanks."

Morse squinted at her. "Something wrong?"

"Everything's fucking hunky-dory." Dorth took off across the parking lot.

"And a good day to you" Morse muttered to himself as he stepped inside the store.

• • • • •

# 058

Dorth made another pot of coffee. She dug out the thickest of her sweaters, a raggedy brown beast, with sleeves long enough for her hands to retreat into, and headed into the shed, ready to attack its accumulated filth.

She was grubbing around inside when the sun burst through the doorway. It blasted light onto the shed wall, illuminating raised-grain boards and odd-dimensioned beams in a stained brown spectrum from caramel to the color of coffee grounds. She rushed back to the house and dug out her pastels. The light cooperated, blowing in and out, dim to dramatic with the changing clouds. The wind flapped and banged the shed door, an unidentified section of metal roofing creaked and moaned in syncopation.

Eisy pedaled hard, turned right below the pines, hands chapped and cold. The house with the new woman in it had a little smoke out of the chimney but there was no sign of her through its kitchen windows. He skidded to a stop in the alley, spraying slush, dropped his bike and stood by a clump of rabbitbrush, writing his name in pee-arcs along the shed wall. He made it all the way to the <u>S</u> in mock cursive when the woman's head poked out the window. Eisy shoved his penis inside his pants and swung the toe of one shoe along the bottom row of shingles, hoping it made something like the same sound; he came down on both feet like a ballet dancer, all the time keeping his eyes on the woman.

Dorth looked from his face to his crotch to his foot to the wall back to his face. "I'm trying to get the colors of the wall right." She held her sketchpad up to the window, beside her face.

"Looks good." Eisy grabbed the handlebars of his bike and was off.

"Bye."

He cut a skidding turn at the street and came pumping past her and her drawing, taking it in as he flew by. "See ya."

• • • • •

# 059

Two Saturdays later Dorth watched from the kitchen as Rudy parked, then met him on the porch. They stepped inside around each other and bungled a combo hug and lightweight kiss.

"Hiya Rood."

"Looks like you're getting settled in." He stayed near the door, his eyes moving around the room.

"I guess. Uh... did you eat lunch yet?"

"Yeah. Have you?"

"I'm not really hungry." Dorth gave Rudy a tour of the house and the shed. It didn't take very long and it didn't make either of them feel any more comfortable. "Want to go for a walk?"

"I guess."

"Let me put on something warmer." She grabbed the brown monstrosity of a sweater and spoke from deep within. "Thanks for coming Rood."

He shrugged and turned away.

They wandered through town, past the store, up and down residential streets, behind the cemetery. Most of the way side by side. Near the river, in the deepest woods they'd come to, Rudy spoke. "I can see why you like it here."

Dorth nodded and swallowed a lump and kept her hands to herself, jammed in her pockets.

They took a combination of skid roads Dorth wasn't quite sure of, back, and came out on the uphill edge of town as the sky turned indigo. Dorth busied herself with a fire as soon as they were inside, then old habits of meal preparation took over. As per carefully spoken and unspoken arrangements, Rudy'd brought his sleeping bag, and spread it out on the living room floor. With much rustling they crawled into their respective beds. "Good night Rood."

"Night."

"I love you, Rudy."

In the morning they shared coffee and a breakfast, half-asleep. Rudy bugged Dorth until she named a few chores that would be easier for two. He helped her rehang the shed door so it would latch. Together they dragged an abandoned washing machine from the front yard to the back porch. Rudy made lunch, potatoes and the last edible bits of vegetables he found in the corners of the refrigerator. While he was still eating Dorth started sketching. He didn't notice he was the subject of her doodling until she was almost done.

"What do you think?" It was Rudy all right; she'd gotten a couple of his moods at one time, into his face.

"I think this is the roughest shit I've ever been through." It frightened him, the way he felt. Empty. Like he wanted to sit, unbothered and undisturbed, for a long long time.

Dorth sat where she was, hands fooling with the rugged bit of pencil, her eyes on the sketch, her heart in limbo.

• • • • •

# 060

---

Pancho knew it was Tía Angie when he heard footsteps on the porch.

"Happy happy." Angie handed him a mammoth bouquet of lilacs wrapped in tinfoil: deep lavender, pale violet, brilliant white. "Your ma around?"

Pancho nodded, sniffing the flowers.

"Is that you, Angie?" Analisa's voice proceeded her as she came to the door. "Oh, when I said they were pretty I didn't mean—"

"You don't want them?" Pancho smiled and held them away from Angie when she lunged.

"You two. Chico, find a vase for them. Plenty of water." Pancho took the bouquet into the kitchen.

"You got time for a walk?"

Analisa shook her head, but Angie cajoled and sweet-talked. Finally Analisa relented, consented to their usual stroll—they followed the first bench above the river to the chipplant, then back through town, avoiding the sight and sound of the Sim.

They were coming up the final hill. For once Angie could easily keep up with Analisa. "You're getting out of shape."

Analisa came to a stop. "I'm pregnant." Analisa took off. "The baby's due in November."

Angie had to trot to catch up, her mind stuttering. "Uh—congratulations."

"I guess so." Analisa blushed this once. "It's not the best time, between me and Jorge. But maybe the baby will change that." They were in front of her house. "You want to eat with us?"

"No, thanks. Daddy's got a cold so I need to make sure he eats something. I mean it, congratulations."

Analisa gave Angie one quick look. "That's kind of you." She started up the porch stairs.

"Take good care."

Analisa turned as she opened the screen door, nodded without smiling.

• • • • •

133

# 061

Morse worked the line out of his reel with his right hand, cast with his left. The water was spring-cold, the sun summer-hot. He worked the rod so the fly danced closer and closer to a slow-moving pocket; he floated it upon the water's surface, let it spiral to the edge of the pool, bobbing. Not bad for the first cast of the year. He pulled in his line and cast again. This time the fly meandered, dawdled, was swept down. Morse cast again. The hard part of living was to keep on trying, endlessly attempting at some level you could handle.

Morse held his breath like a kid as he glimpsed a flicker of shadow. A big fish, a smart one, was there, waiting. His fly disappeared into the suck of the main channel. Morse reeled his line in, switched to a smaller fly, and cast again. It was consequences that were wearying. Consequences that kept coming, way after.

Dorth a case in point. She had so much going on inside her all the time. So at first you wanted to give her a boost up, just to keep her from busting. Then a bigger picture emerged. Like her grand entrance last fall, her wild and woolly drunk.

Morse jerked his fly back and started reeling in the line. Not so much as another glimmer of that fish, not even a nibble. There were two more pools up stream; he'd hit them and time it to be back here when the whole side channel was in shadow.

Nobody ever forgets, everybody's always watching in Raventon, that's what Dorth was learning. If she lived to be a hundred she might pass as a Raventon eccentric to outsiders. But not to locals. The night she'd stayed with him she was so goddamn earnest. She said she'd rather sleep in her car if he was going to try any moves because she was too messed up and too lonely. Then she went on about some painting, trying to make him see something he'd never even thought about.

One foot in front of the other, that part Morse knew how to do. If Dorth was going to stay, she could make some kind of a place for herself. Her arrival had been pretty desperate, but you had to grant her some slack, for eventually landing.

The first pool had shifted during the winter, it caught too much of the river's full rush to hold a big fish. Morse sat on a sunny rock nearby for a minute anyway, warming his numb legs and feet. Dorth wasn't going to stay anywhere until something got nailed down inside her. Something, relating to the somebody who showed up occasionally at her house and never stayed for long. Morse made his way to the big pool he'd been saving.

• • • • •

# CUZ

*Looky-loos.*

*Dorth was one of the very few who stayed. Once the Sim was up and running there were lots of people who hung around Raventon for an afternoon, or part of a week. If the weather or the snow was good, some stayed as much as a season. We'd always had hunters and hikers and hippie types who rented for a while when they weren't playing in the woods. Relatives from over the Pass were a holiday tradition. They did a few chores in their brand new clothes, acted friendly no matter what, made sure their kids stayed close, then about four p.m. Sunday they packed everything into their shiny cars and took off, back to wherever they came from.*

*After the Sim it was different. Friends and relatives you never even heard of came to visit. There were lots of straight out tourists, gawkers who came because of the Simulator and then poked through Raventon, staring like it was some kind of zoo. I remember one man interrupted a marble game to tell us how cute we were, asked could he take a picture? Rancid pitched a marble at his head.*

*Eisy had his own tricks, but there was one I taught him. The looky-loos were always asking for directions, which way to Seattle, or to the Sim, or sometimes to the lake. I started pointing the real direction—right to where the Sim was, across the river; or at the exact mountains between Raventon and Seattle, all technically accurate. No one ever asked which way the roads were. Sometimes one of them would give me a funny look, but they never had the nerve to say I might be lying.*

*So it was only natural we put Dorth through a fair bit when she moved in. I had a slight vendetta because I'd seen her car parked all night that once, at Morse's. I set her up more than a few times, scattered dogshit just outside her front door, Superglued her car locks, flipped her garbage cans. But Dorth fit Raventon in her own strange way. Even with her weird haircuts and strange hours, the way she spent enormous amounts of time in her shed. She knew enough to step back, knew she pretty much had to take care of herself. Rancid took bets on how long she'd stick it out; he was betting she'd stay. Eisy said she was an artist so the odds were by definition unpredictable.*

*Lots of people were all the time drifting through after the Sim opened. The ones who talked the most about staying were the first to leave. Harold was a different story entirely. It was almost like his middle-aged molecules accumulated, until all of him was in town. The only reason I have a clear idea of when he arrived was because he and I had a little run-in. Not even that, an exchange.*

*I first spotted him one afternoon. It was the first summer after the Sim opened, so we still amused ourselves making fun of tourists. He took my regular place, on the bench outside the Frog's Ears and sat there in his plaid shirts, practically all day, every day, from that first afternoon. It's a free country so I couldn't very well tell him, hey that's my bench, now could I? Something more subtle was called for. It didn't seem like he was looking at anything in particular or waiting for anyone. He just sat. I was good at noticing the smallest particulars. I regularly eavesdropped on conversations, knew who ignored whom, what people had in the backseat of their cars when they stopped at the post office to pick up mail.*

*But there was nothing to notice about Harold, he just sat there. Some of the old gents came up to him and told him their same old stories: how many years they'd worked in the mines, how they were born here, what they used to do a million years ago, how much worse the weather used to be (wetter colder drier hotter, depending). It's not that what they said wasn't interesting; I'd just heard it all, way too many times. Harold seemed truly interested, that's what was unusual. He asked questions, tried to piece together their rambling talk until whoever had been going on would wind down. Then there was the long ceremony of goodbyes, hands shaken all around, old men departing step by old-man step. Harold stayed where he was. On my bench.*

*I called him Pinko from the beginning because what I first noticed was his amazing blush. Any kind of human contact, even a passing good morning and he'd flare up, even under his hair. And he kept his coral color for quite some time after a conversation.*

*You have to appreciate how little happens around Raventon to get it, what I did next. I decided I would out-sit him. It's something Eisy taught me; there's a way you can be totally innocent and still bug the living hooha out of somebody.*

*I got to the bench first one morning and pretended he wasn't there. I did this for entire days. It was so boring it was funny. Sometimes other tourists would walk by and make some comment about the nice girl and her grandfather. I monitored the rise and fall of his coloration and knew he could hear them just as well as I did. This went on for so long, I have to admit, I was about ready to give up.*

*He wasn't even looking at me. He just said, "What interests you about this situation?" Not in a mean way. His voice was kind of papery.*

*I'd already decided what I was going to do when he finally spoke to me. But I'd assumed he'd ask a predictably drippy question, like "what is your name, little girl?" or "where do you live, honey?" something like that. My plan was to answer with a Serbian curse I'd learned from the old men. But he caught me off guard, so all I could do was to continue with the total you-don't-even-exist act, as though he hadn't said a word.*

*The next day I figured there was no need to sit by him. I admit it, he spooked me. So I just stayed clear. Pretty soon it was too hot to sit on the bench during the day anyway.*

· · · · ·

# 062

The draft from the window was just cool enough to lull Dorth back to sleep if she wasn't careful. She opened her eyes to mountain ash branches and solid blue sky, rolled onto her back and studied the high white ceiling of her bedroom, the taste of dreams still in her mouth.

Oh frabjous day. A faded friend of a T-shirt, strong coffee with milk, bread with jam; the morning was ripening into a peach of a summer day. Her studio stayed cool until mid-afternoon, so she stepped into it not fully awake and drank her coffee as she leaned on the makeshift table, and read an old newspaper.

"Hard at work, I see." Morse scooted himself onto the stool at the other end of the table.

Dorth folded the paper and tossed it onto a stack in the corner. "Now I remember why I keep the door shut."

"It's an ill wind that blows no good." Morse was off the stool and perusing. He paused in front of the smear of oil on canvas in the corner, dead-eyeing what she had been fussing with for the last week. "Getting closer, no?"

Dorth poured herself more coffee from the thermos and kept her back to him.

Morse studied the painting. "So you hide the good ones, for purposes of germination?"

"Something like that."

Morse turned away from the painting. "Reminds me of tarns."

Dorth sipped at the coffee she no longer wanted.

"On a day when you're mostly in the clouds above timberline, it's wet and cold kind of spooky." He crossed his arms and imitated her look. "Thank you, I'd love some coffee." Swung his arms like a monkey and grabbed the thermos.

"Jesus, Morse. I'm trying to work."

"And I'm trying for a cuppa joe." He picked up an abandoned mug from the worktable, turned it toward the light, blew into it, and poured himself the little that was left in the thermos.

"If you're so into colors why don't you paint?"

"I do." Morse counted on his fingertips. "The loading dock of the store, the Koalnivic's garage..."

"You know what I mean."

"Oh, the artistic bit. A garage door is perhaps lacking in..." he fluttered his free hand "ze context?"

Dorth tossed the last of her coffee out the door.

"But I distract you. Well, in addition to needing coffee, I stopped by to see if you want to get some rock with me this afternoon. I promised Cantoni I'd do a retaining wall with a path, and I thought you might make yourself helpful loading the truck. In exchange for being led to and through some exceptional local scenery, suitable for framing."

"Where?"

"Now that would be revealing the prize, wouldn't it?"

They both smirked.

"What time?"

"Between now and midnight."

"Can we wait until this afternoon?"

"Sure, pack an air conditioner." Morse laughed at her look as he headed for the door. "I'll pick you up about four. I might even spring for a burger or something after, if you deserve it."

"See ya Morse."

He stuck his head back in and jerked it toward the canvas in the corner. "Don't burn your incipient masterpiece in the meantime."

Dorth paced the studio a few times, debated whether to close the door.

The masterpiece huh? Not even close. He was right it was the colors that made it interesting. What it needed was perk time. She flipped a sketchpad to a fresh page and started sketching Morse doing his monkey imitation.

For once Morse appeared exactly when he said he would; Dorth barely had time to grab a water bottle. They headed south on the county road, then cut west on a roadbed posted "No Trespassing" about six different ways. Morse barely slowed.

Dorth braced herself between the dash and the seat. "Whose land is this anyway?"

"One for all and all for one." Morse finally slowed down a little after a particularly loud and raspy scrape. "Nobody who'd mind a little clearing of rubble." He downshifted and Dorth jerked her head back to avoid bashing her teeth. Morse charged the truck into a barely existent turnoff and yanked on the emergency brake. "Pack mules unite." He hopped out and Dorth followed. She caught up to him at the top of a sandy draw, took a breath, and looked around. They were at the base of a crumbling outcrop of smoky-grey-green rock, what was loose ranged from boulders the size of VW Bugs to pebbles.

"Serpentine. Watch out for snakes."

Dorth started to look around and then caught his expression. "In your serpentine mind maybe."

"So. I need pieces somewheres about a foot-and-a-half across, doesn't matter how thick so long as they have one flat face." He picked up a slab. "Like zis, no?"

Dorth rolled her eyes and nodded.

It was serious labor getting the rock down and into the truck. By the time they had it full, tires bulging, Dorth was exhausted.

"This should about do 'er." Morse thumped the last stone in with a flourish. The light was coppery, the sun low.

Dorth wiped some of the dirt and sweat off her face with the front of her T-shirt and came up looking at a rip in Morse's shirt, pale skin exposed at the hollow in his collarbone.

"Pretty evening too." Morse leaned on the side of the truck and smiled.

"Yep. Hey Morse—. I never thanked you for putting me up that night."

Morse narrowed his eyes. "Common decency."

"Not so common, I think."

"You ever tell Rudy about it?" in his same dry voice, with his same smile. Morse climbed into the cab and fired up the engine. "You coming?"

Dorth got in and braced herself for the ride back. This time they took it at a crawl, wincing each time the truck bottomed out.

"*Take me hoooome, country road...*" Morse pulled into the parking lot of the store. "Ready for a burger?"

"I guess." Dorth moved slowly out of the cab, her back and everything connected to it knotted, her hands beginning to throb.

Angie looked up from her book when the screen door opened. "Look what the cat dragged in." Samuel pivoted on his stool, then returned to his beer, unimpressed.

"Good to see you too." Morse took a stool.

Dorth slipped in beside him, feeling ungodly hungry and out of place. "Are you still serving food?"

"Could be."

"May I have a beer please? And a bag of Beernuts?"

"Shit. We want burgers Angie."

Angie drew a schooner and positioned it on a coaster in front of Dorth. "On the house." Turned to Morse. "What if the grill's turned off?"

"Steak tartare will do."

The three of them ended up with cheeseburgers, fried onions drizzled on top, french fries galore. Nothing had tasted so good to Dorth in a long time.

"We got ourselves some world class rock." Morse's enunciation was hindered by his burger.

"Why would you want to do that?"

"Actually it's for one of my clients. Raso Cantoni, Esquire."

"It's beautiful serpentine when you look down into it." Dorth mopped her plate with a fry. "Kind of the color of deep ocean water."

Angie paused. "Did you get this rock where I think you got this rock?"

"Mebee." Morse held out his schooner. "More please."

"Good thing you didn't get caught. He wouldn't like to pay for his own rock."

"She sounds like she knows exactly where we were."

"There's only one place close that has a truck full of rock that looks like you described. Want another beer?"

Dorth reached into her pocket and evaluated by touch what was there in the way of cash. "No thanks."

"I'll spring for this one since you did help some." Morse pointed into Dorth's empty glass and raised his eyebrows in Angie's direction.

"Thank you." Dorth took a sip.

Angie cleared her plate. "Morse told me you got a studio. What kind of painting?"

"Mostly oil. I'm trying to paint what things look like, but also, kind of what you feel about what you see." Dorth took another sip. "If that makes any sense."

"You know about this painting?" Angie reached under the counter and pulled out a picture clipped from a magazine, Dalí's *Persistence of Memory*. Angie pointed to the clock dripping like candle wax. "Seems like other people paint something like what you're talking about."

Dorth didn't know what to say. "Yeah—"

"Let me see that. Please."

Angie handed the clipping to Morse.

"I think that goes a little beyond how a person feels. It looks more like that T-shirt—two fried eggs for eyes—you know, this is your mind on drugs."

Angie ignored him and waited for Dorth's response.

"My stuff is pretty different from his."

"You ever show it?"

"Yeah, I have."

"You want to show it around here?" Angie shrugged at the walls of the store.

"So you're opening a gallery?"

"Shut up."

"Yes ma'am."

"Are you interested?"

"I—I need to think a little."

"Well if you are, let's talk sometime."

"OK." Dorth finished her beer. "Thanks for the dinner."

"Aren't you going to thank me for the beer?" Morse pivoted on his stool.

"I did once. Thanks for the beer, Morse."

"You haven't paid for it yet." Angie wiped the counter.

Dorth left humming. From the porch, the Milky Way stretched like a veil, the more she looked the more stars she saw. She stopped at the pay phone and punched the number she knew best. Stared at the stars while the phone rang and rang and rang.

Dorth slept late the next morning, moved stiffly toward the studio after a second cup of coffee. When she got to the door there was a slab of yesterday's rock, about the size of a headstone, leaning against the studio wall, gleaming green where it caught the light.

• • • • •

# 063

Morse tossed the cardboard box of circuits and switches onto the front seat of the truck, loaded the last conduit into the back, tied it down, checked the list Popper had given him, and went back into the electrical supply house. "Mind if I make a local call?"

The guy at the counter rotated his phone toward Morse.

"Wouldn't happen to have a phone book, would you?"

"White or yellow?"

"White please." Morse flipped through, found what he wanted, and dialed. "Hey, what are you doing right now?"

Rudy wasn't sure who was asking. "I'm, I'm—who is this is?"

"Your minimal acquaintance, Morse Durrell of Raventon. I was down here running around—"

"Oh. Hi."

"Hi yourself. I was calling because you said one time you knew some good record stores."

"Yeah..."

"So. You want to go and take a look?"

Rudy switched the phone to his other ear. "When?"

Morse laughed. "I got a couple hours this afternoon."

In an era of CDs and laser discs, it was vinyl they went in search of that Saturday. Rudy led Morse from store to store, through stacks and racks. They tuned out most of the music played by the usually laconic, usually male, clerks, and skimmed liner notes, evaluated combinations of musicians and compositions, made very occasional purchases.

Morse offered to pay for dinner if Rudy knew somewhere close by that cost less than twenty bucks total.

As they ducked into a Lebanese deli a few blocks away, Rudy wished he'd been slower to come up with a place.

Morse fiddled with his silverware. "I got a question for you, Mr. Rudy."

"What's that?"

"What do you think of Dorth's art work?" Morse pulled out a bandana and blew his nose.

Rudy thought about a lot of things. He'd driven to Raventon to see what Dorth had up in the store and some of it was as good as anything she'd done. He thought about what he knew of Morse. Dorth had stumbled answering, the one time he'd asked how the two of them had met. He had taken note of her pen and ink sketch of Morse. The waiter brought their plates. Rudy watched Morse start in on his dinner. "What are you asking?"

"Shit. I am asking what you think of Dorth's art. I'm trying to make some kind of conversation."

"I think her art's fine."

Morse snorted and put down his knife and fork. "So do I. Mighty fine." He took another bite. "I'll try again. You and Dorth have been together a long time, right?"

"Pretty long."

"Good."

Rudy poked at his food. "Why did you call me?"

"I was in town, and I had some money burning a hole in my pocket, and I was curious to see you on your own turf."

"You know, I hate to eat and run but I need to be somewhere pretty soon."

"You are a terrible bullshit artist." Morse went to the register and paid; Rudy waited for him outside.

"I'm not interested in bullshitting you."

"Jesus. I'll tell you once. We're not in competition. So sometime, if you want to get together, perhaps in a lighter mood, track me down. And thanks for the tour."

Rudy started down the sidewalk.

"I mean it. Thanks."

● ● ● ● ●

# CUZ

Wherever you are, well then, there you are.

Let me be clearer. As long as you are alive (and for a little before and a slight after) your body occupies specific geography: kitchen, bathroom, space-capsule-upon-the-moon. But where are you, my little pretty, when the lights go down, when the curtain drops for the day, when you pause and take a deep breath for station identification? What is the geography of your heart, aka home?

For me, I am on the ridge. Or maybe I am of it. On some late morning, in some October, when the sun's heat makes me sweat and the trees' shadows make me shiver, on that morning I am part of the ridge. Apricot-colored aspen leaves rattle, their grey-green branches sway. Epic ponderosa pine groves stretch uphill, edged with pockets of dark, jagged fir; I find my way to hidden cedar seeps. The ridge is my inholding, my land-of-day-and-night-dreams, the place that takes me in. And when it does, I rest. I rest easy thinking of it now.

Not so long ago I listened to an interview with an autistic woman who thinks in visual images. Say an abstract word and she sees a physical representation, she works from specific images. Eternity for her is a Star Trek window and the space beyond it. Love? She sees weddings and birthday parties.

I am something of the opposite. Mention the ridge and I could not put words to what fills me. A hard part of myself falls away. I recall one twisted branch creaking in the breeze, a particular curve of duff and pine-needled trail, a sandstone lip of rock, a soundless spring fringed with kinnikinik and avalanche lilies; I see all of these when I pause, but what I feel is complete.

Our ridge is a place that has eluded the namers-of-names. It is more than a molehill and less, topographically speaking, than a mountain. It hovers behind Raventon, one part running slightly contrary to north and south, another part not quite east and west. It shielded us, for a long time, with nothing more than an abandoned honeycomb of mines and second growth grown large.

A place gains intricacy, the more you get to know it. As I grew up in Raventon, coyote led me up forested draws, fox led me over, cougar and grouse, beetle and bear and deer all left their prints as well. The ridge and its residents taught me to move almost invisibly. I wandered that ridge, wearying myself, until certain spots are ingrained, until I developed my own way of navigating, far beyond up and down, east or west, past or future. The ridge, by circumstance of birth and supposition and history, is my home, my receptor, my mirror, my beacon in the night.

So let us think back. Imagine fall fading into winter. The ground has absorbed cold rain until it puddles, yards and footpaths soggy. Rain and more rain. To go for any kind of a walk means mud and slipping, the inevitability of water in a trickle down your neck, your pants plastered to your thighs before you've gone a block.

The next day comes in nuances of brooding mist, lingering rain. If you can stand to go out, to look, there is crystalline beauty clinging, everywhere the delicacy of water and wet. But the ridge is hidden, it lurks beyond the fog, at most you can see the first rise of matted green and dark, wet trees. Whole days, weeks, our very lives stretch before us.

In Raventon, we are used to living in this shadow, the light and dark, the dry and wet curve of the ridge. We know this sodden rain as we know our tears, trickling sentiments. We feel the rain and the fog in our hearts and let the weather do our mourning, vague and slow-blooded, too full of a slight dragging hitch. The diehards smile, they savor the tart sadness of the bright early fall; they hold back their tears until these dark rains cover their tracks. And they know winter is coming, know it will bring clean silence and long cold. They are home.

• • • • •

# 064

"The colors I like. But there is so much feeling. They worry me."

Angie stirred her tea for the pleasure of swirling and considered Analisa's comments.

"Like that one." Analisa pointed to *Wish I Were a Magician*. "At first, I think it's happy, with the man and the woman sharing the flower. When I look more, it's like a bad dream. I don't know how." Analisa finished her tea. "But it makes me feel... twisted."

Angie nodded. "They look different to me every day."

"Why did you want them around?"

"I didn't ask to see her stuff when we first talked. Then I didn't get around to looking until everything was up." Angie rocked back in her chair. "They come down in a week anyway. More tea?"

Analisa shook her head. "But why doesn't she paint pretty? She could, you can tell."

"Don't you like to look at any of them?"

Analisa eyes paused on one painting, then another. She pointed. "Maybe that one." *Levitation*. "But it makes me dizzy too."

Angie laughed.

"Everything is making me feel strange these days." Analisa stood awkwardly and took her mug to the counter.

Angie looked closely at her friend. "But everything's all right? With the baby?"

"Oh sure. And Jorge is really happy."

Angie bit her tongue. She knew what Analisa felt was not a subject for discussion.

"Thanks for the tea then."

"Tell Pancho he better get a tarp on his tree house. It's going to start raining bigtime any day now."

Analisa smiled. "As soon as he's home from school he goes out there. He barely comes in for dinner." She glanced at the clock. "I need to go make some dinner now."

"See ya." Angie watched the door swing shut, listened as Analisa's footsteps faded.

Plenty of people saw Dorth's show. Some didn't like to be caught at it. Morse wandered around for a good long time whenever he came in. Minor Haynes avoided looking at any of it directly. When Angie nudged him for a reaction he spun his head around as though he only just noticed there were paintings. "I thought you were remodeling." But Angie'd seen him frown and stare at the one over the cooler, *The Big Disconnect.*

At the end of the month, Dorth insisted upon taking everything down herself. Angie kept herself busy behind the counter, thought about the best way to ask.

"What's the chances you'd consider an offer on that one?" It was a strange cartoony painting of Raventon against the ridge called *Spiritual Relocation.* A tiny blurred figure that almost looked like Daddy was walking toward the store.

Dorth pretended it took all of her concentration to remove a picture hook from the wall. "I'd have to think about it."

"I wouldn't hang it in here, in the store." Angie couldn't say why she thought this would matter. She busied herself with cleaning the grill; Dorth packed up as fast as she could. Both of them were relieved when Dorth finished.

"Thanks for letting me have the show."

"My pleasure. Really."

Next morning when Angie opened the stormdoor, she was lucky she caught the painting that had been stashed behind it.

She hung it next to Momma's picture in her room. The next time Dorth came into the store, Angie tried to bring up the matter of price. Dorth chewed her thumbnail until Angie quit. That was when Angie asked Dorth if she'd do the books for the store. She didn't pause, she didn't give Dorth a chance to say no.

Dorth tried though. Something about not having much experience.

"If you can run your own business you can do the store's arithmetic. It's only once a month anyway. Come by some morning soon and I'll show you the ropes." This time it was Angie who kept her head down. Only she and Daddy ever got so much as a glance at the money part of the store.

• • • • •

# CUZ

Go figure.

Eisy said that a lot to me. He said it when I bugged him too much, he said it to shut me up when I prodded him for more than he wanted to tell. And it never deterred me because he was the only one who could explain so many things.

Go-figure was also a code between us, a signal for when people revealed what a cynic might call their true natures. Eisy said everybody does things in private that are worth seeing. He could get fairly clinical about the details of whom and what exactly they did. But occasionally, even Eisy was surprised.

Once I saw Tía Angie do a go-figure. I thought for awhile she must have known I was watching, but when I described it to Eisy, he said not a chance. What he found interesting was that, given an opportunity for cruelty, Tía stopped short.

I was coming around the wall of the school, singing. She stepped out of the post office. It was late afternoon, and it was Rancid's brother's dog. He'd been lying in the middle of the street, asleep. Out came Tía. The dog stood, stretched each back leg in most leisurely fashion. He came up behind her and started growling, following her close. She turned around and said something to the dog, I didn't hear what, then she kept walking. The dog lowered his head, bared his teeth, he was all set to bite. Which he sometimes did.

The dog was trailing her like he was protecting some national border, making nasty, almost salivating sounds, his teeth snapping extremely close to Tía's legs. She spun around and swung one leg back like she was going to kick him good. Instead she kind of hopped. I thought maybe she'd tripped. She bent over until her face was about an inch from the dog's and she barked.

That dog didn't so much as blink until Tía was almost a block away. Then he let out a couple half-hearted little yelps as though he'd just noticed her.

Eisy said people are usually their meanest when nobody is looking. It was his impression a lot of individuals looked forward to their privacy in this regard. I have never been quite so sure. Overall I mean; there's no doubt about specific incidents.

Then Eisy told me about a nastier go-figure. We were touring Dorth's show. Right out of the blue he told me the whole thing. I went back later to study the painting we were in front of when he told me. **Such-a-One**. At first it looked like a fancy portrait, something that belonged in a mansion or an old movie. But when you looked at it for awhile you realized the lady in it—her tongue had the tiniest fork to it. It was creepy, kind of like one of those pictures of Jesus with eyes that always follow you no matter where you go. I don't think it was this particular painting that made Eisy tell me.

We had walked all the way around the store, looking at everything. I was a little distracted because there was one of Morse. He was walking away, you saw his back and the way he had a kind of hitch in his stride; there wasn't anything drawn in behind him but a couple of lines that made it look like he could go on walking forever.

When we thought we'd seen them all, Tía pointed back by the bathrooms. That's where **Such-a-One** was. While we were standing there Eisy told me about Pancho getting slapped.

The way he told me, with hardly any extra words, just what happened, I had to believe him. The terrible part wasn't the actual slap. It was Pancho's mom. Sure, she was strict and she didn't laugh a lot, but I never thought she would let anybody, ever, hit Pancho. Which was why if it had been anybody but Eisy who told me, I would have started a fight. I think Eisy was almost hoping I might hit him, call him a liar, something. All I could do was stare at that painting. I felt sick, and small.

Eisy said Dorth should have called her whole collection go-figure. I think he was right. Most of the people she painted—she showed their daytime faces at the same time she hinted at something else. It made you want to see a little more to know for sure, to know what they were really like. Even though at the same time she'd already shown you.

• • • • •

## 065

Angie took the last of what was in the coffeepot over to the man who was sitting by himself at the window table. One of the newest regulars, he talked with folks one at a time, took notes, and stared out the window.

Harold looked up from his papers and positioned his cup so she could pour. "Catching up on your field studies of the locals?"

He put down his coffee without taking a sip and turned an even pink to the tips of his sparse and shortcut hair.

"It's nothing to me." Angie went to the end of the counter, put the coffeepot on its burner, and pushed the button for a new pot. Hard.

"Um. That's one way of describing my work. Actually, what I'm studying is the variation in individuals' Experiences at the Simulator. Whether they are local residents or live elsewhere." Harold spoke so softly Angie turned around and squinted to confirm he was directing his mumbling to her.

Straightening his papers, he rocked on his chair so he faced her. "Have you been through it?"

"Nope."

"Do you plan to?"

"Probably not." They each were leery of the other. "You think people are like monkeys in the zoo, Harold?"

"No." He flushed an even deeper pink. "And yes. In the sense we both change our behaviors when observed. I think we are less alike when it comes to how we react to experience. I'm interviewing people about their Simulations because I want to know more about perception. And memory." He paused as though he thought it was Angie's turn to say something.

Which she did. "I'm fifty-six. I got plenty of experience, too many memories, and even more aches and pains. So far everything is basically hanging together in here." Tapping her temple. "Along comes the Sim. Seems like something between Mall-of-America, Disney World, and a therapist. I know to stay away. Because for me, what's inside, whatever that thing does—isn't anything I particularly want to have done to me. Not for amusement, that's for sure.

"You savvy?" Angie leaned over her thick arms to look right at Harold.

He nodded most solemnly, one hand on each knee, facing her. "Entirely. I don't view any of this as entertainment. A colleague of mine named Fred, he—Fred tinkered with too much. And ended up devising the Sim. It wasn't amusing. Some of my own memories, my own aches and pains come from what Fred attempted to demonstrate to me." Harold flicked his hand.

"So now you get paid by MegaCorp to figure out what went wrong with Fred's plan? Did he lose it?"

Harold peered into Angie. "What little credibility I may possess is because I no longer work for MegaCorp. Although I did for many years. And I am truly unsure whether Fred lost or found something."

"Aren't you kind of an old dog to try such foolish tricks?"

Harold blushed.

Angie chose to wade farther into these shark-infested waters. "Back about a light-year ago, when I was so young I—" She grimaced. "Back then I thought I more or less understood people. I thought I could run my fingers through their innards. I was confident I knew what made them tick. Which left me ripe for the windup and the pitch. Which was a punch. Quick as a woodpecker." Angie tapped the counter in time, peck-a-peck-a-peck, her face twisted.

Love and loneliness and lust Angie thought. Experience that.

"So I don't think you have the right to poke around, just because you're interested, Harold. I don't think you or anyone can be scientific about other peoples' lives or memories or whatever. But maybe you got some special training from MegaCorp? That protects you? That gives you special skills for wandering down memory lane?"

Harold laughed. "I wish." He kept laughing, his eyes shut tight, his hands one on each knee, until tears dripped. Until they streamed down his shiny pink cheeks.

Angie stared at him, gaga-eyed. Then snickered. Then laughed with him. She felt something inside herself cut free to float away and something else rip apart.

Harold wiped his eyes with his handkerchief. "Excuse me." He picked up his coffee cup then put it down. "Once upon a time, a long, long time ago, I would have sworn there was no need for protection. That I was professionally capable of wandering wherever I pleased, sampling from the lives of others. I won't bore you with the tedious details, you seem to know what I'm talking about. I was then capable of watching like a hawk. I sniffed the air like a hungry wolf. Like a beaten dog I was acutely aware of the emotional import of each situation. Then I began to understand what Fred was really on to." He held up his hands before she could speak.

"For example, it is not credible to state as 'fact' humans fly unassisted. Nor that animals talk in English, Spanish, Nahuatl; nor that they may speak to us in the same way we speak with each other. Only out there, perhaps in some other culture, can a human have these thoughts. Have these—feelings, these perceptions. And carry them all the way into one's heart. I think of this potential, the possibility—these perspectives—as a place. A land beyond psychological pontification, beyond even metaphor or analogy.

"I drivel on. I have been chasing my own haints. Which has led me to realize they are not the same as demons, or even ghosts. So I think I have become more like you, in that I am no longer sure I want to catch them."

"Do they ever cage you in?"

"Tía Angie, please, can we buy some candy?"

Harold looked over. It was the skinny girl who had occupied the other end of the bench when he'd first arrived. From the way she'd slipped in, he confirmed she had further honed her skill at unnoticed observation.

Angie hoped she hadn't jumped. She hadn't seen Cuz come in, she hadn't even noticed the rest of the kids on the porch, waiting for permission to enter. Angie gave the signal. "What do ya want today kiddos?"

She dipped cones and counted out candies until each of them had something, most of it paid for. Angie stayed at her post until the whole crew went outside.

"Want some dinner?"

Harold's eyes opened much wider. He shook his head. "Ah, no. Well. Actually. Yes, thank you. May I call you Angie?"

"That's my name."

Over a fish sandwich and fries Harold spoke more specifically of himself. Born and educated outside Boston, he had gone directly to work for MegaCorp, at FutureLabs. He made mention of his respect for Fred, references to theories of randomness, his eventual disassociation from FutureLabs, his ongoing interest in the Sim. Harold's manner so gracefully reticent Angie had a little trouble following the exact details of his story.

"Like you, my heart has had its injuries. So I neither seek out nor have I been the target of Cupid's bow for quite some time." He gave a sad prim little smile. "Thank you for a very pleasant dinner."

After closing, Angie grabbed a wool shirt, packed her pipe from the old Chinese ginger jar, and stepped outside.

She struck a match along the railing, watched its rough sparking course, cupped the bowl of her pipe with her palm, and inhaled steady and slow. She sat in the rocking chair and her eyes drifted from the pocket of total shadow under the eave to random stars. Breeze negligible. Frost lurked. Across the river the Simulator glowed. Nothing around her, nocturnal or seasonal, not the frayed rattan poking into her side, distracted her particularly; she sat and let her heart and mind ramble until they settled on one memory without rancor or fear.

It had been a cold day, the kind that let loose the first flakes of snow. In that long-ago fall she and Morse had been lovers. They were in their place way up the river, the place they thought of as their own, and they were lethargic and cozy in their postcoital nest of blankets. "What do you think we'll be like together when we're an old couple?" She'd stroked the hairs on the inside of his calf with the inside of her forearm, resting her cheek on his knee.

"I don't think we will be." He snorted when he saw her expression, tossed down the stalk of dry grass he'd been chewing. "We aren't gonna be no old couple, Ang. You know that as well as me."

"You think we'll both be dead by then?" Angie laughed. "From when I get you to stand even closer to the trains?"

Morse eased his leg away from her side. "Not that. I mean, you're going to go off and do whatever you do. And I'll be on to whatever I do."

"You don't think we'll be, you know—"

"What do you really think? That we'll get married and have babies and run the goddamn store?"

He had her cornered.

She jumped into the river. The water was so cold there was no possibility of breath. Her entire body stuttered, heart a-flutter, skin shrunk until her face felt like a canine's when it bares its fangs. Still no breath, lung-locked, shocked, the pain of cold like a stump. She stumbled and rolled out and fell on the old wool blankets.

Morse was gone. She got her air back in gasps, her feet sawed-off clubs beneath her, her hands numb clumps at the ends of her arms. The first flakes did fall then, melting in her tears.

Words pop into your mouth, you babble on before you're ready, pretty soon, before you have anything thought out, what would have been, inside your head—your heart—what you might have come up with, was gone. Gone with the wind. Gone to the place of your forgotten dreams. To Harold's places, where animals talk with us and people fly.

Harold was the kind of person who put too many names on things.

Angie smiled.

She'd heard once about something called a dreamtime, or dreamingtime. Some explorers' attempt to translate the way another people live in the world. She liked the sound of it. Dreamtime. A dreamtime of things that haven't happened. Or things that happened a long time ago. As though she were half-asleep and half something else, Angie heard leaves rustling, she heard the wind picking up, she was in some other place. A dreamtime in the way most of the time you don't know it's a dream, so you can't get out of it, can't change it until you wake up.

She didn't know how to make it happen any more than she knew how to make it stop.

Talking with Harold, what had she said? What had she meant to say? Words and phrases repeated themselves. The way Harold listened should have made her wary. She'd observed him melt into the Formica while others dished out their lives' stories; she should have known better than to ignore his expertly placed silences. But he'd told plenty about himself.

Angie relit her pipe and the top of the tobacco glowed in the dark. It was

Morse who had touched her. Moved her. She had been the one who'd gone away. And both of them were back now. And back and back and back.

How she would love to fly.

She remembered then, another time; a girl-woman who was herself. Another night on this same porch, in this same town. A small dream. A young man had spoken. She remembered the things Morse had said and what he had not said, the words she had spoken, and what she had meant. What she had meant to say. What would have come of it if she had ever told Morse she loved him?

Angie knocked out her still-burning pipe, locked the door, and walked to the house.

• • • • •

# 066

---

Dorth made herself stay in the studio, and pretended she was working until it was late afternoon and she was cold to the bone. Inside the house she got a fire going, poked her way through a pile of bills and correspondence, washed the dishes, and swept. She even made a batch of soup and had some of it for dinner. The house felt too small, there was nothing in it she hadn't read or rejected already. Then she remembered the coupon and dug through the trash until she found it:

# Try Living Your Dreams!

### THE SIMULATOR® WILL TAKE YOU ON A JOURNEY TO

## the past, the present, and the future,

### USING STATE-OF-THE-ART TECHNOLOGY TO OFFER
### YOU AND YOUR ENTIRE FAMILY EXPERIENCES®
### BEYOND THOSE OF A LIFETIME...

Free child care in our Playdome World for children under 10.
Youths under 15 must be accompanied by an adult.

Dorth skipped to the fine print on the back. Using the coupon on a week night after eight p.m. made it as cheap as it ever got, $27.50. Which was a lot of money, or maybe not, considering she would have a trade-marked, patent-pending Experience.

Fifteen minutes later she made her way up to the last of the pseudo-marble stairs. The whole entryway reminded her of Snow White's wedding dress: perfectly symmetrical, ever-narrowing tiers, leading to the promised land. In this case that was the reception desk, replete with a very good video-simulation of a backlit waterfall. It even had the sounds of falling water, and was there a scented breeze?

The young woman working the desk was engrossed in her homework. She jumped when Dorth leaned forward on the counter to take a better look at the fake waterfall. "Oh—hi. Have you Experienced the Simulator before?"

"Nope."

"One moment please." The young woman picked up a cellular phone. "Don? I need you for an Orientation." Then to Dorth, "Don will be here to orientate you in just a minute."

Dorth looked around, wondering if orientate was generally recognized as a verb. The lobby was pretty much like that of a movie house, except there weren't posters of coming attractions, just velvet ropes looping from chrome post to chrome post, leading in a maze to a descending stairway. A man with a belly that strained his white dress shirt came up the middle of these. "Good evening. Is this your first Experience?"

Dorth nodded.

"Let me familiarize you with the procedures, then." She signed off on a rather extensive waiver and personal profile, then followed him down those same stairs, around a corner and into a small amphitheater. Don gestured to a seat, and she sat, put on the helmet with built-in headset he offered her, and let him strap her in. She was held down by a rubbery web-like frontal suit, tiny prods ever so slightly poking her everywhere. "The first thing that will come up for you is a selection screen. This will help you shape your Experience, using enhancers."

Dorth felt sweat in her armpits and wanted to scratch her head as Don flipped the helmet's visor down.

"Bon voyage" she whispered to herself, and snickered in the darkness. Your First Experience, enhancers, the culmination of your Experience; the terminology reminded her of some junior high lecture on sex.

It began.

She was looking at a kind of neutral, almost meadowy place. The details were not quite in focus. Dorth shifted in her chair and webbing to try and get a better view. The more closely she looked, the bigger the entire scene became, almost like she was falling forward and horizontally. That was when the Mitch Miller voice kicked in, explaining how she could use her eyes to explore or to slow down her motion. The voice asked her to speak, to say "stop" clearly, three times, into the built-in mouthpiece, and informed her that if, at any time, she wished her Experience to stop, all she had to do was say so. The melodious advertising voice went on, explaining all sorts of commands and controls, each affecting some direction or condition of the Simulation-you-are-about-to-Experience. It seemed any aspect could be sped up or slowed down or enhanced in ways she didn't quite understand, and doubted she would remember.

Then came the selection panel:

```
ADVENTURE
PERSONAL EVENT
MOOD ENHANCEMENT
WILD CARD

PLEASE MAKE YOUR SELECTION.
```

After listening to the descriptions three times, she pointed to *Wild Card*. The two words glowed then faded. Dorth wanted to make this gizmo try for just-the-facts-ma'am, she wanted to see its limits. It reminded her of getting her fortune told: don't volunteer any information or confirmation.

Another selection panel appeared:

```
YOUR AGE DURING SIMULATION?
PLEASE SPEAK CLEARLY.
```

She was nineteen when she'd met Rudy. Try that. "Nineteen." Her own voice sounded muffled and far away.

"*Niiineteen?*" asked Mitch Miller.

"Yes."

The Sim went 3-D, with sound.

As best she could remember later, there were four scenes going on at once, it was kind of like there was one in each corner, but there wasn't really a screen. She drifted among the four.

One was all done up in some kind of pioneer motif, she could look down and see her hands and her lap in some made-for-TV version of female frontierdom: calico skirts and she was clutching a little hanky, her chair rattling along. She could smell sage and animal sweat and dust. When she turned she was looking into the interior of a covered wagon, creamy white canvas stretched over wooden ribs, chests and quilts and a couple little kids inside. It seemed like the pioneer menfolk were having adventures out in the sagebrush but she was somewhere else before she could quite be sure if there were actual bad guys or whether her hanky had really turned into a pearl-handled derringer. A low and throaty female voice whispered into her ear *"multi-firing, up to six."*

Then she was in a space battle, all kinds of huge creepy crawlers, a slightly electronic voice telling her to destroy a planet called something like Ranzon. Dorth thought this sounded interesting and was wondering if she could find some way to try for weightlessness when a husky male voice-of-experience reminded her she would soon be vaporized along with the final bits of Ranzon, *"—you must attempt survival or switch to attack mode."* Several wild and cartoony creatures writhed to their death before she ever figured out any exact correlation between their mortal wounds and her own random looks around, or her pointing, or her steering and squeezing of things as they appeared in her hands.

The kill-or-be-killed theme was heavy-handed and seemed to permeate her Simulations. Any sort of benign Experience in these make-believe worlds seemed either unavailable or beyond her abilities as a participant.

Meantime she drifted into a third arena. This one was kind of like a National Geographic special. The Wonders of Planet Earth were indeed wonders, but even when her skin felt truly wet during the snorkeling part, the special effects didn't really cut it. The visuals were more like an Imax special than actually being anywhere, and the whole thing jumped around too much. The flying part was pretty cool but she couldn't control where she was going and then was moved along before she was ready, to other predictably cheap thrills: instant jungle, instant volcano, instant sunset over the ocean.

So as sometimes frightening as it all was, Dorth wasn't ready to say "Stop," the only command or control function she could remember. When she tried verbal commands it was as though she was talking to herself. She couldn't even be sure she had spoken out loud; during the bungie jumping she thought she was screaming, but how could she really tell?

The last Experience was the one she fell into. She'd relaxed during the others, in disappointment. At first, this one seemed too abstract to be engaging. There were 3-D animated visual patterns you could "enter" as a reedy-voiced female went on, something about *"that's the nature of our personal experiences. Each of us is like a single wildflower in a blowing field of colors—"* or some pap like that. Dorth remembered being exceedingly relaxed while the woman spoke, and the patterning around her was amazing. It never actually changed in a way Dorth could track and yet all of it was in motion, modulating with other synchronized sensations: tingling, warmth, cool, minty smells, an almost salty taste. Then the woman said something about no more prompts and Dorth looked to her right, wondering why she wasn't feeling carsick with so much motion and so little sense of equilibrium.

Rudy appeared in front of her and a little below, looking a lot younger and very nervous. He was bent over, looking down, totally engrossed, trippy patterns in kind of a sea around them both but not quite between them. He remained oblivious to her.

"Rudy?"

The harder she looked the more detail she saw, but if she strained to look directly, the edges of Rudy went into more patterns. She felt like she was losing her balance and put her hands out. Rudy looked up and took one of her hands. His hand was incredibly soft. She felt like she was next to Rudy, but couldn't be sure if her eyes were closed or open. She felt his arms around her and she could run her cheek along the flat where his shoulder became chest.

It was Rudy kissing her and she forced her eyelids open as wide as they would go and saw nothing but starry patterns gyrating at first, then a chain of images, almost snapshots or movie clips, of what seemed like Rudy before she'd met him: a little kid pulling his tricycle with a rope; aping a smile from the driver's window of what had to be the van he'd told her he'd had in high school. Then he was standing in the doorway of their Seattle house with his briefcase and a bag of groceries, looking defeated. Meantime, or at the same time, the caressing had become serious lovemaking, somebody's hands everywhere and she heard breathing but also sounds that went with the pictures she was seeing—then Morse's face popped in, then she was looking out over some landscape kind of like the Great Salt Flats, glaring sun and crystal white ground and blue sky—

Dorth was sweating and kissing, she hoped it was Rudy. But it was Morse's voice joking about buying a pickup, then his voice was close to her ear and he was saying what if she did spend the night while her hand was on what she thought was Rudy's chest.

A deep background disco beat distracted her, made her think of the guy who'd worked all night in the darkroom one floor below her first apartment. The next thing she could remember was everything winding down, like a carnival ride when it begins to be over. All the images and sensations sort of spread themselves out, and she was put in a sitting position although she hadn't been aware of lying down exactly. An irritatingly soothing male voice came in under the other sounds, reminding her to breathe deeply. The world around her began to dissolve into little squares of color. New age music got louder and a chorus chanted words as they appeared before her: *Thank You for Simulating.*

Then she was truly back. Don was smiling and helping take the helmet off her head. Dorth looked around and was relieved she still had the web-thing on and felt pretty confident she had her clothes on under that.

"Pretty intense, isn't it?" Don looked pleased with her disorientation as he efficiently unclipped her webbing. "Usually people like a minute or two to readjust. We call it Reentering. When you're ready, the exit is right over there." He nodded to a corner door. She hadn't noticed it when she came in. Or maybe it hadn't been there before. Shit. Don flipped something on the helmet she had worn. She tried to swallow, her mouth totally dry. "Refreshments and souvenirs are available as you exit."

• • • • •

# 067

Angie would have been more comfortable with a sweater. Instead she wrapped her beefy arms around herself and pulled the collar of her flannel shirt closer, savoring the fruity smoke from her pipe. Thick clouds rode the ridge, more were rolling in from the north. She watched the mid-morning sun poke through in brilliant patches, part of the chase-and-be-chased. Without moving her head she also took notice of Dorth's slow approach.

Dorth had a slightly nervous air. The solitude of her work left her overly aware of her footsteps in the gravel, of Angie on the porch, of the distance that was still too great between them for conversation but too small to ignore.

Angie returned to her study of the ridge as Dorth came up the steps. "Ready to dig in on this month's horrors?"

"More or less."

"Well then." Angie knocked her pipe out on the river rock at the edge of the porch and led the way behind the counter, hefting a stool in front of several overstuffed notebooks and bulging manila envelopes. Dorth made herself comfortable while Angie extracted a monstrous adding machine from under the bar. Together they wormed its cord free and plugged it into a yellow extension cord that ran to some unseen socket. Angie made eye contact. "Got what you need?"

"I'll let you know if I don't." Dorth dumped out the contents of the envelopes, sorting scraps and sheets of paper. Soon there was the syncopated and comforting clickity-CLACK, click, click CLACK of the adding machine, addition and subtraction, percentages and totals. The keeping of October's books had begun.

As Dorth relaxed into organizing the mess of numbers before her, another part of her brain was free to roam. She noted the occasional change in handwriting from Angie to her father, the flare of Angie's initials. It was like a spider web, all the people drawn in and through the store's teeming, mismatched, and grandiose business. Almost everybody showed up somewhere; running tabs, making deliveries, services rendered, checks bounced. And she saw herself, swaying like a sea-creature, exploring every window and orifice of a sunken ruin, floating through the many-chambered heart of things. Cash and trade and credit, the web woven to catch every quarter, every five dollar bill. Which led Dorth into some thoughts she had been glad to do the books in order to avoid. That is, her own spider web.

Rudy had departed Sunday in disjunction, to use the mathematical description. Or she had remained, in discord. Which meant they had played patty-cake make-right over the phone for the last five days. Dorth re-tallied the total she had just run.

By lunchtime she was on her way to filling an old cardboard box with curlicues of adding-machine tape. Half the counter and all of the floor space around the legs of her stool held various stacks of papers, most of a case of beer bottles served as paperweights. Locals knew better than to get too close with their burgers or small talk. The few tourists that wandered in were either intimidated or charmed. In either case they left well-enough alone.

When the lunch rush cleared, Angie took Dorth's order for an open-faced meatloaf sandwich and a chocolate milkshake. Dorth worked while she ate; ketchup stains on the books were totally acceptable. Then, with a cup of coffee and the dregs of her shake, she entered column after column of numbers into the red notebook, stapled together one stack of receipts after another. It was after five when she slapped the cover of the notebook together theatrically and unplugged the adding machine.

"Bravo" cheered Angie as she coiled the extension cord, wrist to elbow, round and round. She tossed it behind the paisley curtain of the backroom doorway and went to the cooler door. "What flavor?"

"Dark" said Dorth.

And only after Dorth had taken her first draw from the icy bottle neck did Angie ask whether the books came out ahead or behind.

"Ahead by a nose."

"Does that mean she gets a bonus?" Morse made a beeline from the door to the beer taps and served himself as Angie ignored him, anchored on her own stool, flipping through the notebooks.

Dorth let her mind unwind from the strictures of ledgers and accounts, half-listened to Morse's monologue, and thought about the painting she was working on.

"Here comes Friday night. Heehaw." Morse put on an apron as the front door flapped open for a crew of college-age kids just off work at the Sim. A delegate stepped up and counted out bills for a pitcher of beer and two orders of fries while his pals, in matching monogrammed red and blue polo shirts, sprawled around the biggest table.

"I'll bring the fries when they're ready." Morse handed off the pitcher and a tray of frosted mugs.

The door opened and closed more quietly as Cuz came in, flipped back her slicker hood, and perused the comic book carousel, ears perked.

Morse was surprisingly fast on the fries. He plopped a third order in front of Dorth as he scooted around the counter to deliver.

"You must be paying for these." Dorth ate one fry and reached for the ketchup.

"You're damn right he better." Angie closed the notebook.

"Take it out of my pay." Morse went behind the counter and grabbed a fry as Angie helped herself too.

"I'll take it out of something of yours. Clear out." Angie stepped behind the register to ring up the two pieces of gum Cuz laid on the counter. "Since Morse is buying, either of you girls want anything else?" She looked at Cuz.

"A lemonade please."

"Dorth?"

"I'm OK, thanks." Cuz climbed the stool next to Dorth, pivoted so she could study her neighbor, top to bottom.

Morse served Cuz with a flourish.

"How come you put whipped cream and a cherry on it?" Cuz frowned and poked suspiciously at the red fruit with her straw.

"To add an air of elegance."

"Does it cost more this way?"

Morse laughed. "No. So you don't have to tip me extra either."

"I'm not tipping anything." Cuz downed the lemonade in one long slurp, pocketed her bubblegum, and left as quietly as she'd come.

"Funny kid." Dorth hadn't been able to think of a thing to say while the girl had been sitting next to her.

"Funny till she gets the goods on you."

"Morse, be nice. She's just a kid."

"One of Raventon's cleverest."

Even as Morse and Angie bantered Dorth was trying to find her own category for Cuz. Gun-shy? Dorth couldn't think of a time she'd seen the girl laugh. Wary? Even when she was studying Dorth she watched Morse covertly and constantly, the way a crow waited to see how close you might come.

Angie went in back to get another bucket of iced and sliced potatoes. Morse cleared Cuz's glass and replaced Dorth's beer. "You know what a great honor it is to be an employee here?"

"It seems like about everybody has some kind of a deal going."

Morse leaned down on the counter. "Not everybody gets to add and subtract the big picture."

"Right."

"I'm serious. It is an honor."

Dorth pushed her beer bottle around in a circle. "I know that."

Angie set the bucket practically on Morse's foot, which got him back on the grill and pouring beer while she took orders, worked the register, cleared, and did dishes. Dorth drifted to a corner table, ate a salad, and tried to finish the crossword in an old *New York Times* someone else had started. Rudy arrived in town maybe an hour later, and knew to stop by the store first. "Hey Dorth." He gave her a cautious kiss and took the chair next to her.

"Hi Angie."

"Evening Mr. Rudy."

Rudy downed a plate of nachos; he and Dorth gingerly worked their way from halting small talk to easier conversation. When Angie told Morse she'd had enough of his help for one evening he poured a pitcher to bring with him, and invited her to join them when things slowed down. "It's Friday, Morse. So you know that's a safe offer."

Rudy laughed at Morse's jokes, they got to talking firewood and what it took to heat a house all winter, and when the rains would turn to snow. Dorth made a few jokes, she listened, she tried to stay engaged. Angie joined them between orders, Morse left, she rode with Rudy the few blocks to the house.

Near midnight, after a sweet bout of loving, she could not stand how far apart she had been feeling. The words slipped out in a whisper. "Am I so different?"

"Yes" Rudy whispered back without hesitation. He kissed her shoulder and fell asleep, one arm around her.

Dorth turned away, embarrassed, trying to get at what she had wanted to ask, unwilling to consider Rudy's answer. Dorth knew in her bones she couldn't do the small things that would keep her on the easy side of intimacy, that somehow she was the one always taking leave of others.

• • • • •

# 068

---

"We named her Angelina."

There followed a long pause from the previously existing Angie, who cradled the tiny sleeping girl in her arms. She caught a scent of pure baby smell.

Analisa smiled and gave her friend's arm a squeeze. "Like the sound of a trickle of water, I think."

How little, how much, we all carry inside, thought Angie, long after Daddy had gone to bed. It is the person who must live in the name, who answers to the name given. Join the society of Bobs, of Nancys, of Toms and Dicks and Harolds, of Angelines or Angelinas. A name that had rarely brought her an excess of good luck or good cheer.

The silence of the house surrounded her. It conspired to defeat her and the only place she'd been able to turn her loneliness into solitude was in the woods. But tonight she was tired and there was a hard and bleak rain coming down, lousy with chill and dark. And where exactly would she have gone? Maybe daylight would bring a little relief.

Angie turned off the lights downstairs and went up to her room. She opened the window so she could listen to the blowing sleet. Eventually she resigned herself to sleep, windowpanes rattling in the wind, and she dreamed.

Animal, sluggish and thick and dark. Sowbear with loose teeth and fur gone patchy, lumbering. She was flea-bitten and plodding, a weary grace in her slow, crashing gait. Angie felt the bear from inside: slouching big-blocked motion, isolate delicacy, grumbling pains, the effort to turn her massive head, nose to the wind. For what? She yearned for comfort, a warm den, a rock in the sun. Sour sowbreath; she felt her heart close to exploding... clear sweet air in rough springtime blasts roused her, she tried to shake clear of her stupor.

This animal, this living thing, within her. Huge rough paws, and claws; blood sluggish, long of tooth. Everything else is of some other time, belongs to some other place she cannot quite remember. Maybe it is her dreaming me. And then she was in this same place, the same rock, in a bleak over-wintered time. Something in her heart instantly confirmed; she knew. The old bearess gone into maggoted patches of snow-flattened fur, bones gnawed and scattered, where the ground had melted, not far from the river.

Angie awoke. Her knotted covers leaked cold air. She heaved herself up, tired but not wanting such sleep as this. When she stood in front of the window the beginnings of daylight only made clear how grey the rest of the day would be.

• • • • •

# 069

The weather fed Angie's mood. Rain mixed with snow, sometimes froze, sometimes thawing. The ground stayed muddy and dark, the days short, nights long and cloudy. She avoided Analisa and the new baby, or rather, did not seek them out. Took to wearing clothes she knew looked bad, she off doing the laundry, didn't bother with the dump run for practically a week. Until she could not stand herself.

This black feeling was sucking her in; Angie tossed herself the buoy she knew. She ferociously whirled through the house, starting long before dawn: piled curtains and sheets and towels and abandoned work clothes near the washing machine, ran load after load while she cleaned the refrigerator and wiped every dust-collecting surface.

Daddy emerged an hour before his regular breakfast, pale and bemused. "Cleaning day?"

Angie kept about her busyness, made a list of cleaning goods to grab when she went to open. Over breakfast Daddy volunteered to run the store for the day and she, surprising them both, agreed. He was whistling as he carefully made his way down the road, sidestepping the largest puddles, the frostiest spots. Angie watched through the living room window, then started in on the floors. By midmorning she was on a ladder outside doing windows, her hands stinging and numb, polishing each glass faster than the rain could smear it.

Then she'd had enough. She wished she was away, far away. So she put the ladder in the shed and took off.

As she walked she fell back into her funk. The woods were slimy with mud, the clouds solid and low, she didn't have the energy to slog up the ridge. She retreated, slid her way downhill to the river and its crumbling banks, let the rain find its way through her clothes. Analisa was gone visiting family, Morse would say the wrong thing first off if she could even find him, she knew better than to go anywhere near the store. Her feet led her to the cemetery but she avoided Momma's plot once she was there. Angie walked the streets of Raventon, numb, looking into its houses as though she was a kid and they were candy stores.

How she ended up on Harold's doorstep she could never say.

He answered the door in a robe and not much else, rubbing one eye and then the whole top of his head. "Come in, come in."

"I'm sorry. I shouldn't have just stopped by, it's probably earlier—"

"I don't know about the time. Please. You can leave your shoes there." He pointed at a mat inside the door. "I was up reading too late, I'm afraid. I'll make tea."

She could have left then. Instead she bent over and unlaced her soaked and muddy boots, hooked her sodden jacket on the front door knob, sighed, and followed Harold into his kitchen. She took a seat at his table and looked out the window to a yard, a dripping tree, an old shed.

Harold puttered around making a pot of tea, set out two cups and saucers, slices of lemon, and honey.

Angie started shivering and could not stop.

"You're so cold." Harold surprised even himself with the way he put his hands on her shoulders. She felt much smaller than she appeared.

Not a breath between them. Angie didn't move. She didn't know why she'd come, she didn't know anything.

Harold rubbed down her arms, from her shoulders. She cocked her head to look at him, her eyes wide, skittish as a bird, as a leaf when the wind makes it tremble. Harold wanted to comfort, wanted her to understand his tenderness. He lifted his hand to her face and leaned forward; they kissed.

He never quite let go of her. Delicately, his fingers turned her around, unbuttoned her flannel shirt, careful scientist's fingers returned to her throat. And she stopped shivering. He took her wrists and kissed each of them and she watched him. Then she squeezed his hands in hers, hard; they kissed again and didn't stop.

The love they made was as sweet as children's block-lettered valentines and as hard-driven as if they were in the backseat of a Ford. No leader, no follower; joy of desiring.

Angie: wanting wanting wanting. Somewhere inside she was unbelieving and ready to run, somewhere she was saying and singing so much; giving giving, wanting wanting; willing for an instant to throw away and ignore all habit of holding back. All the mixed-up feelings, the doubts, all of what there was no time for right now.

Harold: he was amazed, caught totally off guard by the force of his own want and need, his lust; the sheer delight made him tremble too.

The merest touch kept them together, exhausted. Neither of them wanted to go back to words. They dozed.

Angie woke first and almost bolted. Harold was still asleep. She took a moment to study him. When she sat up, his hand found hers and held on lightly.

Harold opened his eyes and looked at her and blushed.

Which made Angie smile. She came closer and kissed him. They cuddled and passion crept in and they made love once more, most tenderly.

Totally relaxed and intertwined. A stomach growled, hers. And as much as she wished to lie there forever, letting nothing more in or out of her mind her heart her body, little things crept in, Daddy would wonder where she was, she'd left the cleaning half done in piles everywhere, it would be morning. Sooner or later words would have to be spoken.

Harold beat her to it. "Do you have to go?"

She nodded.

"Then wait for me."

She did. Shocked to see how late it was. Both of them dressed, they walked to the store.

Angie started the coffee pots and turned on the grill and the fryers as soon as they were inside. Without asking, Harold helped where he could. When the grill was hot and ingredients prepped, Angie made breakfast. She sat on the business side of the counter, Harold on the customer side. When Harold looked up Angie couldn't help smiling and neither could he.

Happiness?

Cantoni was knocking at the door, ready to pump gas. Angie unlocked and turned on the pumps and ignored his insinuating tone. "You want gas or not?"

When he'd paid and departed Harold gave Angie a quick kiss and said he would leave her to her work. He was back home and cleaning up the tea things when he heard the clanging bell of his heart, telling him he was in love.

• • • • •

# 070

That night, when Angie finally pulled off one damp boot, then the other, and sat with cup of tea and bag of pretzels in the living room, her body groaned but a there was a funny twist of smile brewing inside her. Daddy was practically his old self. Not one word, not so much as an indiscreet eyebrow, regarding the night before. She offered him a pretzel.

He winked as he took one. "Thank you, dear. Is that your dinner?"

She rocked back in the easy chair, slopping only a small splash of tea into her lap. "Yep."

"If I heated soup would you eat it?"

They ate the soup and some crackers and Daddy even popped the cork off a bottle of wine he'd found in the way-back of the refrigerator. They hardly spoke as they slurped in boon companionship. Daddy took their dishes to the sink, then they played cards, one dumb game of cribbage after another. She was as tired as Daddy when they agreed to stop.

"That was nice, Daddy."

"Indeed. Sleep well."

And she did. She fell into a sleep as easy as that beside Harold. In the nooks and crannies of his body there was a rooty smell that was a balm to her, it made things she didn't even know inside herself stretch out. She fell asleep thinking of the arc down into his hipline, the scrawny hair under his arms and in small patches on his winsome belly, at his breastbone.

She worked a regular day, and another, slept well through most of the next night. In the half-awake mystery of creamy moonlight she thought of Harold, how she hadn't seen him or heard from him since he'd left her at the store. Her mind in its infinite circling knew it was more than conversation and sex they'd shared. And it scared her to the bone.

Once this tailspin started, Angie fell in on herself, gears grinding. She couldn't separate what she'd said out loud from what had passed through her while she'd been with Harold. And like a rat in an exercise wheel, the faster she tried to sort things out, the faster it all came at her.

Angie stood up, flicked on the light and stood before her mirror. She was old: wrinkles like cracks into her face, the drooping of her breasts, varicose veins on her legs, stretch marks all over. She grimaced and looked into her own eyes and affirmed, she was in love.

• • • • •

# CUZ

There wasn't much to do in Raventon, even with the Sim. Even less that wasn't totally predictable. Girls Scouts was a good example. I wasn't the only one who joined just to join; practically every girl in Raventon, grades three through seven, was in our troop at some time or other. The tradeoff for a whole school year of meetings and merit badges, for me, was summer camp. We all went together. That part was gross but we did at least get out of Dodge for two whole weeks. Most of the counselors were strangers, and girls I had known forever could turn into pretty decent camping companions. After we came back, I hung around with a tentmate or two. For the memories, you know?

Which is why I was over at Sharon's house. Sharon at camp was different than Sharon at home, but I hadn't figured that out yet. We were lying on our bellies on some pretty raspy carpet in her living room, playing an idiot board game with the big-screen TV watching over us. Her dad sat near us, in the same huge La-Z-Boy he occupied whenever he was home. Sharon's mom spent a lot of time in the kitchen, her voice floating in with some comment right when you'd forgotten she was even around.

Sharon's parents had these conversations filled with long pauses and non sequiturs. She would lob her comment to him from the kitchen. Unless he felt like he had something smart to say, he would pretend he didn't hear, submerged in his chair, leg rest up, his hand clutching the remote.

Sharon's mom started. "...Guess who Julie Smuthers saw cooing down the hill to the store first thing Monday morning? The queen of the store herself, but guess who she was with?"

"What got Julie out and about that early?"

Sharon's mom snuck a look from the hallway to confirm she had his attention. "It wasn't who you think. She has definitely moved on from the ever-so-handy Morse. She was with that scientist guy."

I bent my wrist the other way under my chin and got poked by Sharon. It was still my move.

"They were holding hands. Julie said they were cute as a pair of baby ducks." I had to strain to catch her last word as she retreated to the kitchen.

Sharon's dad switched channels with a flick of his thumb, five o'clock national news to advertisement, big shiny car. "Yeah, Cantoni told me. He saw her and Pinko in there having a cozy breakfast for two, before the store was even open. So I guess she's not a—"

*"Little pitchers have big ears."* Sharon's mom had returned to the doorway, twitching her head in our direction.

He switched channels again. *"She's a weird little duckie, I'll tell you that. I bet she and the pasty doughboy have their own kind of fun."*

*"Larrrry—"*

*"Not like the fun we have, now is it baby?"* He snapped his chair to upright and headed toward a kitchen rendezvous.

There was a slight clattering of pans and Sharon's mother giggled. *"Larry—"*

*"How soon till we eat?"* Sharon had her own way of participating in their conversations.

•

Try to remember, to revisit or even identify the critical situation, passed. You will know you are getting close when a voice comes up from the very bowels of remembrance: "We are currently experiencing technical difficulties." The projector of memory tries to focus—we strain our ability to recall—from blur blasts sudden momentous clarity—YEOWW! our heads recede into the cushion of forgetfulness. Images zoom in and and out of recognition and recollection and you and I do not have the control unit in our sweaty little palms.

Eisy was the one who snuck me in, the first time I Simmed. Brad Izmenzki was working at the Sim, and he didn't like me Simming then, he never liked to see my shining face anywhere nearby. But good old Eisy had established some kind of trade agreement with Brad, and my free and unaccompanied Sims were part of it.

Other people Simmed for kicks; I Simmed for answers to the same questions I had outside the Sim, questions I was too scared to ask, and yet needed to answer. What did Sharon's parents mean when they said Morse was ever-so-handy? And was he really my father? And if he was then why—I teetered on the lip of a black pit of inquiry, not sure if I wanted to pull back or jump into its gaping mouth.

The protocol for my Simming was this: I waited out of sight until whoever was working reception locked the front doors and turned off the marquee. Then I sauntered over to the employee exit and when somebody came out for a smoke or to dump the trash I sidled in. If anybody asked what I was doing, I shrugged and kept moving. The key was to avoid ever running into Don. He knew there was a fair number of friends-of-employees slipping in, so he never tallied the lumpen figures that ended up in the amphitheater after hours. But if he had known it was me, all of eleven, I would have been out. After I'd Simmed, I was about as low profile as a deer caught in a car's headlights. By then though, it was late, we were all entangled in residual Experience, and Don had gone home.

172

But I get ahead of myself. Each of these Sims was like a forgotten dream, nagging. All I wanted was one clear look at what I glimpsed, not that any Sim is only visual. I knew I was very close to understanding, but I didn't know, I couldn't explain even to myself what I was trying so hard to Experience. It wasn't like I ever generated a situation that explained anything. I had abstract Sims and was left with a mood, a little insight, a lot of questions. One part of me said, hey, check it out; another part said beware, get clear, stay well enough alone. I was distracted at the same time I got better with the controls, and something about what I was doing made me feel guilty, but I didn't know why.

I desired.

And so there we are, with our not-quite-traceable memories. Grind and stutter, eyes on the big screen of our own history, images frozen and beginning to blacken, maybe melting around the edges? Something flickering through. Screeching feedback like fingernails on a chalkboard, amplified and inescapable; is it spine-tingling? And if you were to see so clearly just what happened, would it be like the kickback of a chain saw coming straight at you, panic like a car accident just beginning to happen and you the helpless passenger. Whiplash, neck snap, your brain Jello in its broth, and not even a blurred picture to hold the connection. "I'm sorry, your call cannot be completed at this time. Please—" But you cannot let go, you cannot but wonder and try harder, to recall. Something caught, something jammed, the smooth whir of pure day to day, mechanical operation interrupted: a motor somewhere straining to turn, a whining, a crescendoing shriek, full throttle blocked. Hiccough and cough and clench your fists. Grind and mash metallic teeth, a filigree of soft metal curls onto the ground. The lights come up; you can go home now.

•

Playground bullshit. Everybody's used to it when you're a kid. You play hard, you get hurt.

Playground bullshit. I irritated Sharon not more than a month later, in stating loudly and publicly what was true. Her slip did show, and the part that did was ratty looking. We had spent too much time indoors, the gloom of late fall made us all mean.

Just the facts ma'am. I was bored, and tired of the girls-standing-around scene. Sharon was all dolled up except for this one very critical detail. "Your nightie's trailing, dear." I pointed. Everybody knew I would never wear such a little-girl dress, or a little-girl slip.

"Yeah, well..." Sharon had this incredibly irritating way of chewing her gum in slow motion, mouth open, her tongue rolling around after. "At least I can ask my dad and he'll take me shopping for a new one." A less than gentle reminder to one and all who might have forgotten; there was nobody at my house answering to Dad. "See you and dear Poppá at the mall then." I beat a quick exit, stage left.

• • • • •

# 071

Morse coulda been her father. For there was a time, a fall and winter, just the right number of years ago. And a place, the Pass. Both Morse and Cuz's mother-to-be, had worked there, had spent time together, intimately. Morse was pretty sure it had been exclusively. Morse knew. Cuz was his daughter by force of desire, if not genes, she was his.

Morse's lack of paternal confirmation wasn't a question of indifference or irresponsibility. It was his and Cece's separate and strong-willed ways; perhaps all names for the same thing. Out of their tangled courtship there had come an understanding. If she, Cece Rafferty, was to have this child, then he, Morse Durrell, would stay clear. That much he had agreed to, before there was a Cuz. Cece's vehemence had in the end, or rather at the beginning, driven him off. What he had not considered was that in Cece's mind, his exclusion would be perpetual. Morse wondered later, and always, if he couldn't have somehow carved a place for himself, a bit of a dwelling place more proximate to Cece's life. He also knew she'd never allowed him so much as a toehold.

Morse had managed to be present at Cuz's birth. Cece was staying in Seattle near the due-date, she had picked a doctor and a hospital there. Cece called just before she left for the hospital, more than she'd ever promised Morse she would do. He made his truck go like it never went, ever again, drove like a crazy man all the way from Raventon. Cuz's head was just crowning when he came barging in. Morse never considered himself spiritual, but he was in rapture, right that moment. She emerged, the most amazing and beautiful little girl ever, popped open her eyes and wailed. As that slightly slimy imp curled up to one of her mama's sweet titties, her stand-in poppa and her mama, they had one good kiss between them.

Cece needed her cleanup and her sleep then, and so did baby. Morse crashed in his truck. The next morning Morse and Cece had as big a talk as they ever would, in very few words. There wasn't going to be any name on the father line of Cuz's birth certificate. Non-negotiable. Cece made it clear: any attempt on Morse's part would end in humiliation and further distance. That morning Morse didn't think the span between them was beyond reach; he agreed to all of Cece's terms and never once intended to be more than a heartbeat away.

So when Cece held his promise up to him at his every approach, Morse was stymied. The why of Cece's isolation was in her own heart, he'd always known that; keeping his word to her was what allowed him such intimacy as they'd shared, including the girl child. And the same promises kept Morse outside. In solitude, over time, Morse figured. The best he could do was tip the kid off balance, in loving.

Remorse? People say they understand, but they never do. What they don't understand is, you do something—it doesn't matter what you thought you were doing, how you thought it would all come out. You act—and there will never be a way you can ever change it. No instant replay, no apologies that are anything more than consonants and vowels. And then you get to keep on doing other things, ever after. What's been done is done. And you keep on. Knowing.

• • • • •

# 072

"Goddamn little fucker." The words poured, were purred around a tumbler of scotch in the hand of the terminally irritable Piso. He savored a sip at the bar of the Frog's Ears, staring beyond any one object before him.

Morse thought for a minute before he asked Cantoni's nephew for details. "Is this a recent little fucker?"

The bartender helped out. "That bastard Eisy and some of his delinquent friends."

Morse drank some of his beer and waited.

"They pitched a couple of ice balls in here last night. Got Popper on the neck, knocked over Piso's drink."

"A low blow indeed. Anybody catch 'em?"

They both looked at him. The bartender answered. "Are you kidding? They took off running."

"Lill' fucker. Just wait."

Morse did wait, but he heard no more details that night.

Almost a week later Angie filled him in. Eisy and his cohorts had been as clever as usual. Those in the Frog's Ears called the cops from the bar, but it had taken a half hour for them to gather their thoughts to do so. And what exactly could the cops do? Not much, as the culprits were long gone, and no one could identify an applicable ordinance. Meaning once again Eisy had fostered the taste for out-foxing adults in other youths, and they had all gotten away with it. But it was a humorless bunch they had messed with: barflies and cops. It would take time, but somebody was going to teach Eisy a lesson, that's what almost everybody said. Morse wondered who that would be, and whether Cuz had been part of the fun. He watched the snow shift to rain, he waited for the days to get a little longer, he hoped Eisy had the sense to lie low.

● ● ● ● ●

# 073

Brad Izmenzki had helped Eisy with the snowballs, then led the pack in sprinting for cover once they were sure they'd hit their marks. Brad's problem was that he couldn't quite resist the added excitement Eisy brought to every situation. Which was how Eisy had talked him into allowing quite a number of friends in on Sims.

Brad had been working at the Sim for almost a year, since right after he turned sixteen. He had become more than used to everything about the job: his two Simulator polo shirts, red and blue, his hair cut above the collar and neatly combed, his khaki pants and black shoes. He was bored. Eisy recognized this prime opportunity, and then things weren't boring at all.

Don, the night supervisor, was in the habit of reading everything that came through on the upgrades that were a constant part of Sim maintenance. It came to gall him, the way the techno-mucky-mucks got paid buckets more and ignored all the locals, or worse. Don began to explain everything he was reading to anybody in the break room who would listen. He never once thought of it as confidential information, never even considered Brad might do anything with what he heard.

But Brad told Eisy, and Eisy considered it a challenge. The two of them started making slight alterations in their Sims, squirreling around. They got fast enough they could run six or seven mini-Sims in one night. They skipped all the introductions, set the speed of the Experience so it ran in something like fast-forward, in all ways, not just the picture and the sound. The next thing they wanted to try was to get the whole thing to run backwards. They were plugging and unplugging, checking out each other's Sims, picking every wrong option. It was all a joke, for kicks, they never once thought anything could go wrong.

What they got, instead of a screen that said *"Please be patient, an attendant will be right with you."* —the whole Sim slipped a disk or something and kept going, deeper and deeper. To Eisy it felt like a slow-motion nightmare where he couldn't quite get away and the horrible kept coming, closer and closer.

It wasn't funny at all, even though they weren't plugged in all the way. It was spooky, and fast, and personal things, real people and sex and memories neither of them wanted to remember were jammed together.

When they wiggled out from underneath their sheaths, when both were totally unplugged, there was nothing to say. Brad was crying and couldn't really stop. So they walked home together, not talking. They never talked about what happened that night. Brad called in sick at school and the Sim for an entire week. He and Eisy stayed away from each other, stopped sneaking Sims for a long time.

But nothing really came of it. If anybody official found out, they never mentioned it to any of the peons. Don had a feeling something had happened, but the other ushers did Brad's part of the cleanup, so he never figured out what.

• • • • •

# CUZ

Raventon, we always had our own. Skip the euphemisms; we had kooks, slow ones, and terminal misfits, those maladjusted and those malicious, malingerers, maledictors and malcontents, the overly malleable, the malodorous, me and you on a bad day and on our best days. Other places we would have been labeled, medicated, and perhaps institutionalized according to our symptoms and syndromes; in Raventon we used family names and made slight reference to historical events, situations, and yes, experiences.

Which meant around town we waved to our worst enemies and they waved back. Peering through our curtains we regarded our neighbors: watching, deducing, concluding, prejudging, dismissing, blind sometimes to the obvious and sometimes to the invisible, we took good care, were heedful. The odd ladies were welcome at church group, the silent men were hired to chop wood or rake leaves.

Raventon was its own exact periphery, and had no exit; in this it expressly resembled family.

Fred Mossback, innovator and inventor of the Sim, once he came to Raventon he never left. I first saw him one night when I was lurking around the Sim, waiting to sneak in. He stood by the service entrance, a wad of papers under one arm, and he whispered constantly, oblivious to the rest of us. He was barely taller than me, pale, skinny, and bald except for stringy long hair in the back. He had a badge on a neckchain like the other hotshots who passed through, but I knew he couldn't be an authorized rep. It was almost April and plenty cold beside that loading dock. He stood in the one suit and tie he wore for as long as I ever saw him, waiting, lips moving, gesturing occasionally with his free hand, checking his watch.

I took note of him and hoped for his rapid departure. Not just because he scared me. But also because he moved like a shadow, as elusive as his own ravings. He loitered, barely occupying space. And when it came time to go in, he walked like a drunk, although I never saw him drinking. He never quite went away after that night. He appeared for late-night Sims, and sometimes, early in the morning, I saw him heading up the ridge.

The Fred I saw didn't look anything like the pictures they ran of him later, in the papers.

We in Raventon watched over ourselves. It was a simple prayer and a basic practice, which yielded a complex solution. I watched Fred. Took good care he did not watch me too closely.

• • • • •

# 074

Blustering spring wind and rain and sun mixed and never quite matched. Angie took her smokes in any case, her hair mostly pulled back, self-liberating and frizzled twists escaping around her square face as she stood on the porch.

"Ready or not, here they come, eh Angie?" Morse flung his words at her as he veered around a blue and white tourbus. The Simulator's entourage of visitors had assumed a predictable if slightly irritating part in the general rhythm of Raventon. Hot and sunny vacation days brought them out in hordes; rainy days, chill days, or cloudy skies stanched the flow considerably.

"Like maggots from a cowpie." Angie blew out her last breath of smoke and stretched to the timbers, revealing the merest wisp of greying armpit hair at the edge of her sleeveless Hawaiian shirt. The first of the weekend tour busloads had completed their visit to the Sim and were touring Raventon for cheaper souvenirs.

This busload, like others before, wandered the aisles of the store in clots, seeking something other than groceries or hardware or magazines and comic books. They were irritable and a little jumpy as they studied every can of soup and u-bolt. Since they felt they must buy something, a few bought snacks or one the few Raventon T-shirts Dorth had designed for Angie.

Something from the Sim clung to them like a bad smell. Angie and Harold had had more than a few conversations about this. He dutifully observed numerous busloads and could only say it was had to do with the intensity of their Experiences, and perhaps the two hour busride back to Seattle that awaited them. Angie disagreed heartily. She argued they were tainted, they came in with a layer between them and their surroundings, like the skin on overheated milk. To which Harold challenged her to Experience for herself an actual Sim and the right-after. Angie usually proposed other activities she thought would be more immediately beneficial, and Harold almost always agreed to her agenda.

A few, a very few of the post-Sim tourists did not even come into the store, but sat on the edge of the porch and smiled, staring out at everything and nothing. Angie periodically attempted conversation with them, but it was like talking through a closed window, mostly vague smiles and nods no matter what she said. Angie studied them all, as she studied the scraggly patches of grass and dandelions and fir trees, delivering less than a nod as they filed past, out of the store.

And despite what Harold said, Angie took a moment to air out the store after the last looky-loo bus of the day pulled out. Wondering if she had come to dislike anyone she did not already know, or just become mistrustful of what she did not understand.

• • • • •

# 075

"It was very thoughtful of you to remember us." Analisa untied the ribbon from the present in her lap and made it into a little spool, then slipped a finger under the taped edge of the shiny wrapping paper.

Angie chattered on more and more quickly. It would be no problem if Analisa didn't like this gift. The colors were what had made Angie buy it, but that didn't mean Analisa would want it. Especially because it might not be the right season. Angie twisted her fist around and around the forefinger of her other hand, watching and not-watching as Analisa meticulously unwrapped.

Her gift was a long scarf, the color of clay and rainbow, with a flicker of silver woven through. So soft against Analisa's skin, so thick in her hands.

"It's Scottish wool." Angie couldn't shut up. "It's kind of bright maybe, and I don't know, too scratchy?"

Analisa looked up, beaming, her fingers running over the fabric. "It's wonderful. I thank you."

And that was Angie's present, a smile from Analisa. Analisa put the scarf around her neck, and then Angie smiled too.

"Thank you very much. It is truly beautiful."

Analisa draped it so she could see its colors. The shimmering of a feather, or a seashell. Where she left her hand upon it was already warm to the touch, and softer than Angelina's hair.

"Can I go now?" Pancho's eyes were gleaming as he reeled his new kite carefully across the floor.

"Let's you and me go." Jorge gave his son's rump a nudge with his stockinged foot. His daughter fussed in his lap at the motion, flailing erratically with her fists, yowling until her father stood and walked with her.

Angie said her goodbyes then. Analisa took Angelina from Jorge and they all went onto the porch, the smell of lilacs everywhere. Pancho was jubilant, arcing the kite through its paces at arms length. Jorge leaned against the railing post, thumbs in his new tool belt. "I still don't understand why you wanted to spend your tax refund on us. But we all thank you." Then he grabbed the kite from Pancho and Pancho went for his dad and for once Jorge and Pancho were playing at fighting while Angie took the streets in a traverse above downtown, to Harold's.

• • • • •

# 076

Angelina. To Pancho, she only became more perfect as she grew. Her softest pale brown skin, her coal black hair just beginning to curl, she was a miracle with ten fingers and toes who knew from the first and always when it was her brother nearby. She would swing out a clenched fist and bob her head with her eyes going back and forth from glassy to wide-eyed until she made contact with him.

Pancho held her for hours. Twirled things in front of her. He told her all his secrets; he was her big brother and he would look out for her, always. She would sleep and sleep in his lap, smile when he touched the side of her cheek. When she was crying he could go to her and be close and almost always she would stop.

She was magic, her gurgles and tight clutching hands. Angelina made Pancho full to the brim, with her watching, her touching, her trust in him.

•  •  •  •  •

# 077

Eisy. Out at all hours, uncontrollable and unrepentant was a common view of this terminally curious manchild. Sometimes he snuck around as silent as a skunk, other times he came bombing around a corner, skidding himself and sometimes his bicycle to a stop within inches of some poor and unsuspecting soul. Grinning and gone before you could do anything but jump, he left his victims to squeal or yell or curse an empty sidewalk. He led the other young ones in Raventon on, he proved you could always find something challenging to do. He was gunning for big trouble, was what the barflies said.

There was a summer day, not long after school was out. A hot and breezeless day where everyone but Eisy seemed to be somewhere else, or napping. Eisy was stuck in town. He'd ridden his bike maybe seventeen times around the usual spots, looking and listening, hoping for something of even passing interest. Even Cuz was absent from her usual post, off swimming with a girlfriend. Eisy circled one more time, paused at the lookout spot above Pancho's, the better to observe nothing-in-action. On his way down he stuck some of the gum he'd been chewing onto the side mirror of Popper's truck, stretching a thin strand all the way to the street sign. Eisy watched the whisper of gum-thread drift back and stick to the side of the truck, unwrapped a fresh stick. Then he got an idea. If nobody was around, that would probably include Morse. Eisy zigzagged north, no hands, to Morse's.

No truck in back, front and back doors shut even though it was mighty hot. But Morse was a funny guy. So Eisy cut a brody that sprayed gravel onto Morse's ratty porch, one lucky chunk pinging the bigger of the two windows facing the street.

Still no sign of habitation. Eisy dropped his bike and mounted the porch, peering unsuccessfully around the faded sheet that covered the big window. He pounded. "Yoo-hoo."

Silence. Eisy did a two-step stomp. Not so much as a neighbor's curtains parted. He whistled loudly without any particular tune in mind as he got on his bike and made a show of taking off full steam down Morse's hill.

He was back, on foot, in less than five minutes. He gave the coal chute door behind Morse's house a thump and waited. Heard not so much as a creaking floorboard overhead. Eisy crawled in, lowered the door shut behind himself, and let his eyes adjust. Troops advance; he took a breath and ascended the stairs and was lucky. No one home, every window covered, hours of emptiness refined and tempered to a dim stasis.

The kitchen and living room were all one. Clean mismatched dishes were stacked on a rack by the sink, a small table and two rickety chairs nearby. A huge over-stuffed chair Eisy recognized from his neighbor's garage sale, a few books, a moth-eaten couch, and a braided rug rounded out Morse's decorating scheme. In the bed-room nothing more than work clothes both clean and dirty, old sneakers, a bed and a peach crate with a light and more books on it. The second bedroom was home to what Morse never quite put away: fishing poles and waders, a couple of old packs, a bunch of tools, cardboard boxes stacked precariously in one corner.

Eisy had hoped for at least some weird decoration that would justify the cov-ered windows. He burrowed through the bedroom closet and the boxes in it and found only old dress clothes, some hunting pictures, and a bunch of rocks. He went into the kitchen and opened the refrigerator. Choosing to ignore the burger half-petrified in its Styrofoam case, he removed one of two cans of beer. Nothing to eat in the cupboards either, except ancient Pop Tarts and a few cans of soup and beans.

Eisy sat at the kitchen table and opened the beer. Just as he was taking his third swig the refrigerator motor kicked on, a buzz of adrenaline jangling to his fin-gertips as he choked. He chugged the rest of the beer and left the can on the table, determined to find something of interest.

The bathroom was as stripped down as the rest of the house, a couple of ratty towels, the usual toothpaste and aspirin and soap and toilet paper, no interesting drugs, not even a dirty magazine. Eisy returned to the extra bedroom, thinking the cardboard boxes were his only hope. The first two were predictable and discourag-ing—more books and a bunch of old family stuff, pictures and papers and a baby dress and somebody's rosary made out of shiny black stones. Eisy went into Morse's bed-room. He leaned again the closet doorjamb, slid on his skinny butt until he was sitting on the floor. Where did Morse keep his secrets?

That was when Eisy spotted a scrapbook under the bed. Page one held a sin-gle picture, Aunt Cece, full-out pregnant, haggard but smiling, one hand resting on her big old belly. The picture opposite was Morse holding a baby, a tiny baby without much hair, grinning like he'd won the lottery and caught fifteen trout at the same time. The rest of the scrapbook was newspaper clippings, programs from school concerts, anything that mentioned Cuz: a list of top Girl Scout cookie sellers, a picture of kids sliding off a roof the year of the big snow, Cuz standing scrunched up behind three other kids the year her science project almost won a prize.

Eisy took the book into the kitchen and studied each page as he drank the second beer. He flipped back to the first two photos. Putting out of his mind the lack of any such scrapbook about himself, he reconsidered every exchange he could remem-ber between Morse and Cuz, he thought about what his own father had told him when he'd asked about his aunt, that Cece had had enough hard times up front to make her enjoy nothing happening, every day, for the rest of her life. That was all he would ever say about Cece, or Cuz's possible father, so Eisy had given up asking years ago. Then Eisy thought about Cuz.

Eisy put the scrapbook back exactly as he'd found it. He'd planned, he'd thought it would be funny to leave the two empties on the kitchen table, but now he stomped them flat and slid them into his back pocket, looked around carefully and made sure nothing was out of place from his explorations. Eisy exited via the coal chute doors, reclaimed his bike from the bushes. He biked through town to a trail he knew, and he took that, upriver, to a place where he could watch the water and be alone.

• • • • •

# 078

Any place there was water, she was its royalty. Waterqueen felt Eisy's approach long before she saw him. She had been with the river since it reflected stars, studied its wavering mists as the sun came up, listened and watched as ducks and dippers and a pair of kingfishers worked the water. So she knew Eisy was coming before she heard his bike on the trail and she did nothing to hide or reveal herself to him, but only sat where she'd been sitting, as the riverworld around her adapted to his presence.

His was not a calming or even a playful influence. The deer chose to leave the river and find better cover, the fish took to deeper shadowed pools, even the swallows chose a sunny patch farther upriver; all this before Eisy actually appeared at the bit of shoreline he had in mind. And although he sat as still as a rock for some time, none in the riverworld lost their wariness toward him. Waterqueen felt it too, and wondered what made this young man so dark, wondered why he couldn't play with the river once he was here. Something was knotted. She recognized in him the same hardness that was already building in the summer, some discord that the grace of the river could not subdue, and it made her cautious.

Eisy crouched, he tossed sticks and a few stones into the river, he came to no exact conclusions, and he did not jump in for a swim. He stood with as much impatience as he had arrived with, grabbed his bike and was gone.

Waterqueen wished him well, hoped the undulations of the ride back would soothe him. After the first three stars appeared she made her own way to Raventon, following a trickle of runoff that came from the ridge. She bid farewell to the dusk animals, the otter and the deer; she walked so quietly even the frogs did not pause as she passed by.

Water running through her fingers was best, spring rain next best, but that night listening to the abbreviated and regular shhh-shhh-shhh-shhh of lawn sprinklers would suffice.

Running water could not escape her, puddles called to her, when Angie served her a glass of water she studied the world through it. But this summer... the snowpack had melted fast and furiously, water rushed and flooded everywhere at once, almost more than she could witness and welcome. She cocked her head to find the nearest, merest gurgle, and there had been thousands. Small children apprenticed at her side, learning the rudiments of stick and mud dam building. Her specialty was the placing of rocks so water passing over burbled. Then she gurgled, her laughter mixing with the melody of the water. After the watery rush of spring's thaw it had gotten hot, and stayed dry. Too dry, and too much heat. Tempers were flaring early, and Eisy's discontent was a warning.

Waterqueen got up early, supervised the town crew when there was still enough water to hose down Raventon's dusty streets. She walked the last bit of moistness in the creeks daily, splashed in the street if anyone washed a car. She spent hours by her own faucets, washing dishes, bathing, letting the silky fluid run; the city had no choice but to quietly subsidize her water bill.

She listened for water. It called to her more clearly than her own thoughts and she approached slyly. Locals that summer learned better than to leave the handles on their outside faucets, the town crew knew to find her if they wanted to pinpoint the location of any kind of leak: she would be at the nearest manhole, head tipped to the rushing water.

Water spirit, Waterqueen. She did her best to call the seeps and the fluid to Raventon that summer, she could feel the barometric pressure rising as she saw the water go deeper, and she was parched.

• • • • •

# 079

It rose huge and luminous... a vault of muted alabaster became thousands of tiny full-bodied portraits of humans and animals, holding hands and running in lines upward, like the angels surrounding a medieval church door... but it was not exactly a building, nor a structure, nor a collage.

Dorth woke to flat white light and the quiet hum of her stereo. A dream, perchance a bit of migraine. Sticky with sweat she closed her eyes and tried to return to her dreaming.

She remembered colors like the Oregon coast on a low-tide morning, mud mirrors of wet sand reflecting grey-green light; a pearly quality, a shiny aspect there was no way to elicit from a palette.

The dream had a feeling to it, too. A calm, low-key joy even. The mundane world seeped in; her dream receded as slowly and as definitely as a tide. Dorth was left with an old taste in her mouth and a resonance, her hands curled around air.

She did not make coffee, she did not mess with the decorations and detritus carefully and casually placed around the studio. She went to the one wall she kept blank, propped a canvas on the easel and studied its blank surface.

She set up a second canvas. Dorth shaded and scraped and laid-in one flat flush of migrating oil paint, dusky colors eating into the center of the canvas and pulling outward. She tried sketching.

The dream came to her erratically. She began to enter its chambers, each with its own familiarity, its own light. Doorways in front of her and those she had passed through. It was the opposite of the Alhambra, where windows framed the harsh beauty of the world outside, where the interiors were mind-bogglingly intricate chambers of rugs and tiles and carved wood and stone. In her dream the rooms had no specific detail and the outside was too full, too elaborate.

She wanted to make her representations drop into dimension, like a tunnel of grey blankets. She folded her first sketch, taped others to it until she had a contorted card house. But the surfaces and the light together weren't right.

The day lost its morning freshness, the sun was hot and severe. Dorth pulled the curtains and studied her painting in the artificial twilight. She laughed when she realized she was trying to look with her eyes closed and jerked the curtains open. She was messing around with the gizmos of painting rather than putting down what she wanted. She opened the studio door, hunkered down on the stump outside and closed her eyes. The sun made beaded drifting patterns on her eyelids; she dozed.

Then she was hungry and too hot and it all seemed futile so she grabbed her coffee mug and cleared out before she could hex whatever it was she'd done so far.

In her next dreaming, the edifice was completely smooth, she stroked its walls and doorways almost constantly. Dorth wanted to paint the way the walls pressed in even when they were far away from her, the way she inched her way against them. She remembered the structure as huge and tiny, flat and with depth. And she wanted to paint the whole thing from the inside, to have the light come from within.

She spoke of these attempts to no one. Except once to Rudy, inhaling her fragment of description as she spoke. He gave her a sharp look but asked nothing. She was superstitious of naming it, of assigning words to the overall image or its parts. But she smiled whenever she heard a news announcer speak of 'the big picture.' Because that came closest to a working title, if she'd had to pick.

• • • • •

# CUZ

The center of the river, the shallow part, was glittering in facets as it bumped over a shoal of rocks. The swimming hole on the far side was already in shadow, a simmering surface of slow current and eddies. Eisy and I were sprawled on our towels above the cutbank, watching the afternoon turn into early evening, knowing there would come a moment very soon, when we too would be in shadow, and it would be time to head home. Eisy was plinking rocks into the flume of fast water right below us. I had claimed the only flat spot on the bank and was stretched out across it, facing the river, watching Eisy and his rocks, watching time, because you could see it there, you could watch it go by.

"It's going to be so fucking hot in town." Plink.

"One more dip and I gotta go."

Eisy's next rock was bigger and he pitched it underhanded, in a high arc so it entered with a galumping splash.

I stood, stretched, and dropped down the bank. Jumping in, I swam hard the few yards across the chute, hobbled the cobbled flats, and waded into the shadowy pool. Already I was cold. I swam to the center of the pool without making more than a ripple amidst its shape-shifting surface. With a deep breath I dove under, into the ultimate quiet of mote-dimmed, suspended light, and swam to the lobe of granite that shaped the pool. Shivering I came back across the riffle and the chute, scrambled up the crumbling bank. Eisy kept looking at the river. I put on my battered tennis shoes, hung my damp towel around my neck, and got on my bike, a hand-me-down from Eisy. "You coming?"

"In a little." He tried to skip a rock up the flume and got one hop. "Hey, I was wondering."

I waited, rocking on my bike, forward and back. Swatted a blackfly that tried to bite my neck.

"What's your mom ever say about your dad?"

"What's it to you?"

He turned to look at me. "He's my uncle." Green eyes with a hint of hazel, his brown hair gone blond on the very edges. I could almost see what Sharon and some of the others meant when they called Eisy a dreamboat. My cousin, my best friend.

"Who is?" I could feel a blush rise under my sunburn, the dirt from my towel gritty against my neck.

"*If I tell you something do you swear to think a long time before you do any-thing?*"

*Eisy kept looking at me, and I kept looking at him.*

"*OK. Well. Here's the deal.*" *He picked up a stick and threw it into the shallow part of the water and watched it float, spinning slowly toward the swimming hole.* "*Shit.*"

"*What is it?*" *Everything in me pounded. I saw Eisy, I saw the sun catching in his hair, I could smell the river on me, my hands squeezed the brakes harder and harder; everything was getting louder, whether it was a sound or not. He just kept looking at me. I hated him, for taking so long to say it, for knowing, for knowing how much it mattered to me.*

"*I went exploring. And I saw a picture. I went into Morse's house and I saw two pictures. They were together. He was holding a baby in one. The other one, it was your mom, and she—she was real pregnant.*"

*I took off. I biked over river rock and anything in my path.* "*It's a go-figure. Cuz—*" *I still hear his voice chasing me. I biked back to Raventon and kept going, into the woods, up the ridge, and I didn't slow down until I thought my lungs would burst.*

*My sense of balance—whatever inner ear had been keeping me level and all aboard, teetering ever onward along the path of the straight and narrow—I lost my sense of balance, my pitch. Not because it was news to me. Because he had proof, because now he knew, because he was the only person—I never thought Eisy would be the one to knock me off balance.*

*That was the last time I saw Eisy, by that river, on that afternoon. I didn't wait for him. I never answered him; I couldn't.*

*If a person, say you, were to stay in one place, to learn its ways directly and intimately, would some part of this place work its way in? Nothing dramatic, no magic, not even sleight of hand, but perhaps a shift of the habitual? A wistful tinge, especially certain times of day?* "*I've got you under my skin*" *and it's got you? If this place were Raventon there could be a moonrise as you headed home, a jay's squawks from the garden. Perhaps lunch by a window, beneath an always-changing sky?*

*I have done everything in my powers to obliterate what happened after that afternoon. Faster and faster my recollections rewove themselves into a fabric that might blanket, that could muffle whatever history followed. But I cannot forget.*

*Yet what difference does it make, really, what followed? Perhaps I am not capable of tracing this final dip and swoon, an additional sweep and stumbling bit of*

*circumnavigation, to determine what led where. Whether what follows is one contin-*
*uous surface, present past and future, like a Möbius strip, or whether I am avoiding*
*true connection and relation, I cannot say.*

• • • • •

# 080

It was horrid hot inside the store. Morse and Rudy and Harold were sitting at the big table, hoping the cool of the evening would eventually blow in. Angie threw comments their way between all the other orders. Later, when Harold and Rudy tried to reconstruct their wandering conversation, it was impossible to recall who exactly had put forth the first proposal.

If any of them had been asked at a different time, if the whole idea hadn't come up as sheer speculation over cold beers on a hot summer night, the answer would have been a kneejerk no. Instead, Simming occupied the heart of their entire evening's discussion.

"Shit, we couldn't get in if we wanted to. You should see the lines." Morse refilled his schooner from the latest pitcher. He'd spent the day deferring to such crowds while he helped Popper upgrade the ductwork of the Sim's air conditioning.

"They've got some kind of rush line, don't they?" Rudy'd read about this in a Seattle paper.

"Sure, if you want to be there at eight-thirty in the morning and stand around until whenever there's an opening." Angie's legs ached as she eased into a chair.

They all sipped, and considered.

"Harold, you Simmed for a living, right?" Morse baited Harold. Or tried to.

"Not commercially."

"What—were you a test animal or something?"

Harold looked around to see who was within listening distance. Waldo was at the counter, a table of out-of-towners were flirting with each other. "I participated in some of the modeling. The developmental, um... the test runs of the Simulator. My results were used in the initial certification MegaCorp needed for licensing. Strictly for evaluative purposes. Much different than a commercial Experience." His trademark flush grew daintily into his scalp.

"Hey Waldo, have you gone through the Sim?" Angie spoke to Waldo's back.

"I never been. But you can get in until eleven-thirty p—m—. Because it's a Friday." He rotated on his stool to face their table. "You guys are chicken. I don't have the money. But you, you're chicken."

"Maybe we are." Rudy answered.

"'S the best time, late at night. Hardly anybody around. I think Don's running it tonight. He might cut ya a deal." Waldo was now part of a long conversation, whether he kept his human audience or not.

"Anybody else game?" Morse looked around the table.

Rudy finished his beer. "Sure." Dorth was self-garrisoned in her studio, and would keep working and then drop into bed whether he was around or Simming. Besides, she'd already done it once.

"I'm too tired." Angie preferred her own reality. "And I gotta get tomorrow's order together."

"Are you scared?" Morse was partly interested, partly mocking.

"I don't know." Angie exchanged some kind of look with Harold. "I guess so. I sort of resent the concept."

"How 'bout you, Herr Doctor Professor?"

That brought Harold to a full crimson. "Are you inviting me?"

"Yeah, we're inviting you." Rudy was ready to go.

"I'll pay half for one and all since the Sim paid me today." Morse shocked even himself.

Angie stood and grabbed the empty pitcher. "Last call tonight Waldo. You want to go along? Morse is paying—"

"Hey, wait a minute." Morse hadn't counted on Waldo.

"Your offer stands, does it not?" Angie gave him the eye.

"For half, yeah. If we leave now."

"Let's go then." Rudy was the first one on his feet.

• • • • •

# 081

---

They arrived in Morse's battered truck. Tickets cost more than any of them, especially Morse, expected, but he and Rudy and Waldo were not to be deterred. Harold felt being invited along was too great an honor to decline. Once Don realized Harold knew the ropes and wasn't a snob, the two of them coached the other three on their paperwork, the quicker to get Simming.

Waldo almost panicked when they put all the paraphernalia on him. "What if there's a goddamn fire or I have to pee?"

Morse was brusque. "Just give a yell. It's in Don's interest you don't wet the upholstery. Right?"

Don grunted as he flopped a web over Morse. "You'll be OK Waldo. Just think of your favorite drink and you'll be having it in no time."

Then it was lights out.

From the start, Morse wasn't too comfortable. His sweaty shirt stuck to him, and he didn't like being strapped down where he couldn't move or see or hear. When the first visual came up he couldn't tell what he was looking at—some kind of wavy grass-colored thing, almost like fabric billowing. He tried to sit up straighter, then felt like he was tipping forward; when he leaned back the whole view went back with him and kept going back and back in a colossal flip, all the time a glassy-toned woman's voice recited a lot of terminology. Morse stopped moving any part of himself, he even held his breath. A screen appeared:

```
ADVENTURE
PERSONAL EVENT
MOOD ENHANCEMENT
WILD CARD
```

Well shit. For $27.50 he wanted Adventure.

**PLEASE MAKE YOUR SELECTION.**

He reached up and pushed the simulated button. Into the blender, a-Simming we shall go.

After that everything happened fast. Or nothing actually happened; there were more mesmerizing patterns, a kind of a washing sound. Things separated themselves into sky and water, evolved into an ocean. He was having trouble with his balance because he was on a ship, a good-sized sailboat. Morse sniffed salt air as he clutched the wooden rail in his hands. The edge of the sail above him flapped, snapped a little, the boat had a kind of a rock to it, paced to the swells it sliced through, and they were moving pretty fast. Morse worked his way along the railing to the very front of the boat, braced himself and leaned into where the boat was not yet, caught part of a wave in his face and jerked backward. He laughed and leaned forward again, staring at high clouds, bright sky, the ocean with a million colors in wave after wave forever.

He didn't know how long it was, but after awhile he turned and looked back. There wasn't anybody else in sight, which was a little disconcerting. Morse decided to climb the mast. The rigging swung as the boat rocked, but the mainsail's edge was next to him. The higher he climbed the smaller this boat seemed as more and more ocean and sky stretched in every direction. As he was hanging there, he noticed clouds building in whatever direction the sun was. Morse started down. It was harder to coordinate his descending lurches with the swaying rigging. By the time he was back on the deck and could look around it had begun to rain, a fine mist blowing in sheets. Bigger waves slapped at the boat, broke into white caps splashing over the deck. The weather couldn't have changed so quickly, it was like timelapse photography, clouds moiling into a sky full of darkness and he could barely hold on, the boat was ramping the waves but sometimes sliding backward, he couldn't see anything but a huge wave curling above him. The boat shuddered and the wave slammed him and everything went black.

Morse felt like he was coming to. He tried to move as little as possible, let sensations come and go. Nothing actually hurt. His breath wheezed-and-clicked through some kind of breathing apparatus. When he looked around he could make out a lighted doorway but he wasn't sure he wanted to go anywhere. The space around started to come clear, almost like dawn, but he was in a room, a huge room. What had looked like a door was a side of the room open to a huge stand of Doug fir. He could smell their pitch, there was a trail leading into the trees...

Morse worked one hand out of its glove-like pocket and made a fist. He rubbed his own fingers together, telling himself this sensation was his real hand, telling himself the whole thing was designed for teenagers, telling himself he wasn't scared.

He relaxed slightly and it got worse.

The Joker, right out of Batman, with his painted grin, Joker was doing slapstick with his partner, a meek looking twerp. Except the slaps got harder. And harder. The little guy looked like he was getting hurt. The Joker kept bullying. Morse wanted to go and break it up, he tried to grab at the Joker's oversize collar, he thought he had it in hand and he was ready to punch him when Joker got this really evil grin, *"You're next, you little poppenjay—"* and Morse was instantly terrified.

Joker was going to hurt him in some bad way he hadn't thought of. Morse put his arms out to protect himself, stomach lurching. It didn't matter he could feel his one hand flopping around inside the web.

There were crowds of people he couldn't quite see all around him and they were laughing as the Joker got closer. Morse tried to back up and started yelling—"Stop it. Stop it." He ripped the rest of the web off enough to pull at the helmet part and then that asshole Don came hustling up. "Hey Morse, cool it. This stuff is expensive. What's the problem?" Don guided Morse free from his tangled gear.

"This isn't fucking entertainment. It's sick, is what it is." Morse found his own way out of the amphitheater.

Only when he was clearing Morse's setup did Don realize it had been calibrated to Harold.

Harold overheard a slight rustling and let it blend into the limens and sublimens of his Sim. He was disappointed at how remedial this stock Experience was. Either he'd inaccurately remembered the degree of subtlety built in, or real-life customers had forced MegaCorp to tone down the whole Experience even further. Given the profile information he'd provided, Harold should have been able to pass through the orientation rapidly, instead, the whole mechanism felt sluggish. Harold relaxed, told the voice-of-experience to go away, and enjoyed a Mood Enhancement.

The lights came up slowly. Don unstrapped Rudy first.

"Man, that was really something, the last part." Rudy was looking at his fingers as he wiggled them. "What did you pick?"

Harold extricated himself from his web. "Where's Morse?"

"Hey wake up buddy." Don shook Waldo's shoulder, then turned to Harold. "The one in five thousand."

Harold blanched.

"He bailed. Not more than twelve minutes into the personalized. I should probably check his web and see if it's damaged. He pretty much ripped himself out. Come on Waldo, this is not your bed."

"You mean he quit partway through?" Rudy was having trouble understanding the conversation around him.

"Well, that was one hell of a ride, I gotta say." Waldo was trying valiantly to right himself.

"Yeah, Morse took off. Not to rush you guys or anything, but can you find your way—" Don was sweating.

"Certainly. Gentlemen?" Harold made a small bow and gestured toward the exit.

"Harold, is that normal, to leave in the middle?" Rudy checked his pockets and his seat before he left.

"Not at all. Don was citing the statistics: one Sim in five thousand. We considered an early departure a failure. They almost always indicate extreme trauma." Harold guided Waldo to the exit.

"Shhhit. I bet Morse just didn't want to give us a lift home. He did pay, right?"

"You're all paid for, Waldo."

"That was great. I had about the whole Yukon to myself, and no skeeters. The fish were real fighters. Hey Don—" Waldo looked over his shoulder but Don had remained in the amphitheater. "I never did think about a drink. But I'm mighty thirsty now..."

"Rudy, do you have any idea where he might go?" Harold gently let go of Waldo's shoulder.

"No. You think it's serious? I mean Morse is kind of his own—you know."

Waldo was the first outside. "Well boys, it's been. Tell Morse thanks. " He hoofed it down the stairs muttering something about fishing lures and the midnight sun.

"Night Waldo." Rudy and Harold remained on the landing outside as the lights all around them were shut off bank by bank, leaving starlight and summer night and minimal red neon:

## THE SIMULATOR: A FAMILY EXPERIENCE.

"Your Experience was... positive?" Harold studied Rudy.

"Yeah." Rudy rubbed the side of his head. "Most of the adventure crap was nothing special, but the last little bit was cool. Really cool."

They began the walk back to town together. "I'm glad you enjoyed it."

"Are you going to look for Morse?"

"I don't think that's realistic tonight." Harold glanced at his watch.

"What do you think happened?"

"I would only be guessing."

They strolled and sometimes stumbled to town without further talk. Rudy pondered what he'd just gone through, gawked at the unexpected beauty of the dark; Harold considered probabilities and worried.

They stopped when they came to the street that went up the hill to Dorth's. "Tell Dorth I hope she had a productive evening."

"Sure. Night Harold."

"Good night." Although Harold did not think it was a good night at all.

• • • • •

# 082

Morse was in his truck and out of the Sim's parking lot before he knew what he was doing or where he was headed. He tried to take solace from the familiarity of the dashboard's glow, from the discordant jouncing ruts of the dirt roads that led him upriver, away from the Sim and Raventon.

He parked miles beyond where Eisy had sought similar solace, he walked in to a place he liked to fish when he wasn't feeling right. Sticks crackled as his feet found the trail, when his hands parted the desiccated alder and wild rose. He stumbled and slid down a gravel bank and hunched against it. Shivering and sweating, his head between his knees, Morse listened. Water rilled, sub-aquian rocks clinked, there was enough river-noise to keep everything else at bay. A breath of cool river air, a breath of the always changing matched his every sigh and mutter until he could stretch his legs out, open his eyes and admit the beauty of this night, in this place. There was no explaining why he was so close to tears.

He stared at the band of stars over the river. He sat long after frogs resumed their croaking and he listened, but the water wasn't talking to him this night. So Morse climbed back up the gravel to his truck and drove home. He took a shower but when he got out he didn't want to sleep, he especially didn't want to dream. A dark part of himself laughed; what had he ever known about dreams?

With a towel wrapped around his hips he paced his house, ignoring the pointless backtracks of his wet footprints. Once he had the bottle of bourbon he'd been saving in front of him he didn't want to drink from that river. He sat at the table, played with the light and shadow of his hands on the table, paused when a cricket somewhere chirped.

An over-animated cartoon, that's all it was. The little guy getting beat up didn't even exist so it didn't matter if Morse ran away. He should have started running the minute he saw the Joker. But Morse couldn't forget the look of terror from the little man nor his own pure fear. Why had the beauty of the sailing shifted, why had everything turned on him? Was this what other people did for fun?

Morse tried to trick himself into feeling safe in his own house. He turned a light on in every room, told himself he wasn't pacing. He put the scrapbook on the kitchen table and propped the back door open, hoping to catch a breeze. And he knew for sure, he wasn't going to work with Popper tomorrow, he wasn't going to work on the Sim again. Maybe the whole fucking thing would fall apart.

Maybe he was just scared. Well then, put the Sim on the list of what he wouldn't do, what he ended up running from. All-the-time-running: from Raventon when he wasn't welcome, from Cece when he couldn't convince her to let him stay near, from his own girlchild. He took another look at the bourbon and poured a shot, turned out the kitchen light, and stepped onto the porch. The cricket rasped nearby.

Morse wished he could run all the way to that sailboat, and this time hold on no matter what. Instead he would make an attempt to do something other than run, no matter how pitiful.

· · · · ·

# 083

Morse let himself in after Angie had left to open the store. He was sitting at the kitchen table as Alexander Mettle came downstairs for breakfast.

"Well this is a surprise. A pleasant one." Daddy had just about jumped out of his skin at seeing anybody in the house; he was still trembling, and pale. "I've been having tea lately, but maybe you'd like some coffee?"

"Yeah. I mean no. Tea would be fine."

Daddy steadied himself at the counter and squinted, tried to get a reading from Morse. "What if I made some fresh coffee?"

Morse had to laugh. "That would be good."

Neither of them said anything as Daddy puttered. They sat opposite each other as the coffee maker went through its gurgle and hiss. Each of them drank most of a mug.

"I have a debt outstanding with you, if you recall." Morse spoke to his mug. "I want to pay you back. Make amends."

"Morse, that money, that money was a gift. A long time ago. You know—"

"Just shut up for a minute and hear me out." Morse's knuckles were white. "OK?" When Daddy didn't answer Morse looked up. Sitting before him was an old man, his eyes wide behind his glasses, his hair floating in gossamer wisps; he was shaking. For all Morse knew he shook all the time. "I'm sorry."

"Go ahead." Daddy gave him a weak smile.

"I can't pay the actual money back, to you, right now. I, I've got something else." Morse stood and poured himself more coffee. Explaining was much harder than he'd planned. "I want to do a similar thing, like what you did for me. For one, I want to set up an account for somebody else, so it's there whenever she needs it. But I don't know how."

Daddy was beaming.

Morse was blushing and sweating. "I need you to do me a favor, to help me with the details."

"You're a good man, Morse. I'd be honored."

• • • • •

# 084

Daddy's habit was to get out of bed just after he heard Angeline leave for the store. Since Morse's surprise appearance, Daddy made sure he was fully awake before he eased himself down the stairs, favoring his right hip. He would make a pot of tea and linger until the sun came full throttle through the kitchen window. That was his signal to begin the series of activities he had learned could fill most of each morning. He went back upstairs and washed and shaved and combed and brushed; he put on each garment just so. Straightened the kitchen. Then and only then did he take his walk to the store, as close to noon as possible. Once there he might check stock in the backroom, or pick up litter around the gas pumps, or sweep the porch.

There was nothing that made him useful anymore, even on the busiest of days. His presence at the store was a matter of sociability, his own desire to be, if not a part of things, then on the edge of them. Most summer days he simply took a paper from the counter, left his two quarters, and went out onto the porch to observe whatever lunch crowd passed. When the rush was over he would take a spot at the counter and let his daughter serve him whatever she wanted. But this, too, was more a matter of show, for he was rarely hungry, and his stomach accepted almost nothing without complaint. Without complaint seemed to be the hidden art of old age, Daddy thought.

So he said nothing of the the hard lump in his belly that never moved and never went away, nor of the blood he shat. He knew what these meant. And knew one thing or another just like this would be the end of him.

$$\bullet \quad \bullet \quad \bullet \quad \bullet \quad \bullet$$

# 085

Eisy was the first to smell smoke.

He'd spent the early evening shooting pool. When the new bartender at the Frog's Ears got word Eisy was underage and threw him out, Eisy'd done his best to snag a ride with a couple of the high school seniors on their aimless high speed cruises. When they left him behind he finished his own all-too-usual roamings as yet another scorching Saturday night wore itself out. His father was propped in front of the TV, asleep; his mother must have gone to bed. The residual heat in the house was stifling. Eisy stole a cigarette from the pack near his father's hand and went out on the back porch. He lit the cigarette and watched its glow, smoke rising in a straight ribbon, wavering only when he moved his hand. He flicked the cigarette away half-smoked and looked out at a view so predictable he could tell the time by which few neighbors' lights were still on. A dog yapped somewhere near downtown. Not even the sound of a car cruising, or a cat in heat yowling, relieved the general quiet.

When he first caught a whiff of smoke Eisy thought his cigarette must have caught in the grass and considered the excitement if the whole damn house burned. Then he scuffed at the ground around the edge of the porch, trying to locate and stomp out the smoldering butt. The smell remained elusive. If it hadn't been so hot he might have passed it off as somebody's woodstove burning itself out. He kept poking until he kicked up a bent and pretty fresh-looking butt. It was out but he peed on it to make sure.

He still smelled smoke. He walked around the house but couldn't find any place it got any stronger. Eisy leaned against one of the porch posts, close to dozing. The mosquitoes eventually found him, so he went inside and upstairs to his sweltering room. He took off everything but his underpants, pointed the humming fan at himself and fell asleep.

Next thing he knew the siren was blasting. Eisy pulled his pillow over his head but the howling alarm continued, one wailing cycle after another. He peered out, eyes burning, and he cursed; it was only five-thirty. A return to sleep eluded him, amidst his damp and muddled sheets, so he pulled on shorts and a T-shirt and went downstairs.

His father had made it to bed at some point. Eisy heard an engine crank, tires roll on gravel. He looked out and saw Popper slam his door as his truck came to life and he roared by. There was nothing particularly edible and obvious in the kitchen so Eisy jammed his feet into his sneakers and got on his bike, headed downhill, a few other cars careening toward the fire station, not that there was anything obviously in flames. Maybe for once somebody else had pulled a false alarm. That was when Eisy saw a column of smoke straight up off the ridge, getting bigger and darker as he watched. The first breath of wind, or perhaps it was the motion from his bike, ruffled his hair. The first angry flame curled up with the smoke.

• • • • •

# 086

Angie woke in a sweat, put on the thinnest clean T-shirt she had, and stumbled to the store, sweating some more as the loading door jammed on its track with a screech. She was forcing it, sticky sleep still clinging to her, when the first siren wailed. Keys in hand, eyes bleary, she peered out. Toots came roaring by and shouted and pointed, looking as discombobulated as she felt. "It's on the ridge—" He barely missed Piso's huge bouncing pickup as they simultaneously pulled into the fire station.

Angie saw the smoke then, an almost unwavering rod in the breathless sky. Good thing there was no wind. Probably some asinine weekender flicked a butt while ramming around on his four-by-four. Oughta give Piso and some of the other big-talking volunteers a run for their money. She watched the ancient pump truck roll out, Toots at the wheel, Popper co-piloting, half the town peeling after it in their own rigs.

All of them knew as well as she did, the potential. There were fires on the ridge a lot of years, but they usually came later, during hunting season, closer to the rains. This year the woods were tinder, and had been since July. Angie skipped her morning smoke. The whole crew would come rolling in for food when they were finished, they'd want coffee as bad as she needed a cup right now. Inside the store, Angie realized she's been sniffing at some vague scent of smoke since she woke.

Another siren cycled but who else was going to come running? It must be the new dispatch system, blowing off the siren here when somebody down the valley needed help. The sirens got everybody up and moving earlier than usual; the slight haze of smoke from the fire seeped into the way they asked for coffee. Old-timers came down to top off their tanks, to see if she had yesterday's newspaper, but mostly to wait on the porch. Watching.

Even Angie wandered out when she had a second. By eleven it was clear this was a different kind of fire. None of the crew had returned. Neon yellow trucks with state crews zoomed past town, hell-bent for leather. Some of Raventon panicked, loaded their heirlooms and clean underwear into rigs, and hit the road. The rest stood around watching.

Two county cops and a state trooper pulled in at eleven-thirty. They drove at a crawl all over town, lights flashing, bullhorn voices ordering residents to pack up and leave in orderly fashion. The hackles on Angie's neck went up when she heard these words again and again, like an ice cream cart melody, echoing through town. Those who hadn't turned out to fight and who weren't getting ready to run had their garden hoses out, wetting things down. Knowing there wouldn't be enough water pressure to do much if the fire reached Raventon.

The trooper came back to the store when he'd completed his rounds, adjusted his big-brimmed hat, and started telling one and all it was time to move out. The old guys stared back at him without the benefit of mirrored sunglasses. Before he could continue, Angie announced in a booming voice "Hey, I'm gonna shut down the store. Anybody who wants a ride somewhere, I'm sure Mr. Trooper here will arrange for some carpools. Right?" He nodded and took another look around. A few people started talking to him in the parking lot, the lights on his car still flashing.

Shimmering heat built on this, a scorcher of a summer day. Smoke rode the heat into Raventon, it gathered in a haze that got thicker between things, shifted to a coppery fog. Then came the wind. It started from nothing, pulling, then blowing in gusts. The wind they had all been praying against. Angie herded everyone out to the porch, double-checked both water hoses were turned on, and flipped the emergency shutoff at the gas pumps. The trooper packed five people into his car, promised he'd return with more transportation, and took off into the smoke. Angie headed toward the house in a rough-kiltered jog.

She couldn't find Daddy. She'd been thinking she was looking for him so he could help hose down the roof of the store. Now she just wanted him. She ran through the house, calling. He'd made himself his usual breakfast, his few dishes were in the drain. His pajamas and robe were folded over the foot board of his bed. So where was he?

• • • • •

# CUZ

Smoldering possibility. A bit of cinder, an old leaf, the slightest current of air. Minutes pass, hours, more than a day. A gob of pitch in a pine-needled hollow cradled by a vein of dead root, a sigh of breeze; we have timid wavering flame. Temperatures rise; almost everything has its ignition point. One thing leads to another, energy is transferred, fuels fed upon until there is a new world: fire and the not-yet-burned. A turbine of heat and smoke and consuming flame in a wind tunnel of its own making, a self-fulfilling prophecy.

Change direction. Follow the chain back: effect, then cause. This could be called a history.

Once upon a time, there was a small room in a big city. In this room sat a man named Fred Mossback, damaged goods. He watched light come and go, distinct rays of pure sunshine diffused, dispersed, disappeared. Fred watched this light move across the wallpaper of the room. On sunny days it was a bright rectangle, on cloudy days a suffusion. At night a streetlight came on, casting a rippled and unmoving square.

Fred's mind wandered as he sat, his thoughts drifted and eddied and worked themselves back. He propped a gutted TV casing in front of him and observed the same light through this frame. There had been an earlier time he had seen it all, everything, on his TV, all in one night. In this room it was more than he could bear to watch light on wallpaper.

After a long time, Fred left. He packed his papers from MegaCorp's Lab, two shirts, one tie, three sets of socks and underwear, a toothbrush and a comb and proceeded to the thing-that-had-come-from-what-he-had-seen. He went to the Raventon Sim. Perhaps it was with some hope of seeing something he could bear?

I have decided to spill the beans since the milk is already spilt. No need to cry about either, not now, for tears cannot extinguish and further explanation, especially scientific, would, like water, run through our fingers. You have witnessed for yourself my best accounting, a re-enaction, a hopscotch re-visitation of my stumbling descent. Although the direction of motion has not been entirely downward, in retrospect.

I am tired. The cork has been pulled, the genie let out of the bottle, the carefully constructed model set upon the water and we will see if it floats. Scan the airwaves, broadband casting. Catch shifting cycles, drifting shadows of sound. Float the frequencies, microwave ovens to infrared heaters, radar and sonar, ultraviolet and x-ray. Maybe dislocation is Fred's disease, his vision, his condition.

• • • • •

# 087

Fred talked to himself and his tape recorder, his last afternoon. He was halfway up the ridge, implements and provisions placed in a semicircle around him.

"Invention. Most people think this means something new. But there isn't anything new or old, just habits. We become used to doing a task one way, thinking of things in a certain manner. Inured. Then someone rearranges the materials at hand— reduces, separates, synthesizes—makes some alteration, usually considered to be an improvement. Occasionally this affects the values we assign to time and materials. Much of what we refer to as invention in modern times relates to the registration of trademarks, patents, copyrights. Credit where credit is demanded.

"Is there an ultimate invention? I would suggest ourselves. Or God. Not because I am a non-believer; because any belief wherein we posit the world to be solid and/or predictable involves invention. Let me clarify my own question: What would be the ultimate physical invention?

"If I assume the conservation of energy is correct, the concept of a perpetual motion machine is eliminated. Grand possibilities arise: a cure for AIDS, or cancer, a cheap means of water purification, some kind of defense system that eliminates war... you get the drift. Items of humane import. Of course this list rapidly assumes unwieldy proportions. A conference of industrial engineers would make a different list: an ultimate alloy, a chemical co-processor; high-efficiency crystal generation.

"Which is why this entire line of thought, the consideration of invention, ultimately proves to be unsatisfactory. Let us instead consider the history of "great inventions," or rather, powerful discoveries—the wheel, the lever, penicillin, electricity, the transistor, nuclear fission, the computer chip. What do these have in common? Innumerable applications, relative simplicity, a large and measurable impact upon human behaviors.

"Consider fire.

"It seems ideal in its relation both to inventors and the concept of invention: a bridge between human perception and human control of an existing process. Because of course when we speak of 'inventing' fire we mean its control, the ability to generate and direct it as we choose, when and where we choose.

"I have been asking myself: Is there any way to reinvent fire? To re-perceive fire? For aren't electricity, the neutron bomb, fiber optics—isn't each simply a different application, a reinvention, if you will, of fire? Each involves the transfer of energy between materials; each can be controlled by human action. Yet we choose to think of each as a separate invention.

"Let us revisit the chemical process of burning: corrosion, the lay-person's flickering mass of wood, the reaction of flesh to sun, oxidation, heat generation. All well known.

"Consider the means of generating fire: optically, say, through a magnifying glass. Kinetically, as with a flint and steel, a safety match, a propane lighter. Energy contained or concentrated, then released, leading to the process we most commonly think of when we speak of fire.

"We are now warmed up in our discussion, I think. Heh heh... but is there some other means of generating fire? An interesting possibility, wouldn't you say?

"Given what I learned from my participation in the development of so-called Experiences, and from some of my recent commercial Simulations, I think I understand how energy can be contained and then released—

"But I digress. What about the mythical aspect of 'first' fire? Prometheus steals it from the gods and is then required to pay. Eternally, if memory serves me well. Tricksters throughout the world are credited for the same thievery. Then there is the so-called scientific version, wherein some prehistoric, with grunts and mutters and some portion of scorched flesh, grabbed a bit of burning bush and made it his own. Clearly the taming of flame, what we seem to consider fire's invention, captivates our imagination. My goal was always to use Simulation to explore what we habitually ignore. In this case I have been using it to remove as many assumptions as possible about fire. I should, within the year, generate real flame on the Sim's big screen. I mean concurrent individual visualizations, considered collectively. But again I stray. And in an unproductive manner." Sigh.

"I have with me today the standard, what we might call the obvious materials: matches, a sodden shop rag in a sealed container, a magnifying glass, a bow, rod, and wooden platform, a battery and wired connections.

"'To Build a Fire.' A story by Jack London, of a trial by fire. Let us reflect upon this bit of fiction as I begin with the most physically demanding and tedious of today's procedures. I begin with the bow, wooden dowel, and concave base, into which I have placed a bit of punk." Fred's tape recorder picks up a raspy rubbing. "The... consolidation—" pant "—of my energies into eventual flame." Whirring, whirring "And sooner or later—a smoking—" faster rotational sounds. Panting "—a smoking gun, if you will. Unfortunately, I neglected armaments in today's experiment." Chuff "It is always interesting to use an object in a manner counter to its intended application. Its purpose, as my esteemed colleague Harold Hastings used to say."

Pant pant "Ha. We have—... oh, not quite. Very close, so near to the recognizable transfer of energy we call fire—" puff puff "definitely a burning pain within my neck and in the blistering of my—Yes!

"We have fire. Immutably hahaha. The sad part is that I will now need to extinguish it... a bit more difficult than I supposed, but—... there.

211

"As I—" gasp "—uh, catch my breath—" pant pant "—let us reflect. Body sugars converted to action, friction to heat, in the presence of fuel and oxygen.

"Let us now proceed with experiment number two. A magnifying glass focuses sunlight. I have been particularly looking forward..."

On and on Fred garrulously gabbed, combustion after combustion. Until the shop rag burned hotter and faster than he expected. "Out of the frying pan and into the—" a slight and unexpected explosion. Fred stomping "oh my dear, oh my dear—" his voice becoming distant, his gasps disappearing amidst the crackle and hiss of fire.

• • • • •

# 088
---

Morse found himself a stool at the back bar and ordered a boilermaker when the fierce waitress gave him an opportunity. When he blew his nose he smelled with satisfaction the pine pitch on his bandana. After his talk with Angie's father he'd retreated until there was no more drivable road, and then some; made a base camp and spent days roaming. His jeans fit too tight, even small hills made him huff, so he took his time, zigzagged off the ridgelines, a couple of candy bars in his shirt pocket. On top the wind was icy through his sweated-out shirt. In the side-pocketed bowls, the sun baked him as he wandered through dried out flowers and heather.

One afternoon he wandered into a clump of browned-out ponderosas, nuthatches all over. When he stopped to watch he heard a pileated's hard rapping. He worked his way through the stand until he saw a pair of them, hopping round and round a golden trunk. One look at him and they took off in dipping big-winged swoops that lightened his heart. The last day he followed a deer trail, did his best to hike without a noise, without leaving a full print, and barely made it back to camp by dark. He hadn't seen another human the whole time.

"You want another?" The waitress took both his empties before she asked.

"Just a beer this time." Morse felt good. Everything'd worked out. Mettle had called ahead so the Seattle banker had everything ready to sign. There was a new account in Cuz's name, accruing interest as of five p.m.. He'd been able to do Alexander Mettle a small favor too, as part of things, putting all of whatever it was he had been so worried about into a new safe deposit box. Morse would give him the key tomorrow. But for tonight, he was having a modest celebration, of life and life only.

Morse shifted over to a window-side booth for dinner, thinking about Daddy's ever-dwindling universe, the way he so carefully read and reread every newspaper; his fragile walk. Morse ordered steak and potatoes and salad and pie as the sun finally sank across Puget Sound. Old and getting older, Alexander Mettle was still leading some kind of charge.

Morse was treating himself to dinner, a hot bath, and a good night's sleep. Tomorrow he would drive to Raventon, and settle with Popper about the work he'd skipped out on. As usual, there'd be a few rude remarks; the rest of his crew could conclude whatever they pleased. Things were going to be different.

Over his second slice of pie Morse started watching the flickering TV screen in the corner of the bar. News, all the big events he'd lost track of. A map of Washington came on with a big flashing dot labeled Raventon, the screen shifted to live footage of a huge fire. Morse jumped to the bar and stared.

Roaming and ranting through Seattle he confirmed Raventon was burning amidst confusing reports that the Sim burning too. That was what everybody seemed most excited about, the goddamn Sim.

He tried calling. Sorry operators' voices could not complete his calls; spot fires and smoke and general mayhem had temporarily closed the Pass.

Morse despaired.

• • • • •

# 089

The sky glowed day and night; humans fumbled as they raced, hearts in their throats, as trees popped and funneled into the air-turbine surrounding them. One fire raged into several, several fires into one; spreading racing ranging burn; heat smoke and a roar sucked what was not fire into fire, faster, leaping draws, a canyon, faster, the ridge a-flame, roofs in Raventon smoldering—smoke everywhere. Thick as smoke.

It burned and burned. Pitiful humans raced to one fiery edge, then bolted from it. Other creatures fled: squirrel ran from fire, its tail ablaze, staggered squirrel-fashion into death. Secretive elk bugled and galloped through downtown. Blue jay squawked and screamed, driven back as young ones were sucked into flame.

Shifty smoke, was it stronger? Closer? Coming or going? Morning into afternoon and maybe it was almost evening, the sun reflected cherry-red onto the river. Birds sat edgy in the tops of trees for miles around, called to each other in the endless false and smoky dusk. A pocket of blue sky, a breath of fresh air, then something shifted and it was once again twilight, foreboding. Night and day some other rhythm, from before.

Helicopters. They dropped hotshot crews from somewhere, a local guided them in. Walkie-talkies, CBs, radio stations chattered. Paid firefighters in yellow shirts directed; volunteers took orders. Ghost-eyed smoke-smeared locals ranted, they wept.

Came another day, somewhere, in a place they still counted days. This beast of fire was trapped, surrounded with a line that stretched over rock and mountain, through draw and creek. Then, of its own accord, without accord, satiated, shrunken, the fire withdrew. All but disappeared.

Came the seventh dawn there was ash and smoke and random flickering. The beast was no longer, but do we know where fire goes? Unseen voices told each other with varying conviction, "It's under control. It's over."

Slowly, smoke cleared. Like a heavy fog it rolled back gracefully, abandoning sleepy grey twists in small depressions. The haze between things grew faint and left in its place a smell, a charred residual. A slight sweetness behind the smoke crept in.

A touch of rain, a slow wind. Another day.

Over time as much as was dying, as was already dead, would survive. Big trees still standing would take big time to live or die. The infinity of small beings, their crumbs and burnt flesh were already the new feeding and spawning ground of others. Singed chipmunk emerged from a random tree trunk, blind. Scorched fur and lungs do not give him air-sufficient. In the slow dying-time he tries to eat, to gain moisture, he shits and shits again, he makes his best and feeble trill to another chipmunk. Redtail hawk dives, feasts. Fire fire burning bright. What caused it to light?

A glimmer, a sparkle? A sliver of glass, a bolt of lightning, a cigarette butt, a bit of solvent on a rag? One thing leads to another. A fire seeks fuel. What is not burned dreams of what is burnt.

Ashes to ashes.

• • • • •

# 090

---

Checking for hot spots, the exhausted firefighter kicked through the remains of the Sim. He poked with his shovel, then squirted with his backpack pump. Stirred and chopped and flushed again if anything anywhere hissed or steamed or smoked. He was working his way to what was left of the Sim's concrete-block entrance way, he could feel the heat through his boots and was about to call for the big hose when a body stepped out. A small human, coated in charcoaled smudge, eyes ungodly white. The apparition took one look at the young fire fighter and laughed; staring back mocking him, then it turned and skipped down what had once, some endless days before, been a road.

Only after this creature was out of sight did the firefighter think to yell in a voice high-pitched and peculiar even to himself. "Hey—Wait up. Are you OK? Does anybody know you're here?" And then, finally, to act. He chased after, equipment clanging, not sure where to run. He jumped again, practically out of his skin, when two huge ravens took sudden flight with the same hunched black motion as the person he'd been pursuing, ca-caw, calling.

The firefighter turned and ran back to the rest of his crew. He choked out what he'd seen and then stopped himself from jabbering further before he got pulled from his double-overtime duties, before he got something added to his record about disorientation and field dehydration near the end of an operation. They all searched where he had been; they found no one.

Eisy watched the firefighter go and couldn't help laughing some more, though it hurt his throat. The guy was so pathetic. Eisy had been dozing in a shady corner and the next thing he knew the wall itself was hissing. So of course he practically wet his pants bounding up to see why.

And what to his wondering eyes should appear but an idiot in bright yellow with goggles and hardhat and face mask and tin backpack with hose, looking like an extra in some B-grade Japanese horror flick, staring at him. No good morning, no how-ya-doing, just another goddamn looky-loo. So Eisy'd did his take-a-picture-it-lasts-longer pantomime and ran.

• • • • •

# 091

Brad Izmenzki could remember. Brad could never forget. The workday had started with a smaller than usual opening crowd at the Sim, it was too hot, people were staying home. Don had called the county and was told the fire on the ridge was almost under control. Its smoke kept everybody edgy, some looky-loos even wanted refunds on tickets they'd already bought. Turned out they were the smart ones.

First run, the amphitheater couldn't have been more than a quarter full and three of the staff were sent home early. Nobody minded. Then the first building alarm went off. Don got right on it. He couldn't find anything and told everybody it was a false alarm, all the smoke and the hot day together must have set it off. The only one who might have insisted upon evacuation was one of the three who got sent home early, a grade-school teacher and a real stickler about procedures.

The staff was more worried about the fire up on the ridge. Brad helped Don, they kept looking for Sim malfunctions, for any kind of a problem. But at that point everything checked out shipshape in their little bit of air-conditioned heaven. General maintenance, that was Derek. When the next round of lights and buzzers went off, he came running. To Don's credit, he personally scrambled to the indicated site as fast as he could, which left him with major burns and permanent lung damage.

Nobody had a clue the Sim was a firetrap. Once it started burning all the fake layout made it a more complex building than anybody had figured.

The biggest flaw, the real killer, were the Experiences. No matter what the staff tried to do, those Simming thought the whole nightmare was some kind of imaginary extravaganza, a Simulated fire, not a real one. One of the first ladies out, she came running to complain her Experience was too violent. Sixteen out of fifty-one survived. One couple left nauseated, one guy had to go to the bathroom; it was the ordinary that saved them.

So why wasn't there a universal cutoff switch, an emergency procedure for those Simming? MegaCorp's defense in court was that it was protecting its customers from the psychological harm of introducing fear at the beginning of an Experience, that sending everyone through an in-case-of-a-real-emergency-routine would have set the wrong tone. And MegaCorp got off. It didn't hurt that no one in any of the agencies that crawled all over the building inspecting, ever thought about the actual Simulation, about how during a Sim, a person might not be able to distinguish real warnings. "Standard fire escape and warning procedures were not effective in this context." A direct quote from the decision. Who could have predicted folks would sit there with little embarrassed smiles and let the fire burn them alive? That they'd just sit there waiting for an even more exciting Experience?

Maybe they got one. Afterlife.

• • • • •

# 092

---

Raventon's demised:

### "Daddy" Alexander Mettle

Survived by his daughter Angeline. It will be a mystery forever how Angie did not see him as they passed each other in the hundred yards between house and store. The little that was left of him was found near the register. Angie believed, she was almost positive Daddy snuck around her and stayed, that he'd chosen to sit at the counter while the store burned around him.

### Angelina Maria Llamado

Those who lived onward included her mother, Analisa; her father, Jorge; her brother, Francisco. Pancho had carried her, he had run with her far far beyond the flames, both of them coughing. She died of lung complications in less than a week, as Raventon still smoldered.

### "Eisy" Eiseneers Rafferty

Who gave him life still lived: his mother, his dad. Cuz's grief for him was like a raw sore. Eisy died in a freak accident, a burnt grand fir toppled on him after mop-up on both fires was almost complete. He had signs of dehydration, minor burns, possible fever, but it was a falling tree that killed him.

### Waterqueen

She was killed in the line of duty. She died doing her best. With watering can and a garden hose she tried to keep the post office from burning. Her heart was big, but not big enough for her efforts; her death certificate cited massive pulmonary failure.

• • • • •

# CUZ

---

*After the fires we held a reckoning, a community memorial service. Our cemetery had changed least, its headstones merely scorched, one section of wrought iron fence melted to a snake-like twist. For me, one time through, one ceremony, was plenty. More than enough. Tía Angie made all the arrangements, she paid whatever bills came in from anyone crass enough to charge.*

*Many at the service had seared lungs, burns, singed hair and brows. Attire was modest as we had only what we'd been wearing when the fire started, or what we grabbed as our town filled with smoke and terror. Raventon had done everything to help each other, we had been cowards and heroes, we were grieving.*

*If the fires had been a war, there would have been a bronze plaque. Instead there were four new headstones and a lot of silence as we reckoned our losses.*

• • • • •

# 093

The still-living of Raventon grieved under a daytime sliver of moon, blocking each other from television cameras and the never-ending questions of reporters. Words were exchanged, tears shed; laughter and sorrow in the same mouthful. Those who survived were present as they buried their own. Were they alive?

Angie stood to the side of the crowd, she looked for a certain face and avoided the eyes of everyone. When she spotted Jorge, hair slicked down dark as ebony, his mouth narrowed to nothing, she worked her way over. The three Llamados clumped together as though no one else was even near. Jorge gripped Pancho's shoulders, Analisa, at his side, was in a daze. Angie held out to Pancho the bolo tie from Daddy's safe deposit box. "He had a tag on it. It said he only let you give it to him so he could keep it shiny for a bit."

Pancho's head was down. Jorge gave him a rough nudge and the boy put his hand out. Angie put the silver tie into it. She stroked his cheek and wiped his tears with her thumb. She wrapped her arms around Analisa, hugging her and feeling nothing back, wishing she could serve herself up and have that make anything better.

"Thank you, Tía." Jorge's cheek muscles were pumping. Angie untangled herself from Analisa and shook Jorge's hand in the soft way he'd taught her.

"Friends." Father Mungo cleared his throat and tried again. "Friends. I am here today, as you are, to mourn. It is not for me to offer..."

Angie took Analisa's hand, and she wept. She wept at sky as blue as it could be, she wept for herself alone. She felt someone brush against her and turned away. Harold kicked at the dirt, he blushed, he stood by Angie without a word.

Morse's plan had been no more complicated than to pay his respects, to say hello to the still living and goodbye to those gone. He pulled over at the bridge and walked in from along the river. So he had no idea what a circus it was until he crested the knoll and saw the crowd and the cameras and it made him sick. He ducked below the slight ridge until he found an obscure angle where he could watch and not be much noticed. At which point he saw Harold join Angie and witnessed what he already knew: Harold had a way of getting closer while Morse made such distance greater.

Morse scanned the crowd and saw those he had always known diminished: Sam shrunken and wearing somebody else's suit, hands in his pockets, his wife nearby but separate; Popper with a big patch over one eye and an arm around the slow-sobbing Waldo; Minor Haynes continuously adjusting his tie like it was choking him; flocks of kids clinging to their parents, not one so much as fidgeting.

He kept looking until he spotted Cece and Cuz; mismatched, bedraggled, full to overflowing with sorrow without particular grace. He retucked his shirt, wiped his hands on his jeans, and took the first step.

Cuz slipped from Cece's side, wiggled her way through the crowd. Morse stopped in his tracks, watched as she came up behind Angie and pulled on the back of Angie's blouse. Angie looked down to see a dirty-faced Cuz who kept hold. She was asking in flat voice, so no one else could hear. What about Morse?

Tía Angie couldn't answer what Cuz was asking. "He'll show up as soon as he can. You know that, don't you?" she said. Wondering if there was anything more horrible than the faces she was seeing today, hoping instantly she would never know what it might be.

Morse watched them whispering and edged back. Too little too late was what he had to offer. He dropped down to the river, followed it to the bridge and his truck. Running again, and he knew it.

Cuz and Angie looked for Morse, they asked round. Nobody had seen him since before the fires; nobody had seen him since. No carcass yet discovered that could be his. Angie was beyond trusting her instincts but she refused to believe Morse was dead until somebody could prove it.

In his absence, Angie and Cuz both heard behind peoples' comments, an unspoken litany of everything Morse had done since he was a little boy. Heard this reshape itself and seep into whispering rumor and silent innuendo. That Morse hadn't showed up for work with Popper the day of the fires was only the most recent evidence. The unspeakable found slight shelter in a rhetorical question: Maybe it was Morse who set the Sim on fire? The town that knew him, that had laughed with him, that counted on his strong back and knowing hands, now accused him. Because where was he?

One trick is to take a deep breath of moon, when you first see it in the morning sky. Cast away the me-me-me-me-me filling your ears and clogging your heart, give away the eagerness of pulse and what could be said.

Take a quiet breath. Cast deeper. Look to the trees; the moon; to the elk with ears back, twitching, head angled to catch the slightest scent or breeze.

Dream with your ears and eyes and skin as wide-awake as this. Dream of a time we all would be more wary, a time we all were less chased. A time quiet and sufficient, not plentiful, not of desperate need. Dream fully alert, and if this dreaming comes, cast it like nets but do not take what it gathers; cast again. Hold its crocheted fringe like a long kite string, with a light touch; be its anchor.

Use the names of others if they help to put flesh on the dreambones. On a good day, when dreams visit this world of our flesh, acknowledge them. But do not expect dreams to fetch, or do chores, or provide some filling to your life, some sustenance.

Take a deep breath and know it is sorrow that makes the moon hang crooked.

• • • • •

Fire Report: BIG SMOKY

Date of fire: August 23

Fire protection responsibility: DLR (Dept. of Land Resources)

Person Taking Report: G. Perrs

Report Done on Computer: September 15

general info

    District: Sahaptin Valley

    Fire type: Severe II

General and specific causes (unknown is never an option):

- x    Miscellaneous
- _    burning building
- _    burning vehicle
- _    fireworks (other than children)
- _    sparks from house chimney
- _    electric fence
- _    powerline
- x    spontaneous (other than sawdust)
- _    sparks from car exhaust
- _    sparks from farm tractor
- _    highway construction equipment
- _    land clearing equipment
- _    cutting torch or welder
- _    use of fire (other than logging)
- _    hot ashes
- _    tracer ammunition
- _    burning material from aircraft
- _    equipment crash
- _    woodcutter
- _    tree planter
- _    Christmas tree operations
- _    other _____

<u>Landowner cause:</u>

   (yes/no/transient) <u>no</u>

<u>Discovered by</u>: <u>Raventon resident</u>

Time reported by Air Observer: <u>11:15</u>

1st Effective Control Agency:<u>Raventon Fire Department, (District 11)</u>
Size at Arrival: <u>.2</u> (acres)
Ownership Where Fire Started: <u>Northwest Railroad Inc.</u>
Ownership Largest Area Burned: <u>Northwest Railroad Inc.</u>
Aspect: <u>SW</u>
Elevation: <u>2100-2600'</u>
% Slope in vicinity of origin: <u>40</u>

Weather (some agencies only)
   Wind Direction / Speed: <u>0-20 NE</u>
   Temperature: <u>75</u>
   Humidity: <u>15</u>

Fire Intensity Level (some agencies only)
   Flame length:
      _  0-4 ft
      _  4-8ft
      x  8-12ft+

<u>Suppression Action</u>
People & Equipment
   First Attack by:<u>Raventon Fire Department, (District 11)</u>
   First Attack
         No.people : <u>15</u>
         Equipment: <u>8 handtools, 1 500 gal. pumptruck</u>
   Reinforcements
         No.people : <u>115 (w/standard issue gear)</u>
         Equipment:<u>3 D6 dozers, 3 pump trucks (2x300 gal,</u>
               <u>1x500 gal), 1 helicopter</u>

226

Effective Line (in chains)

    dozer 330

    jeep 70

    hand 320

Assistance Rendered:

    crew name or # Wenatchee 1,3,Spokane 22

Time:

    Fire Started: 15:30, August 22

    Discovered: 05:10, August 23

    Reported: 05:28, August 23

    First Attack: 05:37, August 23

    Reinforcements

        Reqstd:08:42, August 23

        Arrved:09:50, August 23

    Fire Contained:18:00, August 25

    Fire Controlled:11:00, August 27

    Fire Out:16:00, August 30

Financial Accountability: to be determined

Acres: 1925

Timber Type: mixed Douglas fir, Ponderosa pine

Specific Fuel: windfalls,pole size & larger tree crowns

Total Resource Damages:

| | |
|---|---|
| merch. timber vol MBF | $ to be determined |
| timber products | $ to be determined |
| reprod | $ to be determined |
| forage & minor forest products | $ to be determined |
| watershed | $ to be determined |
| wildlife | $ to be determined |
| real property improvements | $ to be determined |
| personal property | $ to be determined |

**Narrative:** (Big Smoky)

Exact cause of fire still under investigation. Report to 911
dispatch by citizen (in-town sighting of smoke, approximately
.5 mile away), appears to have occurred approximately 12
hours later. First responder: the Raventon fire department
(05:37, 8/23). Technically out of jurisdiction. Initial eval-
uation: small brush fire, line of containment established.
State crew monitored response, was called to assist when fire
jumped line, (08:42, 8/23). Wind increased, shifted direction. Extreme amounts of downed timber hampered ground
response, provided fuel.

Raventon evacuated, County Road #309 closed (11:30, 8/23).
Fire plan reevaluated to coordinate response with "Simulator"
fire (11:55, 8/23). Line lost at perimeter of Raventon
(12:15, 8/23). Line of containment established: river to
easterly ridgeline, following along northerly ridgeline, to
County Road #309 18:00, 8/25). See report for detailed times,
response units.

Fire Report: SIMULATOR

Date of fire : August 23

Fire protection responsibility : DLR (Dept. of Land Resources)

Person Taking Report : G. Perrs

Report Done on Computer : September 15

general info

District : Sahaptin Valley

Fire type : Severe II

General and specific causes (unknown is never an option):

X    Miscellaneous
X    burning building
_    burning vehicle
_    fireworks (other than children)
_    sparks from house chimney
_    electric fence
_    powerline
_    spontaneous (other than sawdust)
_    sparks from car exhaust
_    sparks from farm tractor
_    highway construction equipment
_    land clearing equipment
_    cutting torch or welder
_    use of fire (other than logging)
_    hot ashes
_    tracer ammunition
_    burning material from aircraft
_    equipment crash
_    woodcutter
_    tree planter
_    Christmas tree operations
_    other _____

<u>Landowner cause:</u>

(yes/no/transient) <u>no</u>

<u>Discovered by</u>: <u>employee</u>

Time reported by Air Observer: <u>n/a</u>

1st Effective Control Agency:<u>DLR (Dept. of Land Resources)</u>
Size at Arrival:<u> n/a </u>(acres)
Ownership Where Fire Started: <u>MegaCorp, Inc.</u>
Ownership Largest Area Burned:<u> MegaCorp, Inc.</u>
Aspect: <u>flat</u>
Elevation: <u>2100'</u>
% Slope in vicinity of origin:<u> flat</u>

Weather (some agencies only)
    Wind Direction / Speed:<u> 0-20/variable</u>
    Temperature:<u> 75</u>
    Humidity: <u>15</u>

Fire Intensity Level (some agencies only)
    Flame length:
       _ 0-4 ft
       _ 4-8ft
      <u>x</u> 8-12ft+

<u>Suppression Action</u>
People & Equipment
    First Attack by:<u>DLR (Dept. of Land Resources)</u>
    First Attack
        No.people :<u> 25 (w/standard issue gear)</u>
        Equipment:<u> 300 gal. pumptruck</u>
    Reinforcements
        No.people :<u> n/a</u>
        Equipment:<u> n/a</u>

Effective Line (in chains)

    dozer <u>n/a</u>

    jeep <u>n/a</u>

    hand <u>n/a</u>

Assistance Rendered:

    crew name or # <u>n/a</u>

Time:

    Fire Started: <u>10:20 August 23</u>

    Discovered: <u>10:50, August 23</u>

    Reported: <u>11:03, August 23,*</u> see narrative below

    First Attack: <u>11:18, August 23</u>

    Reinforcements

        Reqstd: <u>n/a</u>

        Arrved: <u>n/a</u>

    Fire Contained: <u>13:00, August 23</u>

    Fire Controlled: <u>14:00, August 23</u>

    Fire Out: <u>12:00, August 24</u>

Financial Accountability: <u>to be determined</u>

Acres: <u>n/a</u>

Timber Type: <u>n/a</u>

Specific Fuel: <u>n/a</u>

Total Resource Damages:

| | |
|---|---|
| merch. timber vol MBF | $ <u>to be determined</u> |
| timber products | $ <u>to be determined</u> |
| reprod | $ <u>to be determined</u> |
| forage & minor forest products | $ <u>to be determined</u> |
| watershed | $ <u>to be determined</u> |
| wildlife | $ <u>to be determined</u> |
| real property improvements | $ <u>to be determined</u> |
| personal property | $ <u>to be determined</u> |

**Narrative:** (Simulator)

Exact cause of fire still under investigation. Automatic fire alarm system initiated report (10:20, 8/23), on-site manager canceled first alarm (10:23, 8/23). Further investigation pending on dispatch override of first alarm. Second automatic alarm initiated first responder: DLR (Dept. of Land Resources). (11:03 8/23). Response coordinated with "Big Smoky" fire (11:55, 8/23). High number of casualties related to confusion over internal alarm system, possibly due to entertainment programming. Standard fire escape and warning procedures were not sufficiently effective in this context. Further investigation pending.

******

# 094

The morning after the service, Harold passed himself off at the police road-block as a resident and returned to Raventon shortly after dawn. Against the charcoal black and ash grey of everywhere, anything not burnt was garish: blue sky, the white hulk of a refrigerator, red brickwork of a chimney. White and yellow rocks seemed to have sprouted from the earth overnight.

Harold could project his recollections of crooked gravel streets and rickety houses, of wild rosebushes and grassy ditches, in rough conformity to where his feet took him. But inside him lurked a far-back laughing, a funhouse clattering as he tried to find correlation to what had existed so recently. He walked, and as he walked his mind called forth snatches of conversation, groceries purchased, the flap of the post office awning—the mnemonics of Raventon. The echoing horror, all this was no more, corresponded more accurately point for point to what actually surrounded him: charred timbers, melted siding, ashen debris. He was disconcerted by so much absence. Maybe he was frightened.

Harold came back the next morning and sat on a rock and observed. His thoughts did not make sense so he watched where the town used to be and the rest of him waited. He was sitting there, close to where he was pretty sure Morse's house had been when the store truck arrived, banging through what had been downtown. Angie got out, she wandered down the street until she came to the burnt skeleton of the store, kicked one bit of rubble and then another, paced.

She was facing the ruin, hands on her hips, as Harold approached.

They stood side by side, looking.

"I'm glad to see you, Angeline."

She gave him a quick and covert sideways glance, turned back to the destruction, and nodded, swallowing.

Harold helped make coffee. Angie had a generator and a percolator among all the supplies she'd trucked in. Harold spoke only the few words it took to keep himself practically invisible to anyone but Angie. When it was just the two of them they unloaded the truck, shuffled whatever remains Angie prioritized that minute, that hour. For two days following they met in the morning, at what had been the store, worked or stared, served whatever food Angie had hauled in to whoever came by. They sat in the evenings, nursed beers and a piece of the dark and quiet, Angie streaked with soot, Harold flushed, barely a smudge on his slacks or shirt.

On the third night Angie took a big breath and let it out long and slow;

something broke away. She pursed her lips and studied her hands and in a low voice asked Harold to marry her.

For the first time since the fires they looked at each other directly.

Harold nodded. Then gave her the flicker of a wink, kissed the palm of his hand, and blew it to her.

• • • • •

# 095

Harold and Angie set a date, then continued to work side by side, dawn to dusk. They hauled in two huge generators, ran lights and power tools and a radio, the constant noise a barrier. Each morning they pulled in with another load, each night they drove to Seattle and bought what they needed to fill the truck up again. At the end of the second week they'd cleared a spot big enough to put up three wall tents, a lean-to, and a Portapotty. Unburned oddities were placed on display: a mirror, half-reflecting, half-bubbled into clear glass; a box of safety matches and a hot pad; a toilet seat framing a bundle of singed work gloves.

Angie kept clearing and straightening and improving; Harold helped. She harassed anyone who appeared to be official: insurance agents asking leading questions, media-hungry politicians and their entourages, members of the press. To locals and their friends and relatives she offered lawn chairs and hot coffee from a percolator perched on the toasted remains of a car fender. Even the Red Cross deferred to her logistical genius and followed her directions. Harold was the maitre d'invisible to Angie's tasks and intentions, providing a paper napkin, an extra chair, a steady hand, a glass of water.

They were gone one and one-half days. With strangers as witnesses, they were married by a justice-of-the-peace, and did not kiss before those officially gathered. They went directly to a suite at the Breakwater, overlooking Elliot Bay, and watched the sunset from a couch Harold moved near the picture window.

Angie looked over, Harold looked back, they held hands and sipped champagne and she felt love and fondness and desire. When the sun was fully behind the mountains Angie turned and Harold smiled and leaned forward and that was their first married kiss.

For Harold their lovemaking was like a cool drink of water, like having someone answer him before he spoke. He caressed the soft of Angie's body and its curves; the roughness of her hands and her weathered face. They moved to the bed and undressed each other and their lovemaking crescendoed, all the time eyes opened or closed, Angeline above and below and beside him, around him, sharing sweat and breath and oblivion. He loved her, he loved the slap of their bellies, he loved the touch of her and the feel of her and her touching him. Angie loved him back, pure as cool water, with all her strength. Then they snoozed.

When they finally crawled out of bed they had a room service breakfast, made love once more, then dressed and checked out, ran a few errands and drove to their wall tent. Harold handed her tools or worked at his plywood desk while she designed and constructed. It seemed to him they had been together forever and also that he was as good as sixteen in his desire for her, an urgency not only to make love but to be near her that hit him like a wave when she reached for him. Fireworks: a hug, a squeeze of hands, a smile. They shall be as one precisely correct.

When they returned to Raventon neither of them wore rings. They set up a folding table, a filing cabinet, kerosene lanterns, and installed a plywood floor. Together they built a platform for their double box springs and that was it, they'd moved in. It took time for Angie to reach for Harold, to allow her calloused fingers to rest on the back of his pink freckled hand. When she did, Harold beamed and brought her hand to his lips.

Angie refused to sell anything to those who returned to Raventon. She lent things or gave them away, used donations to buy coffee and sandwich makings. She nagged, and finally the power company ran the first service line. Insurance representatives and electric company linemen and public works guys continued to scurry like insects over what had been Raventon. Reporters drifted away when there was nothing new to report, only another profile of some family picking through rubble, their talk of rebuilding or never returning.

Each day one pickup or another would find its way toward a charred residence, a cousin or a son-in-law or a brother or the sister who lived in Seattle would hop out with a loud voice and forced energy, and rummage. They dug until they unearthed some freakish remnant of an entire household, or until it got dark, or until they gave up. Most locals came by themselves after the first visit. Rummaged a little, stood, and stared from what used to be their yard, or their kitchen, or their kids' bedroom.

• • • • •

# 096

---

Trying to find Dorth's house was odd. Roads were discernible but then what? Rudy and Dorth walked up the hill from the newly graded turn-around. Dorth climbed around alone through the ghostly footprint of what had been the house, studied a melted glob of stereo, the corner of a print unburned under a fan of broken glass, the carcass of a borrowed vacuum cleaner.

Rudy kept a patter, a chatter going. "Jeez. Totally burnt. Here's the handle to the dresser. The whole place looks weird, all shrunken. Dorth? We'll find some way to get you set up again. But I don't think there's going to be much here..." He kicked at something. Or nothing. "Dorth?" He poked with a bit of chrome trim. All the time his eyes flitted to her, seeking some signal they'd been here long enough, that it was time to leave.

Dorth reached into her shoulder bag and took out her sketchbook.
Trees gone, or burned to sliver-boned skeletons, a landscape in black and grey with hard deformed glints, unnatural gasps of twisted color. She drew. She studied with her eyes, directed her hand.

Rudy drifted from one spot to another, probed what lay at his feet, stirred, knocked at standing bits, kept talking. "Look at this, it must have been the pepper grinder," holding out a helix of burred metal, a whisper of stainless steel coming off the top like a molten banner frozen mid flap. When she only glanced at it he let it drop.

The sun dropped behind the ridge and Dorth stopped sketching, her throat raspy. She stared at the shrunken wood-grain of a stump of table leg.

Rudy used his poker to make a circle in the rubble, round and round.

Dorth hoisted her shoulder bag. "Let's go." Her voice had nothing to spare.

Rudy let the poker drop and they made their way out of the open shell of the house, through what had been.

On the drive back to Seattle they had some kind of conversation. But there was a bigger silence, where words and gestures were only minor intrusions. In the morning Rudy called insurance agents. When they returned to where the house had been he started a collection of burnt oddities. Neither of them spoke of the studio.

Dorth filled her sketchbook, used charcoal from the burn. That is what she called it. Never the fires. Rudy never called it anything. He talked his way around its edges, spoke rapidly of objects that had been, of materials and features, he made list after list.

She came back alone. Sometimes before the sun came up. Once she stayed late into the night. The various shades of darkness were no different than anywhere else on a moonless night, the stars distant and flat. She made herself stay. Thought black on black.

Nights in Seattle, in what passed for darkness and for quiet, she curled against Rudy's back, the smell of smoke always with them somewhere. Dorth kept thinking of their love as like that starlight, without clarity. She kept her hands from making absent motions on Rudy's chest, kissed the back of his neck. Tried to follow his breathing into sleep.

After three days Rudy brought it up. "We need to talk about what's next. Dorth?"

"I need someplace to work. Not the garage. Seattle is wrong for me. Way wrong." Dorth crawled into bed. Closed her eyes and pictured iridescent shells, the way light glowed without shadow inside them. Bubbled lacquer, sooted colors; she thought of a carny freak show: step right up and see the horror, the wondrous horror...

Rudy stayed up late that night, kept the TV volume low, flipped from station to station. When finally, in the dark, he slipped into bed beside Dorth he was cold to the bone.

• • • • •

# 097

The sun streamed into the church and the organ played. But what did any of this have to do with Analisa? The priest was a good man but he knew nothing about having a daughter. Nothing about losing her. It was time to go forward, Jorge beside her. All the faces along the aisle, faces from her family and people she didn't even know, all of them stared at her, everything peculiar-looking.

It was left for her then, to walk those last few steps, to her daughter's casket.

"You, you and Jorge, have another baby soon" Jorge's mother washed the dinner dishes, Analisa dried. "There is nothing anyone can do. After a while your heart gets sick of the hurt." The tiny white-haired woman spoke as she scrubbed plates and glasses and silverware. Analisa listened. After all the dishes were done, Analisa went to her room.

She lay down in the dark and remembered another time, in that same church. Standing beside her husband-to-be, repeating after the priest the words they had practiced, speaking in front of God.

Jorge had turned and looked to her as she walked to the altar, that time. She had walked to Jorge, his face confused, and as she did she thought she would faint. A state of grace was what the priest told her.

They prayed, said their words, exchanged rings. The kiss was for all of the ones watching, not between them. Then they were always close together but they could have been in different places except for a quick squeeze of hands. Cake and who knows what it tasted like and it was time to go.

The car they borrowed was all soaped up, cans and stuff tied on. Jorge stopped near the Pass to use the restroom and get gas. Everyone who saw the car made comments and jokes. She asked him if they couldn't get rid of all the decorations, and he pulled over and got most of it off.

The priests taught her chaos was the great void that came before. God used this great darkness, without warmth or heartbeat, to create. After a while your heart gets sick of the hurt.

Pancho came into the darkened room and sat on the bed beside her and held her hand. Panchito, the solemn and silent one.

Jorge did what was expected of him; he went through every motion. Buried his daughter, went to church with his wife and son; he worked days and came back to his parents' house at night, and tried hard not to drink too much.

Jorge felt absolutely responsible.

His boss gave him a day off when he asked. He and Pancho took his brother's truck. He avoided Tía Angie's tents, he drove to the carcass of their house, its excellent foundation mocking him. Pancho slipped out of the truck but stayed near. There was nothing Jorge even wanted to touch. If he'd had anything good to say, he would have said it then, to his son. Instead he sang.

His voice was high, almost reedy. No gruffness to it. Analisa told him once he had a beautiful voice, even though he never got the melodies exactly right.

What he sang was old and Spanish, rough with sadness. Pancho listened. Pancho, Angelina's protector, was without. While his father sang, Pancho remembered the time Eisy tried to get him to fight.

"Aren't you mad? Come on, Punch, let's go. I got some ideas that will show that fat fuck—"

Pancho had scraped at the dirt with a stick, one way, then the other. Smoothed it all over with the sole of his shoe. Roger Koalnivic was definitely not skinny, but he was bigger.

Eisy stuck his head in the space between Pancho's face and the ground.

"I know you can beat him up. Or we could mess with his precious bicycle, huh?"

Eisy especially despised Roger for having such a beautiful bike and hardly riding it. Pancho had seen this desire stain Eisy's face whenever Roger was around; he saw it that afternoon.

Pancho said nothing and Eisy continued to squat beside him. It gave even Eisy a chill, the way Pancho went inside himself, immovable, so Eisy went into one of his monologues. Pancho let Eisy's voice wash over him.

Words and more words flowed out of Eisy. Plenty of obscene and clever combinations using Roger Koalnivic's name, his lineage, what he reminded Eisy of, what he did with himself in the privacy of his own room. Pancho studied the dirt, watched ants emerge and move grains of soil, observed their wobbling antennae.

Eventually Eisy wore himself down. "Hey Punch?" he shrugged into Pancho's side, trying to knock him off balance. Pancho rocked, that's all. When the sun went down behind the ridge and the cool that had winter buried in it settled on them, Pancho blinked. "You're right. He *is* a fat fuck."

Eisy had laughed for days. And Pancho had smiled ever so slightly.

But now Pancho sat alone. Not even his father's singing touched him. It wasn't ice in his heart. Just no heart for it.

Stoneboy. That's what they called him at the new school.     P a n c h o heard the nickname from inside-his-world. He waited. The others got nervous, made lots of small talk, shuffled around, and then left him alone. That was how Pancho knew he'd won. The rest of it didn't matter.

· · · · ·

240

# CUZ

I live with great earnestness, and know this makes me a fool. Others take a different approach. They survive through poise or grace or dignity, or maybe a degree of indifference. Bow their heads, cover vitals and cower, square their shoulders and shake their fists; somehow they continue through all things: Auschwitz, peanut butter, tidepools, and temples; the bizarre path of the temporal.

What makes me more the fool is my desiring. I search for the cosmic in the ludicrously and pitifully human, stand blatant witness when what I love is destroyed, chase after the slightest potential of a dream come true.

Yearning.

I know this is a romantic, a sentimental term. But find a private corner, and consider. Then answer me, in a whisper if you must. Have you ever made a wish, fingers crossed, hoping? Was there never a time you desired what was perhaps not yours to have? Is there no name nor face nor aspiration that comes to mind and heart? It does not matter how fast you rebury this memory; I will look aside if you blush at the very thought, and do not ask you to relive such vulnerable circumstance. I only request you take the most cursory of peeks and see if once, it was you, yearning.

Dorth had dreams. The fires left her sorrowful, tired to tears, right up to the brim and overflowing. But her banging heart was not snuffed, nor withered. It was yearning.

So allow it fair review, that catchbasin for so many dreams.

• • • • •

# 098

Very little still existed to which one could even attach a piece of paper. None the less, flyers appeared:

**Fire, fire, burning bright**
**In the forests of the night**
**And what shoulder, & what art**
**Could twist the sinews of thy heart?**

**W. Blake**

Come and see:

> Thursday, about half an hour before sunset,
> Where First and Nevada used to be.
> (You might want to bring a chair)

First and Nevada, like all of Raventon's streets, was a matter of civility, a social contract regarding what had once been and might be again. A few people smiled weakly at the address, most owned little more than a recently purchased lawn chair.

There weren't many fliers, and yet at the appointed hour it was the biggest assemblage of Raventon's residents since Santa's visit the previous Christmas Eve. Some drove long distances, others wandered over from the cleanup and salvage of their former homes. There was something other-worldly about seeing so many folks from Raventon together with no Raventon around them. A few benches had been set up on the hillside, but nobody felt quite comfortable sitting. They stood in small groups to one side of a big structure covered with tarps. Men's handshakes didn't let go right away, women held on with both hands. Nods went out across the benches. Word was, this thing this night had to do with that woman who had her paintings in the store. Tía Angie'd been the one who talked it up, openly admitting she didn't know a thing about what would actually happen.

The covered object was about the size of a garage, with a much smaller covered lump behind the benches, other scaffolding tacked here and there.

Angie's generators stood nearby.

The sun went behind the ridge. Dorth stepped forward and faced the crowd. "Ladies and gentlemen. Please, take a seat."

Angie jumped in with her natural bullhorn of a voice. "Sit down now. Nothing happens until everybody's settled. Then we'll get a look at what Dorth has made for us."

People joked and bumped and found a place on the benches, or wiggled their chairs close together. Kids ran around the edges of the crowd and the tarped mystery, unsure where the real excitement would be.

Angie gave a nod and Dorth began her introduction. "Thanks for coming. Parts of what follow are upsetting. I hope this piece, all of it together—I mean it as a gift." Dorth walked around the crowd to one of three projectors Harold had wheeled into place.Under his direction a volunteer crew pulled steadily on ropes. Flaps of tarp lifted or slipped away or formed a kind of awning. There were boxy speakers around the edge of where everybody was gathered and out of them came music: a piano playing, a trumpet, an accordion; mournful and regal. A movie screen hung at the very back of a three-sided and ceilinged chamber. The funneled walls flared out wide toward the audience from this screen. As the music got louder, white light shot onto the walls while the screen remained in shadow, sparkling.

Photographs of individual objects flashed onto the main screen, seemed to emerge from the sides, and everything they could see was burning: a house fire somewhere else, a cigarette, a gas stove, a forest fire, a newspaper, a charcoal grill, a volcano. In between these were full screens of flames, then of Raventon as it was. The images alternated, faster and faster; flickering—

Some in the audience shouted, some got up to leave then stood watching. Others shifted on their benches and chairs, spoke with their neighbors, pointed. The names and occasions for the flashing images were shouted out, people yelled at the things they were seeing.

A kind of hypnotizing rhythm synchronized the pictures, the voices from the crowd, and now there were voices mixed with the music. Some of what was said in the audience was amplified. A black-and-white sketch of Alexander Mettle filled the main screen: Daddy at the counter, looking over like you were a little kid. From the left side Waterqueen floated in, with wings and a watering can that sent crystalline beads of water arcing below.

Eisy came darting beneath her sprinkling waters on his bicycle, one hand under the floating feet of the Waterqueen, balancing her on the palm of his hand as he grinned, the wheels of his bike going around and around as her sparkling waters cascaded around him. Only then did you notice one of the side flaps looked like the side of Waterqueen's house, curtains blowing, the shadow of someone looking out. The sketch of Daddy started moving like a flip book, he reached across the counter and put a streamer in the handle grip of Eisy's bike, waved to the parade in front of him that moved but didn't go away. The main screen was getting redder and redder around its edges, as though a colorful sunset was reflecting in, but no, the sky was almost completely dark. The music faded into burning sounds as the back corners seemed to sizzle and bubble, the light on the screen looked like a flashlight shining into a campfire. A corner of the screen began to curl.

"It's burning—" somebody finally yelled, a few people started to leave. The same young volunteers circled the structure with pump backpacks and hoses. Dorth stood to the side, by one of the projectors, her arms crossed. Angie and Harold were beside her when the first of the speakers blew. Most of crowd stood where they were, staring at flames that crept along the edges of the chamber, crawled across the screen, burned as pictures of flames and of Raventon, its houses and streets flipped across—

Then there was only one image. A tiny hand reaching from inside a beautiful scarf, the back of a stroller made it impossible to see more. The flames ate the screen as the shadow of somebody bigger leaned in toward the baby inside the scarf. It had to be Pancho and his sister but the image was gone in the bonfire of what was left.

The sounds from the speakers behind them amplified every snap and crackle and hiss from the fire before them.

Dorth watched, with the rest of Raventon, as the Big Picture burned. Tears shimmered in the firelight.

• • • • •

# 099

---

The silhouette of a man stepped close to the fire. Morse, gaunt and grey, had returned. Those who recognized him whispered and pointed.

Morse began to clap.

The crowd was silent.

Then Pancho, wearing his bolo tie, began to clap too.

Morse and Pancho kept it up, one clap after the other, beat for beat. Until they were interrupted.

"You just show up, and now, in front of all these people—" Minor Haynes rose from his bench and ranted. "It's the straw that broke the camel's back, that's what it is. You should be—"

Pancho clapped twice as fast. Rudy stood and joined in.

As did others from the audience, slowly, until it was a crowd applauding.

Minor sat down, as he explained to those around him, "I didn't mean the performance wasn't—good. I just meant—he, he shouldn't be..." Then resigned himself to a few weak palm slaps. The ovation continued long after Minor stopped.

Some people drifted away, some stayed until dawn, flicking their cigarette butts into the new ashes.

No one spoke much. They made a place for Dorth to sit, amongst them. Occasionally there was the sound of a car door slammed, an engine started, the receding hum and jounce of a truck as it drove away.

It was precisely the straw that broke the camel's back. The mundane accretion of what could have been. And it could have been one glance, not even a look. But Morse saw it. He didn't think there had ever been anything Angie needed that she couldn't get or do for herself; but this once, that look. Morse made himself a gift to Angie. He walked up to her and started to explain.

"I, I didn't—I wasn't anywhere close when I heard about the fires."

Angie looked as though she were going to spit on him. "I never, ever thought you had anything to do with how the fires got started. I—"

Morse couldn't believe his ears. He tried again. "What I'm trying to tell you is, I would have gone—" He would explain himself, this once. "I would have gone in for your Daddy. Or for you, Ang. I'm sorry. I'm sorry about everything." The rest of what he might have said, so much sound, he contained. So much nighttime and starlight but not enough for him.

Angie started after him, she had words she should have said to him a long time ago. But when Morse kept walking she stopped and only watched him.

"And what shoulder, and what art, could twist the sinews of thy heart?"

•   •   •   •   •

# 100

On a drizzling, low-clouded day Angie emerged from their tent. She made a full percolator of coffee but she could tell it was the kind of day everyone finds some reason to stay inside. By mid-afternoon the drizzle had condensed into all-present mist.

Angie talked herself into going for one of her old walks. She had pretty much acclimated to the burnt way of everything since there was no way to avoid it. What she had been avoiding was to go where the big trees had been, through what had been the woods behind town, and up the ridge, to find her way over the paths she'd known and loved best. She had a feeling these, the places she had always known without thought or consideration, would be gone forever the day she went to them and saw nothing but more burnt residue.

It began to rain in earnest a few minutes after she started, almost precisely as she was beginning to savor the sodden calm of scorched branches and clods of dirt, like some Chinese pen and ink drawing. The rain hit the hood of her jacket, added consonance to the suck of her footsteps in the mud, whispered as it hit the ground. Hissing.

Angie crouched in the ash and mud and there was a whispering as raindrops hit ash, louder in one spot. When she knelt lower to try and get her ears close enough to break the sound into smaller bits, the ground was warm to her touch, dry ash spattering the rain, small craters where each drop hit. The fire was still alive.

She thought of something Harold told her when he'd come looking for her, a few days after they'd first made love. With his pink face hidden from her, he told her about the theory of the expanding universe. At first it didn't seem to have any direct connection, but then he got to the part about more and more space, all the time. Space between molecules, within atoms, everywhere, incrementally. Ever expanding distance. His face a furious red, Harold told her he had traveled through this distance to be with her.

So maybe it was your heart that, in stretching, held together what there was in the way of connections and relations, while time and space kept expanding. He hadn't actually said that. He had taken the last few steps through space to hold her. Angie took a handful of the warm ash and headed up the ridge.

· · · · ·

# 101

As for Fred Mossback, inventor, Fred pried open Pandora's box after deducing what was inside. He had not planned to start any fire he could not immediately extinguish. He had planned to experiment with the point of ignition. And he had a theory about telekinetically generating fire that involved the Simulator.

But Fred had lost his edge. Consequently, all his intentions were distracted, some misdirected. Like the mythic cow that kicked the lantern that landed in straw and started the Great Chicago Fire, our man Fred was present, he did initiate part of the fatal chain of events; his one action led to another, and another. What followed floated pregnantly within that first lick of flame.

The Sim combusted, non-simultaneously. It is impossible to logically deduce any connection to Fred's experiments on the ridge, and yet...? A bit of faulty insulation? A defective switch? The circumstantial, or maybe it's the proverbial, chain of events leads link-by-link in one direction to Fred, in the other to fire.

Fred's body was found just before the first snow. He'd made it almost to the top of the ridge before the fire caught him.

• • • • •

# CUZ

People deal with death in different ways, or maybe ultimately all in the same way. You are alive, so you keep moving. If there is true knowledge about death it can only be pinned down by analogy. A butterfly is mounted with flat wings; museums of natural history and anthropology have drawers of dance masks, pottery chards, silky moles with tender whiskers and rigid feet; all specimens, all lined up and labeled the better to compare and contrast.

Eisy died.

I went to the memorial service, afterward I went to his grave. In such sad and sorry circumstances I realized what I was waiting for; Eisy should have been there with me and he was not. And he wouldn't be. We have no vocabulary for our relation to those who are not.

I stopped speaking of him to anyone. How to describe his proximity? How could a bit of Eisy be so near when he was not? Out of the corner of my eye, as close as the elbow-room of a nudge, an almost audible whisper... manifestations with such focus, just beyond my own attention at any moment. How was I, so completely distracted, so positive of his presence?

I skittered back and forth. Never for a minute did I forget him, never did I forgive him, constantly I sought the slightest hint of his presence. In a scary matter of a few weeks I could only remember his face from photographs, his voice from one-liners too often repeated. I could no longer hold him in my mind's eye. Who was Eisy, and what could-he-have-been? A contender? Such a bitter joke. Eisy had always blown the top off any tally; there was and would be no Eisy. Recall that I was twelve. Eisy had been my mentor, my friend, my surrogate big brother and conduit to comprehension.

I knew then and I know now there is an Eisy still present. Glinting Eisy, flash of bike chrome, sharp-directed spit as eloquent punctuation. Nothing present upon direct or circumspect examination. Still and always there is a nagging sensibility, deep within: he should be. A feeling: he is. Call it subjective. Call it foolish.

Eisy died, Raventon was burned into oblivion. No amount of memorialization, retribution, or even spectral visitation can change these matters.

Mom and I settled into a modular home in the sprawl of not-quite-suburban-Seattle, over the mountains from Raventon. From this new home (I use the term loosely) I rode many buses, sometimes all the way into downtown. As engines purred through swooping turns I stared out the window at a million situations, all transient, none involving me. Within a year there was another grand opening for a new Simulator, somewhere north of Seattle. Its exact location didn't matter much to me.

I went alone. It was the same horse-and-pony-show as Raventon's had been, with a cosmopolitan twist. Ever-present security guards made sure no one received more than one T-shirt, they kept kids off the traffic barricades, they divided and conquered any possible spontaneity. Within this orderly scenario, I passed for fifteen and had my first legal and fully oriented Experience.

How directly and transparently was I swept into whatever I could Sim about Eisy. I spent a good part of the following winter and spring in a sad little two-part harmony of disappointing technical imitations and fading memories. My world revolved around Simming, the going-to-go; the almost there; Experience, a tantalizing disappointment; the saving of money for the next.

Most of another year passed. Then my one-time some-time friend Sharon called. She had moved to the south-suburban fringe. We began to call each other regularly. Jabbered. When I mentioned my bus trips she wanted to come along. We first met at the bus plaza downtown. I was hesitant to share my best routes but Sharon was quick to think of new possibilities and our explorations expanded.

We dared each other into new exploits, kept straight faces until we had exited through the warm doorways of department stores, made-over creatures reeking of perfume. Cackling at each other, we washed it all off in the library's restroom, then went our separate ways. Side by side we ordered octopus in a Chinese restaurant, licked its drooping tentacles from our lips. We followed a handsome man in a three-piece suit into a skyscraper lobby, up its elevator, then toured the rest of his building on our own. Eventually, inevitably, we went Simming, although Sharon was never a Sim devotee.

I drag you through this long accounting because of what I Experienced with her. Sharon and I were messing around as we were strapped down; in the spirit of ouji boards and seances and all the hype and tripe of young women seeking amusement and mild hysteria, we agreed to try to visit each other's Sim and say hello.

Undeniably, I Experienced Sharon. Our programs made contact, short-circuited, and mine went way beyond any kind of programmable entertainment. There was no here, there. It all became other. Schizophrenics hallucinate the presence of what is not; I Experienced what is, as though I were not. Out of the kaleidoscope of pretty patterns I witnessed myself from the outside, I saw myself as the sometime side-kick Sharon called friend. Like some rippled nightmare captured in a funhouse mirror, I had a short tour of the world as though I was not myself. Terrorized, I struggled to maintain physical sight of the one I thought was me. I saw her from outside and knew myself from within and this combination was more frightening than the fires, than waiting to hear what happened to Eisy, than being alone. And on this empty plain of sorrow I was not even alone when I realized, when I truly understood, I could *have been anybody. I was Nobody. So much flotsam in the sea of others' Experience.*

*Memories change, altered by desire, perspective, frayed synapse. Finer and finer wires of recalled experience weave themselves tightly around us in an infinitely growing veil, frail as a spider's web and with equal tensile strength, an almost unburstable bubble between us and life.*

*Once launched, like a bird who does not have time to get her wings out for flight, do we bounce into this veil? Does she, that little caged bird, does she sing?*

*There was a time I postured and positioned myself as captain of my soul. Words, those chunky lettered carriers of thought, used to be my scaffolding for the climb. Now I am more interested in precision. If I feel myself to be flying, what do you see? Is there magic? Is it all make-believe? Truth, tailspin, lost talisman, technical stuttering, aftershocks, consequence. Is it possible before and after have the same drift as magnetic north or where the sun rises? That perhaps the cardinal directions are from the gyroing of this life, this place we call home?*

• • • • •

# 102

---

They met at the Pike Place market, overlooking a glassy Elliot Bay. Cuz, at sixteen, was so balanced on the cusp of womanhood it was painful to look closely. Her breasts blossoming, her hips with something between a swagger and a sway; she walked to the restaurant with an assurance so fierce it was almost a taunt to harm her. Except she was nervous too.

They were to meet at a restaurant as old as the market, with dark wood and a dark entryway, windows and booths at the back, breakfast and booze served twenty-one hours a day. Cuz checked her watch and walked past its doorway several times, adjusted and relocated the shoulder strap of her purse, flicked her not-quite-blond hair, and finally, stepped inside.

She didn't see him right away, thought maybe he had chickened out. But the waitress led her back, past the counter of old men with too much time and not enough coffee, past the window booths she had seen from the door, to another room of booths.

Morse stood and nodded with a wry smile that she couldn't read, sat down when she did and lifted his water glass. "Happy birthday."

"How do you know it's my birthday?"

Morse took a long drink. "How do you think?"

"This was a bad idea." Cuz ducked her head, used her hair as camouflage.

"You're the only one I ever saw born."

There was a lot of silence after that.

When the all-business waitress returned, pad in hand, Morse ordered a sandwich, looked at Cuz, and said to make it two.

Beyond the patchwork of roofs and parking lots, sunlight glared on the bay as a freighter made its slow way toward the port's orange cranes. The restaurant smelled of fried fish and old cigarette smoke, the clatter of dishes, snatches of conversation, and the worn bearing on a ceiling fan took the place of any small talk between them.

Morse hitched himself out of his chair enough to pull out his wallet. He extracted an envelope and held it out to Cuz.

She looked at his hand and his face before she took it.

Morse had nothing to do but watch.

Cuz lifted the flap, removed the papers inside, and read them. "You think money is what I need?" She tossed it all on the table.

Morse shook his head and rolled his eyes. "It's part of a painful tradition, I guess. A Raventon tradition." He realized Cuz wasn't even listening. "That's just the ice-breaker. This is what I really want to give you." He handed to her a photo from his shirt pocket, colors muddied by time, emulsion cracked. A much younger Morse, no young man, even then. He was holding a tiny baby. "That's you. And me, of course."

Cuz rubbed her finger around the battered edge of the picture and drank it in. Morse in a mis-buttoned workshirt, his hair bushy, his eyes wilder. Holding this baby like she weighed nothing, like both of them were floating on air. Cuz studied it until she could see it with her eyes closed and then she held it out to him. "If you're my Dad why didn't you ever ever do anything?" She couldn't stop her voice from shaking, she couldn't stop her tears. But she could stare at him, her sometime father.

Morse studied the scars along his fingers, the dirt lurking under his thumbnail. "It was a deal I made with your ma. To stay clear."

Cuz's mouth had an ugliness Morse never wanted to see. "Nope. She told me."

Morse's had a much more practiced sadness to it, what might have looked like a smile if you didn't know him. "What a person tells—" he swallowed. Swallowed again, Adam's apple sliding up and down. "It's foolishness to think you might—" He took a drink of water. "You're the reason I moved back to Raventon. So I could at least watch you. And you put on a good show." He rubbed his eyes. "Whatever your ma tells you, you listen to her."

Cuz held the photo out further.

"If you want it, that's yours."

Cuz looked at the picture again and put it on top of the papers, halfway between them.

The waitress delivered their sandwiches.

"Why did you call me now? If you made this big promise to stay away?"

"Yeah." Morse nodded. "That's a good one." He was memorizing this young woman, the part in her hair, the shape of her fingers as she played with a french fry. "When I turned sixteen... For me—... I declared my own emancipation. So I was thinking, if you're even a little like me, this might be the time." He bit off all the words he'd practiced. He knew now nothing he wanted to say was what his daughter needed to hear. He reached out and put his hand on hers, and she didn't pull away.

Cuz swiped at her eyes with the heel of her free hand, then a paper napkin. She looked sometimes at Morse, sometimes at the picture, sometimes out the window. "It's too late."

What Morse finally said was "Too late for what?"

When he had been younger, he would have tried to convince her. He would have pretended there were words to make it right.

When she was older she would have found enough comfort from him, found

253

succor in this one day, this one holding of hands. Instead she looked at the photograph and wept.

Instead he brushed her cheek and continued to hold her hand, and let her cry.

• • • • •

# EPILOGUE

Rest. Then begin again.

Humans being the-ones-with-words, the namers. The first name: Other. What is not me. Thou. Point and label each thing, each other, as though by applying a name you can peel some part off and make it separate.

Laugh once for the space between each name and what it names. Laugh again for each thing having so many different names. Save the biggest chortle for Time, the thing and the name, the all-too-human desire for order, before and after. And the laughter fades.

All my life, dreaming. All our lives and the place we live in, that is our name together. Rock stone earth sky water. Rain fern river frog sage bug and bubble. That would be our name too.

You who read this, therefore are human. We smell flowers, quench our thirst and get thirsty again; we dream and wake from our dreams; we remember.

If you want further accounting we must go backward.

One person; two. Me, you, us.

Some gathered together. Comes the business of settlement, in many places, of towns. Appearing like freckles, like blisters, like clouds on a windy day. Proceeding with great industriousness. Proceeding to change many things previously named. Proceeding to rename old things.

"Clearing land" means the taking-away-from-a-place. "Settlement" means bringing-in, the placement-of-human-made-things-on-a-cleared-place.

In one freckle named Raventon, documents were dated; these were signed and sealed in another, more official place. Giving Raventon another name: incorporated.

All the time more humans. More names. "Settlement" means some-humans-always-staying. Clearing the land of others. Croatians and Scots and Appalachians and Athabascans, white ones and black ones and dark ones and light ones, cruel and crude names they all have for the colors they are not. All the time more arriving. Each one with a dream, or several. Some articulate, which means the out-loud-spewing-of-names-other-humans-like-the-sound-of-on-all-that-is-and-is-not. Others quiet. Which means you didn't hear.

At the place, the freckle, called Raventon: a lattice-work out of tules and leather and shanties and brickwork. Each more cloven from the earth than what came before. So much all-too-human in one place. So many dreams bumping into each other in one valley. Frequencies of communication pass through the air, the soil, the water. All of us together we make some combination of imagination and location we call home.

Only a frecklonomist would continue to observe Raventon in particular, only a human would seek names for the phlegmatic details.

All-of-us.
All-of-us dreaming.
All our lives dreaming.

*We run...*
like a gazelle, at the shot of a gun, run for your life with the real Bogeyman right behind, like Roadrunner after her beep-beep—run all out, bound, leap for your life, panting, with a pounding heart—

knees pumping, lances held high:

*Plant:*
seed in the ground, ourselves, brace our feet stalwartly, ready to meet the Whatever—hold fast while all the tensile twang of life and life only backs up against the Unmoving—

Perhaps we climb together, the teetering pole: stand at the precipice and together we jump? we vault?

*Perhaps we fly?*

• • • • •

# ABOUT THE AUTHOR

Born and raised in suburban Minnesota, Ellie Belew migrated west. She has lived in a former Burlington Northern Railroad mining town in Washington State since 1989.

Her fiction has appeared in small literary magazines, her one-act play, *Predominantly Blue*, was selected in competition for performance in Portland, Oregon, and her articles have appeared in a variety of trade journals and newspapers. She edited and contributed to *About Wallowa County* (Pika Press 2000). Another book by Belew, *Fully Involved*, will be available in November, 2003. It is a history of the Washington State Council of Fire Fighters, to be published by that organization.

Belew is currently working on a new novel that overlaps some of the events and characters in *Run Plant Fly*.

For further information please visit www.elliebelew.com.